Tracks of Deceit

ALAN MORRIS & GILBERT MORRIS

ADVENTURES
Katy Steele

TRACKS OF DECEIT

Tyndale House Publishers, Inc.
WHEATON, ILLINOIS

Cover illustration copyright © 1996 by René Milot
Author photo taken by Bill Bilsley copyright © 1996

Scripture quotations are taken from the *Holy Bible,* King James Version.

Library of Congress Cataloging-in-Publication Data

Morris, Alan B., date
    Tracks of deceit / Alan Morris & Gilbert Morris.
        p.   cm. — (The Katy Steele adventures ; 1)
        ISBN 0-8423-2039-3 (SC : alk. paper)
        1. Frontier and pioneer life—West (U.S.)—Fiction   2. Private investigators—
West (U.S.)—Fiction.   3. Women detectives—West (U.S.)—Fiction.   I. Morris, Gilbert.
II. Title.   III. Series: Morris, Alan B., date   Katy Steele adventures ; 1.
PS3563.087395T73   1996
813′.54—dc20   95-46656

Printed in the United States of America

03 02 01 00 99 98 97 96
 9   8   7   6   5   4   3   2   1

TO CINDY

Noble wife, best friend, and gift from God

"For I cannot be

Mine own, nor anything to any, if

I be not thine."

CHAPTER ONE

A Little Drama

Y ou can go in, Miss Steele." The clerk, who rose as Katy entered the outer office, was a tall man with a cadaverous face and a sepulchral voice. He wore a plain black suit and looked more like an undertaker than anything else.

"Thank you." Katy Steele stepped past the desk, and as she opened the door and entered, a thrill of excitement rushed over her. *Mr. Warsham wouldn't have called me if I hadn't been chosen for the job!* she thought.

She had been rejected so many times that hope had almost left her, but the note that had arrived earlier asking her to come by the office of the Williamson Laboratory had brought it all back with a rush. She had dressed frantically, taken a cab to the downtown section where the laboratory was located, and was slightly out of breath from dashing up the stairs of the three-story building.

"I came as soon as I got your note, Mr. Warsham," she said breathlessly, but then she saw the face of the director and knew instantly that she was not going to get the job.

Leslie Warsham, director of the Williamson Laboratory, was an able scientist but a poor poker player. He could never manage to keep what was in his hand from being reflected in his features. His round face was morose as he rose to greet Katy. He had smiled

1

constantly when interviewing Katy earlier, but now a gloomy air rested on him—and he refused to look her in the eye.

"Ah—Miss Steele," he said in a jerky tone, then paused. He fumbled with a button on his coat and then swallowed hard. "I—I'm afraid I have bad news for you." He licked his lips nervously and finally managed to lift his eyes to her.

He saw a woman dressed in the plainest of clothes and the most sensible of shoes. She was tall and inclined to stoop somewhat, as though ashamed of being so tall, and the shapeless brown dress concealed her figure. Her thick ash-blonde hair, which was tied up in a rather ugly knot, formed a widow's peak on her broad forehead. She had strong features, including a squarish face, high cheekbones, and a determined chin. She would never be a real beauty; her features were too strong for that. She would have been attractive enough, but lack of care made her look older and less winsome than she actually was.

Katy had been so certain that she would get this job. In a bitter tone she demanded, "Is it because I can't do the work—or because I'm not a man?"

Mr. Warsham squirmed, and then honesty rose in him. He faced her squarely, having to look up into her face. "My dear Miss Steele, I will not trifle with you. You are a brilliant student, but my staff raised such—serious objections that I was forced to—to—"

"To hire a man—I understand." A streak of blind anger erupted deep in Katy Steele, but she fought it down. She had been subject to fits of rage as a child but had learned to control them as she had grown older. She had overcome them so well that her friends and even her family never imagined the mindless rage that sometimes exploded in her. "Thank you, Mr. Warsham," she said stiffly, her face tight and expressionless. She turned and marched out of the office holding her head high.

Warsham followed her, wringing his hands and stammering, "Miss Steele—wait! Perhaps we can—"

But the outer door closed, and Warsham stared after her, disturbed by the incident. He liked the young woman and had wanted to hire her. But he was a weak man, unwilling to fight for such a cause.

"She would never have worked out, sir."

Warsham glared at the sour-faced clerk and snapped, "Suppose you tend to your own affairs, Jenkins!" He reentered his office, slammed the door, and experienced a vicious thrill when a picture of his uncle, the founder of the firm, fell to the floor. As the glass shattered, Warsham thought, *There, you old buzzard! Good enough for you!*

———

Katy turned blindly when she reached the street, tears rising to her eyes. Blinking them back fiercely, she tightened her lips and made her way along the sidewalk, unaware of her surroundings. A gusty wind snatched at her hat, but it was pinned tightly with several ivory pins. It whipped her skirts, but they were long and thick, impervious to the gales. Overhead, dark clouds were rolling in from the west, and soon a few fat drops of rain tapped at her cheeks, but Katy paid them no heed.

For over an hour she walked the streets of Sacramento, reliving the appointment. It stung her spirit like salt in a raw wound, and she demanded bitterly, *Why do you let it bother you so much? You should be used to it by now!* But she was not accustomed to it and would never get used to it, she well knew. She prided herself on having an analytical and rational mind, but at times like this, her emotions seemed to sweep all her objectivity away. Now, as she moved down Washington Street, she realized that more than anything else she wanted to bury her face in her hands and sob aloud.

"Miss? Miss?"

Startled, Katy pulled her thoughts away from the shame of the rejection. She glanced up to see an elderly man slumping against

3

the wall. He was wearing a worn, outdated brown suit, and snow-white hair fell beneath the brim of a derby. He was trembling, Katy saw. When she hesitated, he slid down the brick wall he was braced against.

Katy looked around but saw no one close enough to help. Quickly she stepped beside the old man, asking, "Are you ill?"

"I . . . don't—" The man's lips seemed purple, but his face was flushed. A thick beard and mustache covered the lower part of his face. His eyes were dark, though Katy could hardly see them as they were almost shut. He gasped and grabbed his chest in an alarming fashion, and his eyes rolled upward in his head.

"I'll get a doctor!" Katy said, fearful that he was having a heart attack. She turned to go, but he lifted his head, plucked at her sleeve, and whispered something she didn't catch. "What did you say?"

"Help me . . . get to my . . . room," the sick man gasped. "Donner Hotel . . . right down the street . . . there."

Katy saw the hotel sign but was uncertain. *I can't leave him here alone. I'll get him to the hotel, and they can get a doctor.* "All right. Let me help you." She pulled the man upright and was surprised to see that he was taller than he'd seemed, a few inches over six feet. "Hold on to me," she commanded. He put his arm over her shoulder, and his weight came down on her. "Careful now—just walk slowly."

"A spell . . . I've had them before," the man gasped. He dragged his feet over the sidewalk and once nearly fell, but she caught him. "Can't make it," he moaned, but she held him tightly.

"Just a little farther." She was relieved when they came to the door of the hotel. She saw that there was no clerk and asked, "What's the number of your room?"

"Room? Oh—207," he whispered. "Don't know if I can . . . climb the stairs, miss."

The stairs did turn out to be difficult. Katy had to struggle to get him up each step, and they paused at the landing to let him rest. His face was drawn, and his mouth fell open with pain and exhaustion. Feebly shaking his head, he muttered, "Let me . . . lie down!"

"No, you've got to get into a bed!" Katy redoubled her efforts, and by the time they reached the top of the stairwell, she was afraid the effort was too much for the old man. But she half dragged him down the hall, and when they came to room 207, she asked, "Where's your key?" She took it when he retrieved it from his vest pocket after much fumbling, then managed to open the door without letting go of him.

The room she found herself in was a sitting room. A lamp was burning low on a table beside a horsehair sofa. A door to the left—evidently leading to the bedroom—was covered with a brown drape of some sort. "Come along, we'll get you to bed," she said, moving toward it.

"No . . . just let me rest . . . on the sofa!"

He looked so terrible that Katy agreed. He slumped down on the horsehair sofa, and Katy lifted his feet so that he lay down. "I'll go for a doctor," she said and turned to leave.

"No! Don't . . . leave me!" Fear had washed across the old man's face, and he nodded at the table where a pitcher of water stood. "Just a little . . . water."

Katy quickly poured a glass of water and held his head up as he drank it. "I've got to get help. Do you have any relatives?"

"No, not here." He blinked and whispered, "My name is Samuel Bronte."

"I'm Katherine Steele."

Bronte leaned his head back and breathed deeply. "I'll be all right in a few minutes. If you'd just wait—"

"You've had these attacks before? What does the doctor say?"

"Says I'm getting old." Bronte lay silently, then presently began to talk. His speech was slurred, and he lost track of what he was saying, as old men sometimes do. He spoke of his daughter in San Francisco several times, seeming to long for her.

"You should go to her, Mr. Bronte," Katy said, "if you have no relatives to take care of you here."

Bronte put his hands over his face and shook his head. He said nothing for a long time, then muttered, "I want to . . . but I don't have . . . money for the fare."

Katy hesitated, then said, "The fare to San Francisco can't be all that much."

"Only nine dollars . . . but I . . . I don't have it."

"Well, I do." Katy reached into her purse and pulled out a few bills. Thrusting them into the old man's hand, she said firmly, "It will be a loan. You can send it back to me when you get to your daughter's house."

Bronte lay absolutely still, the bills in his hand. Katy thought he meant to refuse them—but then he lifted the bills high and called out loudly, "How about that, Brinkley? Does that do it?"

Katy was startled at the change in Bronte's voice, which was no longer feeble, but strong and resonant. Then when he jumped up from the couch in one smooth movement, a smile on his face, she knew that something was terribly wrong.

A sound of muffled laughter to her left caused her to whirl around, and she saw the brown drape abruptly part, and a man stepped inside the room. Instantly fear washed over Katy, for though the newcomer was well dressed and seemed respectable enough, the thought of being in a hotel room with two strange men paralyzed her.

Brinkley was smiling broadly, his small dark eyes gleaming. "Well, Sam, I guess you win the bet," he said to Bronte. "I never thought you could pull it off!"

"You're a good loser, Brinkley." Bronte was smiling now, but he turned to Katy and saw that her lips were tight, and she was staring at him with fear in her eyes. "Now, don't be afraid, Miss Steele—," he began, but Katy whirled and started for the door. "Now, just a minute," Bronte said quickly. "Let me explain this to you—"

"Let me out of here!"

The man called Brinkley had stopped laughing. He was a self-assured man of forty with slick black hair and a mustache, and a bold light in his dark eyes. "Let me explain this to the lady, Sam," he said. "It's just a little bet, miss—no harm intended." When he saw that his words meant nothing to the woman, he smiled and waved a well-manicured hand, "Look, it's kind of a joke. You've got a sense of humor, I hope?"

"Please—let me go!" Katy said tersely. She normally did not give in to fear, but the surprising turn of events took her off guard. She had heard of women being kidnapped off the street and used for immoral purposes, and now she feared for her life. Pulling her arm loose from Bronte's grasp, she said in a determined voice, "I'll scream if you don't let me out!"

"Why, Miss—Steele, is it?" Brinkley said quickly. "Look, just listen for thirty seconds. I'm sorry we frightened you, but this is all on the up-and-up." He waved his hand at Bronte saying, "Show her what you really are, Sam."

Bronte reached up and pulled the white mustache and beard from his face, then withdrew a handkerchief and scrubbed heavy makeup from his features. The cloth came away smeared with flesh-toned and dark hues. Katy gasped when she saw that the wrinkles that had made the man seem very old had disappeared. The white eyebrows went next as Bronte said with a smile, "Don't feel badly, Miss Steele. You did a noble deed, coming to the aid of an elderly man." He carefully peeled off what Katy saw was a white wig, and she saw that Bronte's hair was shoulder length, black, and slightly curly.

Brinkley chuckled. "You see, Miss Steele, Sam here is an actor. He wants me to back a play for him."

Katy stared at the face of Bronte, who said quickly, "This is

7

Mr. Charles Brinkley." He smiled, and his white teeth gleamed against his dark skin. He was, Katy judged, in his late twenties. "It's pretty hard for an actor to get backing, but with your help, it looks like I've made it."

Brinkley laughed and shook his head. "Well, I don't know too much about acting. Not in my line. And when I sink money into a venture, I make sure things are in my favor. So I made a little deal with Sam here. I told him he'd have to prove to me he could really act! Sort of take a test, you see."

Katy was beginning to understand a little more clearly. The fear was leaving her, and for the second time that day, she felt anger trying to take her over. "And what exactly was this 'test'?"

Brinkley caught the diamond-hard note in the woman's voice and grew alarmed. "Why, I'll let Sam tell you about that. It's really his deal."

Bronte had also noted the offense in the woman's hazel-green eyes. *If she wants to make trouble, she can do it,* he thought abruptly. *Women like this sometimes have husbands and brothers with guns.* Aloud he said smoothly, "Oh, Mr. Brinkley said he wanted to see if I could act out a role. If I could convince someone—a stranger—in the part, he'd back the play."

"Sure, that's it," Brinkley said nervously. He was not a timid man, but there was something in Katy Steele's expression that made him wish he'd never agreed to the plan. "So I told Sam it would have to be a hard test. What we decided was that Sam would have to convince some woman he was sick and get her to help him to his room—a respectable woman, you understand?"

Bronte saw the eyes of the young woman fasten on him and said hastily, "Part of the test was the woman had to offer me money. It sounds pretty silly now, but no harm done." Still the eyes bored into his, and he added lamely, "I'd like to have you come to the play—as my guest, Miss Steele. . . ."

His words trailed off as he saw her whirl and head for the door without a word. He exchanged a troubled glance with Brinkley. The two men stood there until the door slammed, and Brinkley cursed angrily. "See what a fool thing this was! She could have both of us in jail!"

"It was your idea, Charles!"

"Go after her." Brinkley pulled out a white handkerchief and wiped his brow. "You call yourself an actor—well, act your way out of this thing. Now go make that woman happy, and don't come to me until you've settled it!"

Bronte stared down at the smaller man, eyes growing narrow. "You're looking for a way to welsh on the bet, I see. You wait here. I'll calm her down—then we can talk." He moved to the door, and as he left the room, his mind was working fast. He ran to the stairs and saw that the woman was just turning toward the lobby. Taking the stairs three at a time, he crossed the lobby and caught up with Katy as she reached the door. "Please—Miss Steele," he said urgently. "Let me speak with you for just a moment!"

"You have another act for me, Mr. Bronte?" Katy's voice was flat, but a river never ran colder than the tone she used on him. "You don't care who you hurt, do you?"

Bronte was already ashamed of what he had done, and the sight of her pale face and the slight tremor in her lips sent a wave of regret through him. He hesitated, unable to find the words he needed—which was unusual for him. He was very quick witted and had talked himself out of many tight spots, but the sight of Katy Steele's strained face silenced him.

"Pretty cheap fun, wasn't it?" Katy demanded.

She went through the door and started down the steps, but Bronte rushed to cut her off. "Miss Steele, please forgive me, I—"

Katy just wanted to go home and try to forget the rotten morning. "Mr. Bronte, I ought to have the police on you and your friend, but what I want the most right this minute is for you to let me pass, please." Bronte did, and Katy walked away tight lipped and feeling miserable.

Bronte felt a sudden touch on his elbow and was so startled that he wheeled around quickly. He found himself facing a large, red-faced man who was watching him with a pair of cold blue eyes. "I'm Manning, the owner," the big man said carefully. "I don't stand for funny stuff in my place. Check out of your room, Mr. Bronte—and don't come back."

Sam Bronte could not meet Manning's hard eyes. Suddenly he was weary and sick of himself. "All right," he said quietly. "I'll clear out as soon as I get my clothes. No trouble."

When he returned to his room, he found Charles Brinkley waiting nervously. "Did you get it straight with her?"

"She's gone," Bronte answered shortly. "I don't think she'll make trouble."

Relief washed across the smooth face of Brinkley. "Well, that's good, Sam." He pulled out a cigar and lit it with a kitchen match. When it was burning, he blew a plume of blue smoke upward, then nodded. "Blasted fool thing to do! I don't let myself get caught fooling with decent women. Good way to get killed."

Bronte saw the other man move toward the door. "You want to talk about the play, Charles?"

Brinkley squinted his eyes, studying the other man. "Come and see me in a week or so," he murmured. "A venture like this, it needs a lot of thought."

When the door closed, Bronte stared at it, his eyes growing hard. "Well—so much for that," he whispered, then turned to pack his clothes, knowing that he'd missed the chance he'd worked so hard for.

———⊰⊱———

Outside, the dark clouds closed in on the street, but Katy took no notice. She was struggling to thrust the deceitful incident to the back of her mind and examine the failed job interview. Three times before she had been turned down for similar jobs because she was a woman, and this fourth time she was taking it more personally. *What will it take to be hired to do a job I would love?*

For the past few months, she had been teaching first through sixth grade at a local school and had recognized from the start that she was not cut out to be a teacher. She was intelligent and knew the subject matter well, but she couldn't seem to break down a barrier that existed between herself and the children. They sensed an aloofness in her and responded to it by distancing themselves from her. She couldn't seem to overcome their mistrust of her. *I was never a happy child myself—no wonder I can't get on their level.* The thought was an enlightenment, and she felt her eyes water. She knew it was self-pity that gripped her, but the tears still came.

Stopping to retrieve a handkerchief, she noticed a small red-haired girl wearing a yellow dress rolling a hoop down the sidewalk. As she approached, the girl skillfully snatched up the hoop and stared up, asking, "Lady, are you all right?"

Katy stared at the girl, wiping away the tears. Her throat was thick, but she managed to nod and summoned up a faint smile. "Yes, I'm fine."

"You don't look good. Are you sick?"

Katy swallowed hard but said, "It's nice of you to notice, but you'd better be careful of strangers. You never—you never—" And then she could say no more and so stepped past the child and hurried down the windy street.

The girl's voice came to her, floating on the air. "I ain't afraid of no strangers—not me! I can take care of myself!"

The wind was rising, and the keening sound grated on Katy's nerves as she moved down the street. Gusts of wind picked up pieces of paper and hustled them along the cobblestones. From the west came the muted roar of a stronger gale, and the shadowy street seemed to close in on itself, or so it seemed to Katy as she made

11

her way along. A sudden bolt of lightning clawed its way across the sky. She stared at it, waiting for the thunder. She always did that, having learned that she could tell how far away the lightning was by allowing one second for each mile.

One—two—three—four—five, she counted to herself, and when the hoarse voice of the thunder boomed, she listened to it, thinking dully that the storm was five miles away, but coming toward the city. Her feet felt heavy, and as she moved along she seemed to hear the voice of the young girl—proud and defiant: *I ain't afraid of no strangers—not me! I can take care of myself!*

"She'll learn better when she gets older," Katy whispered, a bitter note in her voice.

The lightning flickered again, and she pulled her coat more tightly around her throat as she headed toward home.

CHAPTER TWO

Two Are Better than One

The thunderstorm broke as soon as Katy opened the gate of the small picket fence that fronted a two-story stone house on the edge of the Sacramento business district. Taking her skirts in hand, she raced up the walk to the front steps as huge raindrops began to fall.

Inside the small foyer she removed her hat and coat, still mired in her dark mood. She couldn't help thinking how typical the dark rain was on a day like this. Turning from the closet, she almost ran into her aunt.

"Oh—Aunt Agnes, I didn't hear you come down." Katy stepped back uncomfortably from the tall figure of Agnes Teller. It had always disturbed her when her aunt seemed to materialize in some sort of ghostly fashion.

"I was in the kitchen making myself a sandwich," Agnes replied. She was the older sister of Katy's father—a tall, angular woman with iron gray hair pulled back into a tight bun so severe as to look painful. Her smallish brown eyes never seemed to miss a detail, and she had a permanently pursed mouth. She was an altogether imposing figure—never comfortable to be with.

"Well, I'll just go change into some dry clothes."

Katy started for the stairs to her room, but her aunt's thin, rather nasal voice probed at her. "Katherine, the least you can do is tell me the results of your interview." Somehow Agnes had the ability to make Katy feel guilty, even over small things, and there was a harsh light in her eyes as she added, "You might have a little consideration for others, Katherine."

Katy turned and started to respond when a blinding flash of light accompanied by crashing thunder came through the small window in the front door. She jumped at the noise, and she thought she could feel the house vibrate. But Agnes had not moved a muscle. She stood there, the corners of her lips pulled down in a frown, and Katy knew she could not put off the subject. "I didn't get the job," she muttered, staring at the pattern in the worn carpet.

"I *knew* it!" Agnes exclaimed almost triumphantly. "I still can't understand why you even had your hopes up. Your place is in a schoolroom teaching children, not in some smelly laboratory working with men!"

"Aunt Agnes, I can't spend the rest of my life trying to educate little heathens! I was meant to do something more with my life." Katy had hoped to avoid her aunt. She was tense and upset as it was, and Aunt Agnes usually intensified the feelings. Katy knew she didn't deliberately provoke her, but the end result was still distressing.

"Katherine, come and sit down." Agnes turned and walked abruptly to the parlor, which was dark as usual. A single whale-oil lamp cast an amber glow over the well-kept old furniture. Katy sat down on the horsehair sofa, which seemed to have been designed for the torture of the human spine and, glancing at her aunt, thought grimly, *Here comes her it's-a-man's-world speech.*

"It's a man's world, dear," Agnes started, "and men still have a hard time accepting that a woman can perform certain tasks that have been inherently done by them." She paused and drew her thin lips into a line, her eyes glinting like flint. "We do not encourage this way of thinking, but we must adhere to it. I learned very early in my marriage to Fred that it was perfectly acceptable for him to

14

attend scientific conferences—and drink and womanize all night!—just as long as I stayed in our home and took care of my domestic responsibilities." Her eyes glinted with anger as she remembered her years of enduring Fred's free lifestyle. "That's why I have taught you not to draw attention to yourself where men are concerned—to save you from a life of pain and heartache such as I have endured."

Katy's mother had died during childbirth, so her aunt had become her surrogate mother. For as long as Katy could remember, Agnes had always dressed her in drab, loose-fitting clothes. She didn't find out until she started school that other girls were allowed to wear anything besides brown or gray dresses that were bulky and hot in the summertime and constricting in the winter.

For some reason an old memory surfaced in Katy's mind, and even as Agnes spoke on about the dangers facing a young woman in the evil world, she thought of the time when her father had purchased a beautiful, stylish white cotton summer dress for her to wear to a birthday party for a girl who lived down the street. Katy was sixteen years old, and her father had even allowed a boy named Micah Davis to take her. The party had gone well, and Micah had been a perfect gentleman until they had found themselves alone in the kitchen at one point. He'd tried to kiss her, catching her totally off guard, and when she'd resisted, his efforts doubled in intensity. Katy's hands tightened as she thought of that time—and how she'd jerked away and run all the way home and pulled off the white dress. Weeping and sobbing, she had told Aunt Agnes about it, who had replied, "Now you know what to watch for, Katherine. Boys are the same as men—only wanting to possess women as they would a pretty bauble and do with them as they please!" The incident had affected Katy deeply, and she had never been alone with a boy or man since. Not that the opportunity had presented itself very often; men sensed the remote and cringing little girl inside and shied away from her.

Agnes saw her shiver and said, "Go upstairs and change clothes. Your father will be home shortly."

Katy considered telling Aunt Agnes about the incident with Sam Bronte but quickly dismissed the thought. Though her aunt was a well-meaning woman, she wasn't the type that would listen to her feelings—the details of the event would only bring on another lecture.

As Katy climbed the stairs, hearing the familiar creak in the third and fourth boards, she instinctively stopped midway. Her eyes lifted to the painting of the mother she never knew hanging on the opposite wall across the hall. Great, brown doe eyes stared back at her as Emily Steele, forever sitting on a crimson divan in a fine room, half smiled at her. Katy's father had had the painting commissioned right after they had learned they were to be parents. Katy again found herself searching her mother's middle as she'd done countless times, seeking a sign of the growing life inside her. However, there was nothing of the infant Katy in the painting—nothing except the glow on her mother's face. John Steele was proud of the fact and told anyone who saw it that the painter had no idea Emily was expecting a baby. But guests that saw the beautiful woman invariably made comments like "What a radiant woman!" or "She certainly had a glow about her, didn't she, John?" Katy's father would visibly swell up with pride and tell the story of a simple painter, the only one John could afford at the time, who'd perfectly captured his dear wife in the prime of her life—the hope, the happiness, the desires, and most of all, the maternal shine.

What were your hopes for me, Mama? Katy asked the portrait for the thousandth time. *What were your dreams?* She shook her head faintly and continued up the stairs, thinking darkly, *Whatever they were, I'm sure they didn't include an unmarried woman with no hint of a future living with her father.*

Pickles the cat was curled up on Katy's bed. The red tiger-striped feline stretched lazily when the bed sank from Katy's weight on the edge. "What a life, Pickles. Nothing to do but try to keep from falling off a bed all day." The tomcat had earned the name from his love for crunching sweet pickles. He would subsist on them if given the chance.

After scratching him between the ears for a while, Katy rose and crossed her immaculate room to the window. The storm had passed by and left the street coated with reddish mud. As she watched, the sun broke through. A few boys from surrounding houses appeared, and for some time she watched them play baseball, their shrill cries rising to her window. The sport had so grown in popularity that all over the country a person would be hard pressed not to find boys playing it.

Katy moved to her large mahogany dresser and picked up the *Sacramento Sentinel*. It was dated October 12, 1867. It was three days old, but she'd noted an editorial she wanted to keep. Her father was a detective for the fledgling Central Pacific Railroad, and she was interested in anything concerning the Central. Sitting down in the straight-back cane-bottomed chair in front of her dressing table, she read the article:

> All citizens of our fair state must be proud of the building of the transcontinental railroad, for it is an endeavor that will benefit all Americans. We in Sacramento have a special pride in this mighty work, for the offices of the Central Pacific are in our city, and the officials of the line are all Californians.
>
> However, it has come as a disappointment to all thoughtful citizens to see that the construction of the railroad has been marred by corrupt and savage competition between the Central Pacific and the Union Pacific. Only last week a half-built bridge only ten miles out of Sacramento collapsed, and Mr. John Steele, a detective for the Central Pacific, has stated that evidence proves that the bridge was deliberately destroyed.

The Union Pacific—commissioned to bring the rail across the country from the east—has been charged by Leland Stanford with sabotage, while the spokesman for the Union Pacific, William Durant, has filed countercharges against the Central Pacific.

This editor cannot lay the blame on either line, but we do ask that the officials of both the Union and the Central lay aside such vile practices. The building of a transcontinental railroad involves enormous amounts of money, and where that condition exists, corrupt men will rush in. We insist that the leadership of both construction companies put aside any personal interest and observe sound ethics during the building of the railroad.

Katy began to feel somewhat nervous about her father's return. As a detective for the Central Pacific Railroad, he could almost set his own hours. He was, however, often called away east, where the railroad was being built slowly but inexorably toward a meeting with the Union Pacific Railroad that had started out from Omaha, Nebraska. The Central had bogged down in the Sierra Nevada Mountains—ninety miles away—and was having to use black powder to blast away rock and stone in the sides of the mountains to create a path for the rail. John Steele was often called to Cisco, the small city that had sprung up around the supply depot for the railroad. The rivalry between the UP and the CP to see who could get the farthest the fastest (and get the most government loan money in so doing) was so intense that her father was constantly having to investigate sabotage in some area around the rail.

Katy put the paper down and began undressing, thinking of her rejection that morning. *Papa will understand,* she thought. *No one understands like he does.*

Out of the corner of her eye she caught a glimpse of herself and turned to a full-length mirror. She spent less time before her mirror, perhaps, than any other twenty-five-year-old woman in Sacramento. But now she examined her face carefully, noticing the pronounced widow's peak in her ash-blonde hair. She had beautiful hair but kept it pinned back as Aunt Agnes had taught her. Her face was square, with heavy brown eyebrows, a straight, slightly upturned nose, high cheekbones, a determined chin, and a flawless complexion. She would never be beautiful enough for the stage; there was too much strength in her face for that.

Stepping back, she considered herself at full length. Katy was tall for a woman and many times found herself looking down on men from her five-foot-eight-inch height, which she found to be a handicap instead of an advantage. Her 130 pounds were well distributed, but she herself thought too much of it lay in her shoulders and hips. Actually she had a fine figure, but she was never happy with her appearance. She sighed, turning away from the mirror. *Well, having a man to put up with for the rest of my life is the last thing I should be worried about!*

Slipping into a simple brown dress and a long white apron, she made her way down the hall to a room at the end. She opened the door and immediately noticed the rats were bothering the rabbits.

Her Uncle Fred had been a scientific genius who had insisted on having his own laboratory in his home. Had he been a frugal man, he could have afforded to buy his own factory from the money he had made from discoveries, inventions, and patents. But Uncle Fred had had a weakness for the bottle and strange women—the former having killed him a little over a year before. But the alcohol could not dim the extremely sharp mind he put to use on scientific discovery. His special interest had been a field called *pathology*— the study of deadly diseases. How many hours Katy had spent in this room as a little girl, watching, listening, and learning. Everything had fascinated her, from the myriad of beakers to the sometimes horrible smells his experiments provided. Katy had been like a sponge, soaking up everything with her adolescent mind, and at seventeen she had attended Mills College for Women at Oakland and breezed through the science courses easily.

She looked up at the daguerreotype over the line of test tubes and smiled at the round face in the mahogany frame. There was an impish look in the small eyes of her uncle, and Katy thought of the years she'd worked for him as a student and assistant. He had been highly immoral—a fact he never hid from her. But for four years he had poured his immense knowledge into her. After his death, Katy had been forced to look for employment, but she remembered with longing the days she'd spent in this place with him. *I wish you were here, Uncle Fred,* she thought, moving away from the picture.

Katy kept rats and rabbits for her own experiments, and today the rats were running all over their cages, fighting and rolling around, making the rabbits very nervous. As she was feeding them, she heard a deep voice from behind her. "Playing with your pets, Gabby?" Katy started and turned, finding a playful smile on her father's face.

"Papa!" she exclaimed and rushed over to him to give him a hug. "First Aunt Agnes sneaks up on me and now you!" She looked up into his laughing hazel eyes and felt the familiar rush of love that always flooded her when she hadn't seen him for a while.

John Steele chuckled and said, "How is Gabby today?" His pet name for her had come from Gabriel, the archangel. He had called her his "little angel" until he had seen how big she was going to be. One day when she was nine, he had said with a serious look, "You aren't going to be my little angel much longer." Katy, hurt to the core, had asked why. "Because, the way you're growing, you'll have to be my big angel! I'll call you Gabby, for Gabriel, the biggest angel of them all!" Katy had squealed with delight, and from then on her father had called her nothing else—except for Katherine when he was disciplining her.

"I'm fine, Papa; how are you?" Then, not giving him time to answer, she asked, "How long are you home this time?"

"Just for a day or two. Looks like things are getting worse with the railroad instead of better. I have to go back to Cisco on Thursday." Katy's face fell in disappointment, but her father added quickly, "But I have someone I want you to meet." He turned toward the hall and motioned. Through the door came a short, elderly Oriental man. His head was shaved except for a small round patch of hair at the crown of his head from which sprouted a two-foot-long ponytail. He was dressed in a very plain dark blue coolie outfit that all the Chinese workers for the railroad wore. Katy had seen some of them arriving from China by boat when she had been in Oakland. "This is Chang Li. He's going to be our new houseman."

Chang bowed deeply and said, "Nice meet you, Miss Kahtee."

"Thank you, Chang. It's very nice to meet you," Katy answered, smiling at his extreme politeness.

"Chang was just getting too old to be throwing railroad ties and rails around. I knew Agnes could use some help, so I asked him if he would come to Sacramento to work for a while," John said. He leaned toward Katy and said quietly, "His wife and daughter were killed in an explosion at the depot. They were in the wrong place at the wrong time. I am so sick of these sabotages!" His eyes flared with anger.

"Chang, I am so very sorry!" exclaimed Katy, making a mental note to discuss the newspaper article with her father later.

Chang bowed low again. "Many tanks, Miss Kahtee, but it happen very long time ago. Wife and daughter with Jesus now."

"Why, Chang, it was only six months ago!" John said in surprise.

"Seem long time. Jesus make Chang pain go 'way, mostly."

John shot a glance at Katy, then looked back at Chang. "Why don't you let Agnes show you around the house and where you'll be staying?"

Chang bowed once again and said, "Chang wish to tank Mistah John again for job."

"Don't mention it. You'll have your work cut out for you having to put up with my sister all day long."

Chang bowed to Katy and left.

Katy looked at her father with questioning eyes. John said, "He recently converted to Christianity from Buddhism. He expresses his faith in a far more demonstrative manner than we're used to. I hope you aren't uncomfortable with him."

Katy and her father had attended a rather formal Methodist church for years. Katy had accepted Christ as a girl of fourteen but had never seemed as happy in her faith as John would have liked. She had attended services and even sung in the choir, but somehow she seemed isolated from the real life of the church.

"Of course not," Katy answered. "Chang's refreshing. He sure doesn't seem like anyone we see at St. Matthew's on Sunday morning," Katy remarked. "Do you think he'd want to go to church with us?"

John Steele considered the question for a moment. "You could ask him, but I believe he would be out of place. I'm not sure how the elders would react to having not only a Chinese but a fanatical one at that." While John liked Chang, he knew his peers were too used to the status quo to embrace such a novel new member.

"Oh, Papa! What's more important? Not upsetting some stuffy old men or making a new friend feel welcome?"

"You do have a point, Gabby," her father conceded. "And since I'll be out of town this weekend, it will fall to you to introduce Chang to the congregation. That way," he continued with a smile, *"you* can have the pleasure of upsetting the 'stuffy old men'!"

"It'll be worth it, Papa. Chang seems so sweet."

"That sweet man almost killed the poor fool that set that bomb. Took a rail hammer to him after we caught the fellow! It took three men to pull him off." The memory troubled him, and he shook his shoulders slightly in distaste. Glad to change the subject, he asked, "So, tell me about the interview."

"It was very short and not sweet."

"Didn't get the job?" asked John.

"No, Papa, and I'll never try for another one!" Katy shook her head fiercely. "I'll just keep teaching until I'm old and gray and keel over at my desk!"

"Now, Gabby, you'll find the right job someday. It's just a matter of finding where you're supposed to be in the scheme of things. Providence will find you a place."

"But even if I do, Papa, no one will hire me because I'm so plain and clumsy!"

"What?" John exclaimed, shocked. He took her in his arms and cradled her head on his shoulder. "Where is all that coming from?"

Katy sighed deeply. "Oh, Papa, I'm just having a bad day. I didn't mean it."

John pushed her away to arm's length and said, "Now listen to me very carefully, Gabby. You are a very pretty young lady and have absolutely nothing to be ashamed of." His eyes bored into hers with an intensity that surprised her. "There are a few things I disagree with my sister about in raising you, and one of them is the way she seems to have made you feel about yourself. I know I haven't been there for you very much—no, no, it's true. But I'll promise you right now that things will be different in the future, starting when I get back from my next trip. It's about time I started training a new man to take over anyway."

"Are you feeling all right, Papa?" Katy asked instantly.

"Yes, yes, I'm fine, but it's about time to think about retiring. We need some time together—you and me." He smiled at her and added, "How about another surprise?"

"What is it?" Katy asked, already feeling better. Her father never failed to bring her out of her doldrums instantly.

"How about lunch with Huntington, Stanford, and me tomorrow?"

"Oh, that would be wonderful! I've been wanting to meet them ever since you began working for the Central."

"It's a date, then," John said. He put a finger under her chin

23

and lifted her eyes to meet his. "And no more about homeliness, OK?"

"Yes, Papa," Katy said, smiling.

"Good. Let's go have some dinner."

———

As Katy went downstairs the next morning she was met at the foot of the stairs by Chang. "Good morning, Chang. I hope you slept well last night?"

He bowed deeply, saying, "Slept very well, Miss Kahtee, tank you. Much bettah than listening to many people snore in big tent!" He smiled and showed big, white, horsey teeth. "Miss Kahtee like breakfahs?"

"No, thank you. I don't eat in the mornings usually—and my father and I are going out for an early lunch. Have you seen him?"

"He in office. Please excuse." He bowed and went back into the kitchen.

Katy went to her father's office and opened the door without knocking. The room had a permanent tobacco smell, pleasing rather than offensive since John Steele favored a pipe while he was working. A wing-back chair rested behind a huge Sheraton desk. Made of black walnut with carved wheat ears as ornamentation, the desk had been his father's, who had purchased it in London during the 1820s. Many times when her father was away for extended periods, Katy would come into the office to sit behind the massive desk. The room exuded masculinity, and she felt close to him when she entered.

John was standing at his desk with his arms braced on either side of several documents. He did not hear her come in, and as she watched him for a moment, he brought one hand to his chin and rubbed it gently. Katy knew that was his way of showing anxiety. He then grunted and shook his head.

"Big problem, Papa?" she asked.

He looked up, startled, and said, "Gabby!" Nervously he began to gather up all the papers, actually dropping a few. After retrieving them all, he shoved them in a drawer at the top of the desk, pulled out a key, and locked it. "I didn't hear you come in."

"Is something wrong?"

He stroked his chin, glanced at the drawer, and said, "Why, no, not really. I was just finishing something I've been working on all morning. Are you almost ready to go?"

Katy pressed on. "Papa, I've never seen you use the lock on that drawer. Are you sure you don't want to talk about something?"

He came around the desk and said, "I'm fine, Gabby. I've just never had papers that important in the house before, and I don't want them misplaced when Agnes or Chang clean in here."

She nodded uncertainly, then managed a smile. "I see—and yes, I'm ready."

"Fine. I'll get my coat and hail a carriage." He left, and Katy looked at the desk once more before following.

They chatted all the way downtown, and Katy felt relieved when she saw no sign of nervousness in his manner. The cab stopped in front of a large brownstone building, and he helped her out, saying, "This is the Bull Ring, Gabby. It's a good restaurant, and most big deals get settled in here."

The restaurant was lavishly decorated, with hanging crystal chandeliers and velvet curtains. The crowd was sparse, but everyone was immaculately dressed, making Katy feel slightly uncomfortable in her older but clean blue hoop skirt. The maître d' approached with a smile. "Good morning, Mr. Steele. Mr. Huntington and the governor are right this way." He smiled and led them to another room that was beautifully furnished and had only four tables. At one of them, two men stood upon seeing John and Katy.

"Good morning, John," the taller of the two said with a deep, booming voice. He was barrel-chested and gave the impression of enormous self-confidence.

"Good morning, Governor," John said and turned to Katy. "My dear, let me introduce you to Governor Leland Stanford and Mr. Collis Huntington. Gentlemen, Katherine Steele."

"An honor, Katherine," said Stanford. "I'm so glad you could lunch with us."

Then Huntington took Katy's hand. "How nice to finally meet you, Katy. John has told us so much about you I feel we're already acquainted." He spoke with a heavy northeastern accent. Katy remembered reading somewhere that he was from Connecticut. He had a stern look, with a graying beard and strong face. The top of his head was bald, and what little hair he possessed circled his pate in a half-moon.

"Thank you, gentlemen. I'm very pleased to finally meet the most famous men in California!" Katy said rather breathlessly. She took her seat, feeling overawed and uncomfortable because of the pure magnitude of these men's reputations. Both men had been merchants in California and had gotten wealthy from the booming gold rushes—Stanford in hardware, Huntington in dry goods with Mark Hopkins, another owner in the railroad. Stanford had been elected governor in 1861 and had served three years before finally becoming president of the CP. Huntington was vice president of the railroad and was considered the most influential man in Washington.

Huntington dismissed the compliment with a wave of his hand as they all sat down. "Nonsense, my dear. In some circles we are considered infamous, especially in the camp of the Union Pacific! Speaking of which, John, any news as of yesterday?"

"No. All was going well when I left."

Stanford turned to Katy, his eyes suddenly stormy. "The UP will stop at nothing to slow us down! It seems there is some new strategy being carried out lately, with our own workers behaving treacherously."

Huntington sipped his coffee, then shrugged. "Strictly among the Irish laborers, Leland. The Chinese have exceeded every ex-

pectation of character and ability. Not to mention they're a better bargain from the business end of it, working for lower wages than the Irish."

"You have to hire more guards," Stanford said grimly. "John, this destruction has to end."

John Steele spoke carefully. "It's not a matter of hiring more men, Mr. Stanford. There's just too much area to cover. The most important matter right now, in my opinion, is to hire an assistant that I can train in helping me weed out the saboteurs before they strike. I can't track down every rumor I hear about by myself. There are simply too many."

Both men looked at each other and seemed to come to a conclusion without a word. "Very well," Huntington said. "Get right on it." The waiter brought coffee, and Huntington took a careful sip. "And, John, remember you've been a thorn in the side of the Union. They might have decided to go after you—so watch yourself."

Katy looked at her father, suddenly alarmed. John noticed and said, "It's all right, Gabby. I take precautions." He turned to the men and said, "I don't think they'll focus on one man. They only seem concerned with the rail itself—but not caring who gets hurt in the process."

Katy blurted, "I read in the *Sentinel* the Union claims of the Central sabotaging *their* construction." She was simply trying to join in the conversation but immediately wished she had kept her mouth shut. All three men turned to her swiftly, her father in surprise, Huntington in contemplation, and Stanford with the frightening icy eyes she had noticed earlier.

Huntington snapped instantly, "We do not condone that sort of behavior, nor do we practice it!" He was staring at her with an appraising look, as if noticing her for the first time.

"I'm s-sorry, I d-didn't mean to imply—," Katy stammered.

Stanford leaned forward and was suddenly all smiles. The quick transformation had been remarkable. He was a handsome man,

27

obviously accustomed to handling people. "Quite all right, Katy. It's a logical question, but please let us put your mind at ease. The sabotage can be laid at the door of the Union Pacific. There is no wrongdoing on our part." He was smiling but seemed to continue to regard her warily.

"Shall we order some lunch?" John asked, smoothly trying to change the subject.

"Yes—and John, go ahead and hire an assistant," Huntington said. "The best one you can find." They turned to other matters of business and political gossip, and they went out of their way to include Katy in the conversation. She said little but listened carefully, learning firsthand how the giants who controlled history conducted business.

After the meal was over and they'd stepped outside, John said, "Let's walk home, Gabby."

They had only walked a block, Katy's arm through his, when he gave a little chuckle. Katy looked up at him and said, "What is it, Papa?"

"I was just thinking how much you are like your mother sometimes." He smiled while remembering something. "One New Year's Eve we were at a policemen's ball. Your mother and I were talking with the chief of police, the mayor, and their wives. The mayor had presented me with a commendation for bravery earlier—I had stepped in front of a bullet meant for him, from some man who had it in his head that the mayor was the devil incarnate—which was probably close to the truth! Your mother was reading the document, and she looked right at the mayor and said, 'Why, this occurred on Bayside Street! There are nothing but houses of ill repute in that area! What in the world were you doing down there, Mayor?'"

John Steele laughed aloud and squeezed Katy's arm. "Before that time, I had never heard the sound of twenty conversations stopping at once. The mayor looked like he'd swallowed a particularly bad-tasting bug. I guess he suddenly realized his marriage and political

career hung dangerously in the balance with twenty pairs of eyes goggling at us. He stammered, 'Ahem—my *dear* Mrs. Steele—that was—ah—right before the election, and there are definitely votes to be won in *that* section of the city, as in any other.'"

"What else happened, Papa?"

"Oh, everyone tried to ignore it, and after people had resumed their chatting, she turned to me and asked, 'At three o'clock in the morning?'" John laughed a deep, throaty laugh at the memory. "So you see, Gabby, this was not the first time I've had to sidestep touchy situations."

Katy put a hand to her forehead and said, "I can't believe those words just slipped out like that. I've never been so embarrassed!"

"It's all right, dear. I'm sure neither man will consider you anything else but a sharp woman. You do have a very quick mind about you, Gabby." He frowned and shook his head, adding, "I'd hate to see it go to waste doing something you can't stand for the rest of your life. Please don't get discouraged and quit searching for a job in the scientific field."

"I won't, Papa. But it seems hopeless."

"And do we have any thoughts of entertaining suitors anytime soon?" he asked with a glint in his eyes.

"All I want is a career right now," Katy said rather sharply, but she thought, *I haven't seen suitors beating my door down.*

"Well, I know a lot of people. We'll find something for you, Gabby."

Katy stopped him with her arm and gazed into his eyes worriedly. "About this danger they were talking about . . ."

He smiled and patted her arm affectionately. "Oh, don't you worry, Gabby. I can take care of myself."

The words hit a familiar note in Katy, and suddenly she remembered the little girl in the street, who had said the exact thing: *I ain't afraid of no strangers—not me. I can take care of myself!* The memory brought back the pain she felt after the confrontation with Sam Bronte. She considered telling her father about it but decided he had enough on his mind without taking on her problems.

—⊶⊷—

"I should be back in about a week. Remember what I said about taking time off so we can be together more? How about going to the theater? We haven't done that in years."

"Oh, yes!" Katy hugged her father, looking up at him with a sudden smile. The two of them had spent most of their time together since their lunch with Stanford and Huntington, and she said, "This has been wonderful, Papa—doing things with you."

Steele stroked her smooth cheek, saying, "This is the way it's going to be, Gabby. As soon as I get that assistant trained, we'll have all the time in the world."

"That would be wonderful, Papa!" The two of them stood there, reluctant to end the fine time they'd had.

Finally Steele said, "I'm thinking of a verse my mother taught me—don't know why, but it just popped into my mind."

"A verse from the Bible or a poem?"

"The Bible, of course." Steele's eyes grew thoughtful, and he said quietly, "Your grandmother was a great one for reading the Scriptures."

"What was the verse, Papa?"

"I don't know where it is, but it says, 'Two are better than one; because they have a good reward for their labour. For if they fall, the one will lift up his fellow: but woe to him that is alone when he falleth; for he hath not another to help him up.'"

Katy touched his cheek. "It's a good verse, Papa. And you and I are like that. I'll never have a husband, I don't think—but I've got you and you've got me."

"Don't really agree with the husband part," Steele said slowly, "but you and me, we've got to help each other." He leaned down and kissed her cheek, whispering, "I love you, Gabby!" Then he turned, picked up his suitcase, and walked to where the cab was waiting. When he was inside, the cabdriver said, "Hup, Babe!" and the horse started off.

Katy waved, calling, "Bye, Papa!"

John Steele put his head out of the window, waved at her, and called out, "Remember—two are better than one!"

And then the cab picked up speed. It veered and turned the corner, and Katy felt a strange heaviness come into her heart. The feeling was not unfamiliar, for she felt it every time her father left. But knowing he would be home more often in the future brightened her spirit somewhat.

The hours at school seemed to drag by on leaden feet. When she finally left and made her way home, she was terribly tired. *I never get tired of working in a lab,* she thought as she went into the house. *I think doing things you hate wears you out.* She ate the supper that Agnes and Chang had prepared, praising the houseman for it, but retired early to her room. She attempted to read a scientific paper by Alexander Graham Bell printed in *Scientific American,* but found her mind wandering restlessly and instead sat in a chair, staring out into the night.

The black velvet sky was paved with glittering stars. She thought of the small sum she'd saved toward buying a telescope, but that lay in the distant future. Constellations fascinated her, and often she found herself wishing she had someone to share them with. *I'm so lonely, Lord.* The thought appeared from nowhere, and she was shocked at the intensity and desire that sprang from it. *What is your plan for me? I feel so . . . empty.* She felt her eyes well up with tears, and instead of fighting them, she let them come. Leaning her head against the high-back chair, she closed her eyes and felt her loneliness roll down her cheeks, a constant river that tingled and somehow comforted her.

She came awake with a start when a knock at the front door broke into her sleep. Glancing at her clock, she wondered, *Who could that be at one o'clock in the morning?* Hurriedly going downstairs to the front door, she asked, "Who's there?"

"It's Lyle Davis, Katy." Davis was a construction engineer for the railroad and had become one of her father's best sources in finding rumors of wrongdoing on the rail. He had also become his friend.

Katy opened the door. "Lyle, what is it?" One look at his face, and fear closed like a cold fist around her heart. "Is—is Papa all right?"

Davis stepped in and closed the door. He was a rangy man with iron gray hair and a pair of steady black eyes. He hesitated, then said, "I've got bad news, Katy."

For one moment Katy could not speak. Her throat closed, and she felt that her heart would burst out of her chest. "What's the matter?"

Lyle considered what to do; then a resigned look came over his face. He bit his lower lip, hesitated, then shook his head. "Katy, I'm sorry. Your father is dead."

"No!" Katy whispered. "Are you—? There must be—" But she knew there was no mistake, knew from the look on his face and the certainty that no one would play a joke as cruel as this. She shook her head at Davis, and suddenly his face was receding as if in a tunnel. And then bright lights seemed to go off in her head. She felt herself slumping, but she fell into a deep, black pit that closed around her—and then she knew nothing.

CHAPTER THREE

I Guess We Need Each Other

Chang Li had known many sorrows. Besides his wife and daughter dying, he had lost his mother and baby brother to pneumonia when he was only ten years old. His son had died fighting in the Taiping Rebellion back in China. Each tragedy had affected him so deeply that he had thought he would never recover.

He sighed and shook his head, pouring the tea he had prepared. He knew exactly how Katy was feeling and only wished he could ease her pain. But he knew that God was the only one who could do that.

It had been two days since the terrible news. Katy had stayed in her room for almost the whole time. Chang had taken her meals but, on returning for the dishes, had found everything but the liquids untouched every time. She had kept her curtains closed and had stayed in bed, occasionally opening the curtains to sit and stare out the window at nothing.

Chang knocked on her door, heard a soft "Come in," and entered. She had opened the drapes this morning and was fully dressed, sitting at her dressing table. Her hair was pulled back in its usual severe way, and she had dark circles under her puffy, bloodshot eyes. "Good morning, Chang," she murmured listlessly.

Placing the tray of tea on the table, Chang bowed and said, "Good morning, Miss Kahtee. Look very well today."

"Thank you, Chang, but you're not a very good liar." She took the kettle and poured some tea. "Will you join me?"

"Yes, please." He brought the chair over to the table, sat down, and took the cup she offered. He was uncomfortable being treated like an equal with a white woman, for no one in America except John Steele had treated him as such, but he felt she wanted to talk.

"Chang, I want you to go with me today to prepare my father for . . . burial." She faltered a bit at the last word but took a deep breath and went on. "I don't want to go by myself, and I don't want to take Aunt Agnes with me. And—there's one other reason. I want to look for a . . . reason for my father's death." Chang looked confused, and she said, "I just can't believe he died from a heart attack. He was just telling me last week how good he had been feeling, and he seemed so—so—healthy!"

Chang patted her hand, sensing she was close to tears. "It all right, Miss Kahtee. Chang thinking same thing last night. Mr. John very—very—"

"Robust?" A blank look. "Strong?"

He almost came out of his chair, nodding excitedly. "Yes, yes, strong, very strong! Many time Mistah John help rail gang lay track when he have nothing else to do. Very strong man!"

Katy looked deeply into the old man's black eyes and said, "So you were surprised when they said it was a heart attack?"

"Yes, Chang not believe at all," he said seriously.

Katy nodded her head, and a determined look came to her eyes. "Chang, I'll have breakfast this morning—a big breakfast—and we'll go down to the undertaker together." He rose and started for the door. "Oh, Chang?"

"Yes, Miss Kahtee?"

Uncertainly, she asked him, "Do you think Papa is in heaven?"

The old man's face softened, and he nodded with certainty. "Oh yes, Miss Kahtee. On way from railroad Mistah John ask Chang many question about God, about why I so happy about being

Christian. Chang try to answer every one, saying Jesus not just in church, but in heart. Then Mistah John ask Chang to pray for him. He say he have very big problem that need fix." He firmly nodded his head again. "Yes, Miss Kahtee, Mistah John with Jesus now."

Tears spilled from Katy's eyes. Somehow she was happy, sad, and comforted at the same time. "Thank you, Chang," she said softly.

"Miss Kahtee," Chang started, then hesitated.

"What is it, Chang?"

"Why ask about fathah? He say he Christian for long time."

Katy sighed deeply and couldn't meet his eyes. "I'm just not sure about anything anymore. Even myself."

"You take Jesus in you heart before?"

"Yes, when I was younger."

"You still feel Jesus in you heart?"

Katy considered this for a moment, then nodded. "Yes, except when I'm really depressed. Then I just feel . . . empty."

Smiling, Chang said, "He there even then. You just not try find him. That when he most want to help."

"So it's all right to doubt sometimes?" Katy held her breath, waiting for his reply.

"Everyone doubt sometime, even Chang. But Jesus waiting when we ask him to help. Undahstand?"

"Yes," Katy whispered. "Thank you, Chang." The magnitude of her relief was overwhelming. For the past few days she'd been so absorbed and numbed by her grief that she had only felt apart from God and had wondered if she really was a Christian. Now, she realized that she hadn't sought his help to get her through the horrible time; she'd only stared out her window and let misery take its course.

Chang watched her dawning realization and felt a surge of joy. He hadn't known Katy long, but he recognized a sweet spirit and was drawn to her. Bowing, he said, "Go make breakfahs now." With a smile he was gone.

Katy thought, *Oh, Papa, I hope you are happy! But I miss you so much!* She wiped her eyes with a handkerchief that she suddenly realized was her father's, and that only made her cry harder.

After a few minutes, she made herself get up and go to her father's room and pick out a black suit. The undertaker had offered to dress her father, but Katy had requested that she be able to perform the task. Familiar sights and smells in the room caused her heart to sink, but she silently prayed for strength and managed to keep from crying. She chose his best suit and went downstairs.

After breakfast, Agnes came home. Katy had completely forgotten that she was supposed to go with her to see the lawyer this morning. Agnes came in the dining room, set down her purse, and announced, "Katherine, we must talk."

"Good morning to you, too, Aunt Agnes."

"Yes, good morning." She ignored the sarcasm in Katy's voice. "Your father left a very small estate—the house and a small savings—and willed that it be divided between us equally." She waited for a reply from Katy and then, getting none, continued, "I have been thinking very hard about what we should do and have decided that we should start taking boarders. The house is plenty large enough to—"

"No!" Katy said forcefully. "I won't allow it!"

Agnes put a hand to her breast and opened her eyes wide. "Won't allow it! Young lady, you have no say in it! The decision has already been made."

Katy recoiled as if struck. She had not even considered what they were going to do without her father's income, but a boarding-house was the last thing she wanted to consider. This was her father's house and would not be a home to strangers.

At that moment Chang came in, hearing loud voices. Agnes

whirled on him immediately. "And your services, little man, are no longer required in this house!"

Chang looked at Katy, bewildered.

"Aunt Agnes, no! This is Chang's home now. You can't just throw him out!"

"I can and I am," she said, turning her steady eyes on Katy. "John, God rest his soul, was doing a favor for an old, broken-down man. We no longer need, nor can we pay for, his services."

For the first time Katy saw Chang with something besides his usual smiling, helpful face. Now he was angry. "Chang work for no pay! Help Miss Kahtee—"

"I've made my decision, and that's that," Agnes said, turning to leave. Over her shoulder she said, "We can talk about it after you've seen that this is the best way."

Katy and Chang looked at each other in disbelief. Katy felt as if her whole world were crumbling around her. Her aunt had been in mourning much like herself for the past two days. She had stayed to herself in her room, never checking to see if Katy was all right. And now all of sudden she acted as if she were lord of the manor and of everyone in it. *I can't stay here any longer!* The idea frightened her but at the same time seemed so right.

"Chang, are you ready to go?"

"Yes, Miss Kahtee."

"Then let's go. We'll worry about this later."

In the carriage Katy thought about it further. She had always been so cautious in her life, doing everything Aunt Agnes had told her without question. Now she felt as if she were trapped in a corner with only one way out. *I'm a grown woman. I can't live under her rule.* Feeling strangely confident, she glanced out the window and saw they were stopping outside a large clapboard house with a sign hanging over the door: Cyrus B. Claxton, Undertaker. The lawn was well maintained, with a flower bed that had been stripped of its plants for the fall.

Upon entering, they found Cyrus B. Claxton to be a short, bald man with an unnerving habit of blinking furiously behind his thick glasses. With a very high-pitched voice, he said, "Miss Steele, I believe? Please let me extend my condolences. I hear your father was a very fine man."

"Thank you, Mr. Claxton."

"Let me say again that this is a highly unusual practice. I am always allowed to dress the deceased for burial," he tried to smile soothingly, but his blinking was driving her mad.

"I understand. However, this is the way I wish to say good-bye to my father. If there is a serious problem, I'll be glad to have him transferred down the street to Mr. Workman's parlor."

If possible, this caused even more blinking. "Oh no, no, Miss Steele! Please, right this way!" He started toward the back of the house. When he noticed Chang following, he said, "Your man will have to stay outside." When he saw Katy's eyes, he shook his small head with many blinks and muttered, "Never mind." He led them to a door and motioned them inside. "Let me know if I can help you in any way," he said, then left.

The room was sparsely furnished with a desk and chair, a few chemicals and instruments on a counter, and four tables lined against a wall, one of which held a body covered by a spotless white sheet. Katy thought she had prepared herself to be clinical and detached when she entered the parlor, but immediately tears sprang into her eyes. Somehow the stark white of the sheet in the neutral-colored room caused bile to rise in the back of her throat. She turned away and leaned on the desk, suddenly weak. Chang draped the suit over a chair, took her arm, and asked worriedly, "Are you aw right, Miss Kahtee?"

"I . . . I . . . don't know if I can do this. I thought I could, but now . . ." *Get ahold of yourself, Katy!* She tried desperately to keep from losing control altogether. Then she remembered the first time she had watched Uncle Fred dissect a rabbit. She had only been about six or seven and had been very upset. He had smiled at her and said, "Don't worry, Katy. This is only the husk of what was a rabbit. The real rabbit has gone to bunny heaven and is very happy."

There was quite a difference between her father and a rabbit, but the memory triggered a calming concept. Wiping away her tears, she thought, *This is not my father. He is with God now and will never be unhappy again.* She turned to Chang, who was eyeing her carefully. Trying to smile, she said, "I'm all right. Shaky, but all right, and this needs to be done."

Chang nodded but kept his hand on her arm just in case. As they started toward the table he asked, "What we rooking for?"

"Any sort of bruise, cut, or scrape. Anything out of the ordinary—" She'd taken a deep breath and drawn down the sheet to uncover his face, when she stopped abruptly. "Chang, look at his face! It's slightly blue! That's not normal in a heart-attack victim."

Katy started to pull back the sheet that covered the rest of the body but hesitated with her hands in midair. She took another deep breath, looked at Chang, and pulled it back. The body still had on long-handle underwear, Katy noticed, but she was more concerned with the upper body. She reached behind the head and started feeling her way down to the neck. At one point she stopped and said, "Chang, there's a lump here. Help me turn him over." Together they rolled the body on its side, and Katy inspected closely under the hairline. There was a deep red discoloration. "OK, let's put him down again."

When they had laid him back down, she said, "He was definitely hit with an object soon before he died. Probably knocked out cold from the looks of it." She peered at the front of the neck, then began to roll up the sleeve of the left arm. Chang started on the right arm. Katy heard a sudden intake of breath from the little Chinaman and said immediately, "What is it?" He looked at her and pointed at the crook of the arm. There was a small hole with a tiny bit of discoloration around it.

Katy's mouth dropped open as she scampered around the table to examine more closely. "That's a needle injection mark! Papa never took any medication!" She straightened up slowly, looking at the far wall without seeing it. The implications were astounding yet undeniable. *There's no doubt about it now. Papa was definitely murdered!*

A look came over her face that Chang did not like. "Miss Kahtee? What mean?" he asked. Her eyes had narrowed to small slits, and her full lips had compressed into a thin line. Her previously pale face was flushed with color.

She turned to him, and he involuntarily stepped back. "I'll tell you what it means, Chang—on the way to the police station!" With one more look at her father's face she turned abruptly and started for the door. Chang had to hurry to keep up.

——➤◆◄——

The local police building was a two-story brick building that fronted Park Street. The first thing Katy noticed as they went through the door was a level of activity she had never seen before. People were constantly entering and leaving. There were individuals seated along the wall and standing in line at a high-level desk where a very harried officer was seated.

Katy walked right up to a passing policeman, grabbed his arm, and said, "I want to report a murder."

The startled officer bit back a sharp reply when he saw the look on her face. Pointing to a hallway, he said, "Right down that hall, second door on the left."

Picking her way through the throng with Chang in tow, she found the door open. They went in without knocking and found a mountain of a man standing at a desk reading a document. Abruptly, Katy said, "I need to report a murder."

She had his full attention. Brown eyes wide, he said, "Where?"

"Well . . . at the funeral parlor," she said lamely.

He chuckled. "There's a body at the funeral parlor? This is not exactly news."

"No, what I mean is—"

"Why don't you sit down and start slowly?" He sat down himself, the chair protesting with a groan, and picked up a pencil.

Katy sat down and took a deep breath. Chang remained standing, uncomfortable being in a police station. He had heard about the police beating Chinese just for fun. He didn't want to be here, but he couldn't leave Katy.

She began, "My name is Katherine Steele, and my—"

"You're John Steele's daughter!" he said, pointing the pencil at her with something like awe. "I used to work with John when he was with the police. By the way, my name's Rizzo, Frank Rizzo."

"Oh, you knew him? It's so nice to meet you," Katy said with relief. "I've found—"

"I was so sorry to hear about your father's heart attack. He was one of the finest men I ever worked with."

"That's what I'm trying to tell you, Detective Rizzo. My father didn't have a heart attack. He was murdered."

"Murdered!" Rizzo said, shocked and sitting up instantly. "How do you know?"

Katy quickly told him about her discovery. He was very attentive and didn't interrupt, nervously twirling the pencil as he listened. "So, you see, someone knocked him out and injected some sort of poison that attacked the circulatory system. That's the only explanation for the bluish tint of his face. He died from lack of oxygen."

Rizzo looked down at the pencil. "How come you know all this science?"

Impatiently, Katy replied, "I've had some medical training at Mills College, and I was tutored by a great scientist. Could you please tell me what you'll do about this?"

Rizzo stood up and started reaching for his coat. "Get to the bottom of it, first of all. I need to inspect the body myself to make it an official homicide. Then I'll get back to you later this evening. Could you give me your address?"

Katy gave him the information, then asked, "Could you tell me why this wasn't investigated before today?"

He looked uncomfortable, tugged on his tie, then said, "We don't have much jurisdiction where the railroad is concerned. John died in Cisco, and there isn't much of a police force there yet. Someone with the railroad brought his . . . body to Sacramento."

"So what can you do?" Katy asked.

"Like I said, I can have the cause of death officially declared a homicide. Then I'll just have to throw it back to the railroad powers that be. I can't go to Cisco to investigate. I'm sorry." He put on a bowler that had been resting on his desk. "Besides, it looks like whoever catches this killer will have to be as smart as your father was—if not smarter."

Katy went to bed that night very depressed. *Papa murdered!* she thought. *Who could possibly have wanted him dead? Could it be the Union Pacific? Did he find out who was behind all the sabotage, and they found out and shut him up?* She sighed and turned on her side. She had always known his job was dangerous, but it never occurred to her that he would be killed.

Aunt Agnes was still determined to prepare the house for boarders. She had already contacted a building contractor to tear down a wall between two small rooms upstairs in order to make a larger apartment. When Katy had protested, she walked away. Katy thought that whatever tenderness Aunt Agnes had held in her heart had died with her brother. Katy knew she could not tolerate much more of her.

Lyle Davis had come calling in the evening. He had visited every day since the tragedy, only this time he had Detective Rizzo with him. Davis was very distraught at the news of John's murder. Rizzo himself, having known John and liked him, was angry after seeing the unquestionable evidence. Davis assured her that everything would be done to find the killer or killers. Rizzo said there were probably more than one because John had had a reputation for being able to handle himself quite well in a scuffle.

Katy remembered that bright, sunny day when she and her father had been walking after their lunch with Huntington and Stanford. *Don't you worry, Gabby. I can take care of myself.* She had been walking with her arm through his, and everything had been so right.

But you didn't take care, Papa! She rose up on her elbow and hit her pillow once, and then again. *Now no one will ever call me Gabby again.* She buried her face in the pillow, crying, and fell into a fitful sleep.

Later, she dreamed of her father. In her dream, they had been at a neighbor's party when Katy was sixteen. John had told her she was officially a young lady now and he would be her escort. But in the dream her father had been dressed in the suit she had taken to dress him in today. His face was tinged the same bluish tone it had been in the funeral parlor, and he was rolling up his sleeve saying he had a riddle to tell. Everyone gathered around to hear, not surprised at all that a dead man was about to entertain them. Even the sixteen-year-old Katy saw nothing out of the ordinary. "When is a corpse not a corpse?" he asked, showing his arm. There was much consulting, and they finally gave up.

"I know," Katy said in her dream.

"When?" they all asked in breathless anticipation.

"When it's a murdered corpse!" she said triumphantly. The neighbors applauded at how clever Katy was. Her father looked at her and smiled.

"By gum," one of the men said, "she's as smart as you some- times, John." And everyone agreed enthusiastically. Then she awakened with a start.

The dream left Katy feeling slightly sick with revulsion. But no matter how nightmarish, how very disturbing the experience had been, she sensed the forming of an idea in her mind.

———————

Theodore Sedgewick peered distastefully at his mud-spattered shoes. The rain had momentarily stopped, but the ominous clouds overhead promised more. While looking down, he noticed a spot on the lapel of his expensive black suit and surreptitiously rubbed at it with his gloved hand while listening to the preacher continue:

"Our brother, John Steele, knew the Lord in a special way. When his beloved wife died twenty-five years ago, he came to me with a heavy heart, his spirit buried from wave after wave of despair. . . ."

Sedgewick was careful to keep his face a mask of mourning. Deep inside, he couldn't care less about the man in the polished oak box about to be lowered into the ground. *Another casualty for the cause—my cause,* he thought with a dash of pride.

". . . left with only a baby girl. John was ignorant of how to raise a child, as most men left on their own would be. But looking at Katherine today, I have to say he did an admirable and capable job of it. Emily looks down on you today, Katherine, with her husband by her side at last, from the loving and everlasting arms of our precious Lord. . . ."

Dark, piercing eyes studied Katherine Steele. At forty, Sedgewick was keenly feeling his mortality, since he'd never married and had produced no heirs. The desire for a son had crossed his mind more and more lately, but he knew it would have to be a special woman that bore the child for him. Miss Steele was dressed in black, of course, but the dress was tight at the bodice, revealing a shapely waist. She was tall for a woman, with a presence about her that bespoke a shyness, yet confidence as well. Youthful, yet mature. *How old did the preacher say she was? Twenty-four, twenty-five? A bit old to train, but not too old to learn.*

Sedgewick shook himself, drawing a strange look from the woman standing next to him. He stared down his prominent nose at her until she looked away. *Nosy old hen.* Turning his gaze back to Katy, he examined her face more closely, even though he'd just this second ruled out a romance with her. It would be a risk, and Sedgewick had taken the biggest risk of his life on the Union Pacific Railroad. He was left with only caution.

"I pray the grace of our Lord Jesus will comfort you in this terrible time, Katherine. You stand at a crossroads, much like your father so long ago, and the decisions of the next few weeks will shape your future. . . ."

Katherine Steele was either unaware of the words being spoken to her or she chose to keep her eyes on the casket, for she made no acknowledgment. Everywhere in the crowd of forty or fifty people was the heartfelt grieving only found at funerals. But the proportion of tears seemed high to Sedgewick. *What kind of man was this John Steele to have so many close friends?* The concept was beyond him since he could not claim a true friend—not one.

About the only person *not* crying was the daughter herself. A strange calmness enveloped her, as if she had already come to terms with the tragedy and knew exactly what to do and how to handle it. *Remarkable.* He saw her jaw clench momentarily, accenting the strong lines of her features, and he admired her beauty. Her physical features weren't beautiful—pretty, but not beautiful—but combined with her self-evident dignity and bearing, Sedgewick suddenly thought she was the most desirable woman he'd ever seen.

". . . man with many friends, including those he worked with at the Central Pacific Railroad, as evidenced by their presence here today. Never did I hear an unkind word about John Steele, and heaven is enriched by his spirit today. . . ."

I see you hyenas over there! The famous men themselves, the Big Fat Four, looking to get fatter on government money. Well, not if I can help it! Huntington, Stanford, Crocker, and Hopkins were in the forefront of a mass of lesser employees from the railroad. Huddled together with their black suits and umbrellas, they looked like a huge, swollen bug on the green landscape. Directly behind Crocker, he saw a familiar face staring at him. *Don't make a move, you fool. You don't know me, remember?* The man continued staring at Sedgewick, who saw with alarm the corners of his mouth starting to rise in a smile of recognition. Sedgewick gave an almost imperceptible shake of his head, and the man turned his attention elsewhere. Sedgewick would have to speak to the idiot about that.

"Proverbs tells us, 'In the way of righteousness is life; and in the pathway thereof there is no death.' Our brother John has not died; he has continued his life in another place—a place where we cannot begin to understand the magnitude of his happiness and peace. May the Lord bless you and keep you. . . ."

The box was slowly lowered into the ground as an old woman standing beside Miss Steele began to break down uncontrollably. The younger woman put her arm around her in a gesture of sympathy, but also with an unmistakable detachment. Each of the Big Four spoke to the women, followed by some of the employees, including the man Sedgewick knew.

Knowing it was chancy but unable to resist, Sedgewick made his way to the daughter. His legs took him as if they had a mind of their own, while his mind urged him to turn and leave. Before he knew it, he was standing in front of the girl. "My condolences, ma'am," he said humbly, removing his glove and taking her hand briefly. Her touch was cool to the point of being cold, but her handshake was firm. Her eyes were a strange mix of hazel and green, and they searched his face for recognition, found none, and after a passing nod of her head, moved on to the next mourner.

Sedgewick felt an unusual excitement at her touch—a confirmation of the black secret he held in his heart: *I ordered the death of your father, young lady, and you just shook my hand as if I were the man next door.*

———⟶⟜⟵———

"You want to what, Miss Steele?" asked Leland Stanford.

"I want to work for the railroad, Governor." Although he wasn't governor anymore, he still preferred to be addressed that way. "I want to find my father's killer or killers—and I want to serve the Central Pacific as a detective." Katy's head was held high, and her chin was set stubbornly.

"Miss Steele, your father's funeral was just this morning, and I'm sure you feel bad about what has happened. But I believe that with time you will see that that would do no good and that you will accept your father's death."

Katy recognized this attempt to dissuade her. "This is not a whim, Mr. Stanford. I am resolved to see this case to its conclusion."

Stanford himself was astonished. His normally confident manner and personality were nowhere to be seen at the moment. He was seated behind a very large desk. He liked his desk—it intimidated and showed his power. Right now he could find no comfort in it at all. He was leaning on it, face thrust forward in Katy's direction, eyes narrowing. "Miss Steele, I'm afraid that is out of the question." He leaned back in his swivel chair and smiled a smile without warmth.

Katy knew how slim her chances were before she had even entered the huge office. She also knew her power of persuasion would have to be its sharpest. With an effort she bit back the urge to snap at him. Instead she asked evenly, "Could you please tell me why?"

Mistaking her meek tone for surrender, Stanford said with his usual confidence, "There are many competent and well-trained men I can put on the job. Some of them are already looking into the matter in Cisco—a town, I might add, that is very unattractive to ladies such as yourself. The criminal element is very rough and has no qualms about using firearms."

"My father taught me to shoot when I was a little girl. And as for your competent men, why didn't they find the evidence of murder? Why did it take an untrained lady to discover that?" Her voice had unintentionally risen as she talked, and she immediately settled herself down. She knew it wouldn't accomplish anything to upset him.

Stanford sighed. "Miss Steele, there was a definite oversight in the handling—"

"Oversight!" Katy exclaimed, no longer able to hold her frustration down. "This oversight almost allowed a killer to go free as the wind! Governor, someone has gone to a lot of trouble to hide my father's murder." She looked down at her purse and took a deep breath. "All I want is a chance to find out what happened. Just a chance." She looked pleadingly at him.

"But you have no investigative experience, no police training whatsoever! How could I even consider hiring you? Please try to see it from my point of view, Miss Steele." He stood up. "Now, if you will excuse me, I have a lot to do today."

Katy had hoped it would not come to this. She stood also and said, "If you're not too busy tonight, try to read the evening edition of the *Sentinel*. There will be an interesting story on the big, powerful Central Pacific Railroad refusing to grant a simple request from the grieving relative of a recently murdered employee." She wheeled and started for the door.

"Just a minute, Miss Steele," Stanford called sharply. Katy looked at him and saw that the icy glare she had seen at the luncheon was back in his eyes. He came around the desk, never taking his piercing eyes from her. "Apparently I have underestimated your determination." He paused and seemed to have an idea. "You have a deal—on one condition."

Katy, surprised she had won, asked, "What is that?"

"You'll have to hire a man to help you—a tough one. I won't send a woman out there to do this job unprotected."

"But I told you I could shoot—"

"Miss Steele, shooting whiskey bottles on fence posts is not the same as shooting a man. This is my only requirement, and I will not budge from it. If you can't accept that, off to the newspaper you go."

Katy realized she had no choice whatsoever. Even if she had gone to the papers, which she didn't really think she could have done, she felt sure that Stanford would get final approval of anything to be printed. Why he had given in at all was really a mystery to her.

"Very well, Governor. Thank you."

"Let me give you three names." He took a pad and pencil from his desk and jotted the names down. "Give these men an interview of your own and choose one. But I must inform you they will not be forced to work with you. I can't go that far! You'll have to use your own charm and persuasion to hire them." He was smiling, and Katy was not sure if he had intended a slight or not.

She turned to go and said, "Thank you again, Governor."

"Miss Steele," he said when she had opened the door. He moved to stand over her and said softly, menacingly, "Don't ever try to blackmail me again." His hard eyes followed her out the door.

When he was sure she had left the building, he went to Huntington's office down the hall.

"You what?" Huntington cried when told of what his partner had done. "Have you lost your mind, Leland?"

"On the contrary, I thought it was a brilliant solution to a sticky situation. Especially when all three of those men will be told by me personally to turn her down."

49

The beauty of the plan dawned on Huntington and he smiled. "So she can't say she didn't get a chance!" he said.

"Of course." Stanford looked down for a moment. "John Steele was a good man. I can't allow anything to happen to his daughter."

Three days later, Katy went downstairs for breakfast. Aunt Agnes had gone ahead with the plan of establishing a boardinghouse. There had been paperhangers, painters, and all sorts of repairmen busily making the house ready. Katy had been awakened each morning by banging hammers and loud voices.

Agnes was in the sitting room reading the *Sentinel*. She looked up when Katy walked in. "Your ad in the classified section hasn't exactly brought them running to you, has it?" She had a gleam of triumph in her brown eyes. "In fact, not one caller!"

Katy had been turned down by all three of the men on Stanford's list. All had "other things going" that made it impossible to work with her. Katy thought there might be the hand of Huntington or Stanford in the refusals, but she would not give up. She'd decided to advertise, and when she found the right man for the job, she intended to take him to Stanford and have him hire them both.

Agnes spoke again, sarcastically reading her ad: "'Wanted: Man for dangerous investigative work. Must be of high integrity and familiar with firearms. Must furnish references.' Maybe there just aren't any men in Sacramento with high integrity!" Katy wanted no part of her aunt's taunts today. Agnes finally said, "Katherine, why don't you just give up this foolish idea of being a railroad detective and start cooking for the boarders?"

"Aunt Agnes, I won't cook for a bunch of men when I get home from teaching. We've been through this before." She put her hands on her hips. "Besides, don't you want to see Papa's murderer caught?"

"Of course I do, but I sure don't see how you're the one to do it. You have no experience whatsoever."

50

"You sound just like Leland Stanford," Katy pointed out.

"Then Mr. Leland Stanford has more sense than I ever gave him credit for!"

Disgusted, Katy spun around and left the room. She found Chang in the kitchen cooking breakfast. She started to set the table, roughly slamming things around. When she set a plate down too hard, it cracked right through the middle. She stopped, sighed, and sat down in one of the chairs.

Chang had been watching her out of the corner of his eye; now he looked at her and smiled. "It be all right, Miss Kahtee."

"I wish I were as confident as you are," she said forlornly.

"If God want all this to happen, it happen."

"Yes, I suppose so," Katy said. "Chang, if everything does work out so that I am hired, I want you to know I'm taking you with me."

Chang had been pouring scrambled eggs from a skillet to a bowl and stopped immediately. He turned slowly, looked her in the eye, and bowed deeply. When he straightened up, Katy saw that his dark brown eyes were warm. "Chang tank you from bottom of heart. Chang not know where he going."

"I just can't let her throw you out in the street. And I need you, too. You're very wise."

"Not very wise," he said and smiled. "But do know it time to eat!"

That night Katy sat on her bed and tried to think of what to do next. Her spirits were lower than they had ever been. "Please help me, Lord," she whispered. "Thank you for taking care of Papa. I know in my heart he's there with you. I just wish I had had more time with him here. But Chang says this is all part of your plan, even though I don't understand why Papa had to leave. Please guide me. I don't know what to do anymore, and I'm tired. Maybe I should give up and let the officials do their job. I don't know if you still do this or not, but could you please give me a sign as to what I should do? Thank you for listening, Father. Amen."

Katy sat on her bed and took two deep, drawn-out breaths. She felt her muscles relaxing as they hadn't in days. Her mind was no longer confused, and her emotions, which had left her teetering on the edge, were calm.

There was a knock on her door, and Agnes came in. "There's a man downstairs to see you—about your advertisement." She sniffed disdainfully. "Looks like the sort you don't need."

"Who is it?"

"I didn't ask his name," she said stiffly and left.

Katy ran to her mirror, straightened her hair and clothes, and went downstairs. When she entered the sitting room, she stopped in shock. "You!" she breathed.

"Good evening, Miss Steele," said Sam Bronte. He stood twisting his hat in his hands, looking very nervous. His clothes were rumpled, with more than one stain on his coat, and he was in dire need of a boot shine.

"I have nothing to say to you," Katy snapped and turned to leave.

"Please, Miss Steele, hear me out—it will only take a moment. Please!"

Hearing desperation, Katy stopped and stared at him. After a pause, she nodded and said, "Very well," then sat on the sofa, her back rigid.

"Thank you." He looked at a nearby chair but remained standing since she had not invited him to sit. "First, I wanted to apologize for that day. It was a stupid thing to do."

Katy looked down at her hands for a moment, then raised her eyes to his. "Apology accepted," she said coldly.

Bronte nodded. "Secondly, I read about your father and wanted to extend my deepest sympathies."

"Thank you," Katy said, still miffed. "Anything else?"

Bronte noted her angry expression and shrugged. He hadn't expected a better reception, but the results were disappointing anyway. "No, ma'am, I guess not. Good evening to you, Miss Steele."

Katy had a sudden thought. *Could he be the answer to my prayer?* "Mr. Bronte, can you shoot?"

Bronte stopped, puzzled, and said, "It's Sam. And yes, I can shoot. I grew up in Tennessee, and there you learn to shoot before you learn to walk."

"Did the play you and that man were working on turn out?"

"No. Brinkley welshed on the deal, and I lost my temper and punched him. He had me put in jail for assault and battery. That's why I'm late about your father." Bronte cocked his head to one side, wondering where all this was going.

Katy remained silent for a moment, considering, then took a deep breath. "Sit down, Mr.—Sam," she said. Grateful for her acceptance, Bronte sat quickly and clumsily. Katy related everything that had happened, starting with her visit to the funeral parlor. Bronte listened thoughtfully, nodding every once in a while. His light blue eyes never left her face, and Katy felt uncomfortable at first with their intensity.

When the whole story was out, he considered Katy strangely, as if not believing what he'd just heard. "You actually want me to work for you after that dumb stunt I pulled?"

"I don't like you, but I do need you."

He stared down at his scuffed boots, thinking hard. Finally he smiled. "Then I guess we need each other, Miss Steele."

Midnight Encounter

From the stern of the Painted Lady, Katy and Sam gazed out on the banks of the Sacramento River. The brilliant sunshine and cloudless blue sky had brought many of the townspeople out for a day of enjoyment. They saw people enjoying picnics, men tossing horseshoes, and children playfully sticking toes in the cold water of the river.

"What are those long, hammer-looking things those people are waving around up there?" Sam asked curiously.

"I think they're called croquet mallets. It's a new lawn game that just came over from England."

Sam grunted. "I wouldn't want to make my opponent angry. You could knock a man's brains out with one of those things."

Katy glanced at him. *Only a man would think of something like that.* She looked down at his clothes with a smile. He wore a cream-colored suit, a bowler, and carried a cane. Katy had discovered that Sam was quite a dandy when he had money for clothes.

Sam was aware of the look and asked, "Do you like it?"

"It suits you fine," she answered, still smiling.

"I don't think that answered my question, but I guess it'll have to do," he said, smiling also. "'Your voice is ever soft, gentle, and low. An excellent thing in a woman.'" Bronte was, Katy had discovered, fond of quoting Shakespeare, and now he added to that compliment by saying, "That's a pretty dress—brings out the color of your eyes."

Not accustomed to compliments from men, Katy mumbled, "Why, thank you." She was still uncomfortable with him. They both felt that they had been thrown together by fate rather than by their own choosing, but Sam had a way of adapting to situations that she could only hope to have.

Sam gazed at her, asking, "Are you nervous, Katy?"

"A little."

"You're not still miffed at me about yesterday, are you? I mean, it's not my fault Leland Stanford liked me so much."

"Liked you? He acted like you were his long-lost son!" Katy had expected the fight of her life talking Stanford into hiring the two of them. But Stanford had seen Sam in a performance of *Macbeth* the year before and had complimented him no end. "It was like watching some sort of reunion."

"I always like to meet my admirers," he said with a smile. "But seriously, wasn't that better than having to beg for a job?"

"I felt like I wasn't even there!" Katy frowned. "And then when he made that remark about me being in no danger with a 'good' man like you, I felt like gagging!"

Sam said soberly, "Well, at least you accomplished what you set out to do. You're a railroad detective." Taking her arm, he said, "Let's go meet Mr. Strobridge's boys."

At the other end of the main deck, James Harvey Strobridge remarked, "This is a fine ship, isn't it?" Thirty-seven years old, over six feet tall, thin, and tireless, he had developed a lofty reputation as a driver of men. He had lost an eye in a construction explosion, rushing in too soon before all the blast charges had gone off. Consequently he wore a black patch over his right eye. Profane, sarcastic, and high-tempered, men shrank from his wrath. His word as construction superintendent could be questioned only by Charles Crocker himself.

"Yeah, it is," his construction foreman, Ringo Jukes, responded. "How did Mr. Crocker come to own it?"

"Oh, he'd ridden on one in St. Louis once and really liked it," Strobridge replied. "After he came out here and made his fortune in the mercantile store he ran during the gold rush, he just decided to have one built for himself. He asked me if we'd like to have our meeting here, and I jumped at the chance!" Charles Crocker was part owner of the Central and a stickler for organization, and he insisted on his superintendent meeting with the engineers every few months. He believed the rail operation worked better if everyone was aware of what the other sections were doing. John Steele's funeral had created a natural time of meeting while everyone was together.

Noticing Katy and Sam approach, Strobridge said, "Ah, our visitors are here. Gentlemen, let me introduce Miss Katherine Steele and Mr. Sam Bronte. Miss Steele is the daughter of John Steele. She and Mr. Bronte have been hired as detectives to find the murderer and to hopefully put a stop to whoever's giving us trouble on the line."

Katy observed a stunned silence among the other six men. The first to snap out of it was a man about her age who had a broad Irish face and sandy hair that seemed to defy a comb. "My name is Michael Yeats, Miss Steele. I'm terribly sorry about your father. If there's anything I can do to help, please let me know."

"Likewise for me," said a handsome, dark-skinned man with prematurely gray hair. "My name is Cole Price." He shook Sam's hand.

"Let's sit down," Strobridge said. "I must admit that I was skeptical about a female investigator," he began. Katy thought, *Here we go again!* "But after talking with Mr. Stanford, I'm convinced that with the help of Mr. Bronte she should get to the bottom of all this."

Michael Yeats asked, "Miss Steele, do you have any leads yet?"

Katy shook her head. "I only remembered a few days ago that Papa was working on some sort of mysterious papers at home right before he died. I don't know where he kept his key, so I'm having one made, but the locksmith said it would take a while since it's an unusual lock."

"After that, we'll be coming to Cisco to see what we can find there," Sam put in.

Cole Price raised his eyebrows. "Cisco? Not much of a place for a lady. Do you have a place to stay?"

Katy and Sam glanced at each other. "Not yet," Sam replied. "Will that be a problem?"

"Maybe not for you, but for Miss Steele. . . ." Price trailed off.

"There's only one place to stay, and you could hardly call it a hotel," Michael Yeats said thoughtfully. He was in his environment when a problem arose, and he put his whole being into solving even the smallest of problems. Snapping his fingers, the worry lines on his broad forehead disappearing instantly, he said, "I've got it! She can stay in my caboose."

Katy shook her head, confused. "Caboose?"

"Yes, my office is in a caboose on an off track. I have a small bed in it because I sometimes work too late to go all the way back to Cisco from the head of the track." A concerned look came over his face. "It would be a far cry from what you're used to, I know, but—"

"No, no, it would be fine," Katy quickly reassured him. "In fact, it sounds quaint."

Cole Price smiled at her remark. "Quaint? Funny, that's not the word I would use to describe Michael's office. The outside may be quaint, but the inside? The word *ghastly* comes to mind—"

"All right, all right!" Michael interrupted. He leaned toward Katy earnestly. "I assure you it will be spotless, Miss Steele."

"Thank you, Mr. Yeats," Katy said, inclining her head. His bright blue eyes held hers for a moment longer than necessary. All of a sudden, feeling very embarrassed, she looked away—

straight into the laughing eyes of Sam Bronte, who hadn't missed the lingering look.

"Well, that's settled then," Strobridge said. "Now to business. Ed, will you take notes?" Ed White pulled a pencil and paper from a bag he was carrying and appeared eager to write. A small, bookish-looking man, he lived for writing down facts and details.

Kern Gentry and Jesse Boylan also prepared to write, taking notes for Cole Price and Michael Yeats. Gentry was not accustomed to being someone's assistant, as he often told anyone who would listen. His heavy black eyebrows frowned at the injustice of having to do "women's work," as he called it. Jesse Boylan was only twenty and eager to move up in the CP but was aware he had to start from the ground up. Michael had taken a shine to him and wanted to help him any way he could.

"Cole," Strobridge began, "we're about to get bogged down in the Sierra Nevada Mountains, and I'd like your advice on how to handle the delay in laying track. Do we simply shut down while the blasting is going on—or do we start clearing a way on the other side of the mountains while we wait?"

Cole Price prepared to answer, but Yeats broke in suddenly. "Shut down, sir? How can we possibly even consider—"

"Michael!" Strobridge said sharply. "I could have sworn I called on Cole."

Yeats looked down at his hands and said sheepishly, "Sorry, sir." Katy almost grinned at the boyishness of him. He looked like he only had to shave once a week and had a whisper of a mustache.

Price, with an amused glance at Yeats, said, "I have to agree with Michael, Stro." Only Strobridge's closest friends could address him this way. "This is, of course, depending on the winter over there." He took a penknife from his vest pocket and started peeling an apple. Thirty-five years old, he was a Southerner that claimed distant kinship to the Confederate general Sterling Price. Serving in General Braxton Bragg's engineers, he had seen action through most of the war from Tennessee to Virginia and finally in Georgia. He had the unfortunate displeasure of knowing that almost everything he had had a part in constructing was blown up or torn down by the advancing Union armies. He had told Michael once that this was one project Sherman wasn't going to order blown up.

"Yes," said Strobridge, starting to peel an orange taken from a fruit basket on the table, "and depending upon the Big Four's finances. Ed?"

Ed White puffed himself up importantly. "Mr. Hopkins and Mr. Huntington are a little worried about the possibility of a harsh winter. If production slows, that means the Union will be able to gain that much more ground on us."

Strobridge nodded to White and looked to Yeats. "All right, go ahead, Michael. You look like you're about to come out of your chair wanting to say something."

"Thank you, sir," Michael said with a grin on his broad lips. "But I don't see how we can even think of stopping! This is the greatest undertaking this country has ever seen, and to think we could just shut down and burrow away for the winter is beyond me." He leaned forward eagerly, his eyes gleaming. "The war took so much away from the country—hopes, dreams, loved ones—and this project is just the remedy to restore faith in American ingenuity! I say keep going no matter what." He sat back in his chair, slightly embarrassed at his own excitement.

Ringo Jukes spoke for the first time, turning to Katy and Sam. "You'll have to excuse Michael. He's so timid about expressing his opinions you hardly know he's there sometimes." Everyone laughed and Michael flushed. "And, Mr. Strobridge, you just say the word. I'll have the Chinks digging tunnels and laying track fifty miles on the other side, if you want it." From his expression there was no doubt this would be done if he so chose. He had dark, empty eyes that gave away nothing. His wiry frame had compact movements; he had no wasted motion about him, but at the same time he exuded raw energy that could explode at a moment's notice. Katy had not seen him smile since she had arrived.

Strobridge nodded, satisfied that his construction foreman was his usual reliable workhorse. He popped a slice of orange in his mouth and spoke around it. "The decision is ultimately up to the Big Four. It's their money that will be lost if we get severely bogged down in the mountains. The government only pays by the mile, and while we're inching through mountains, the Union Pacific is laying three or four miles a day in open plains. Stanford will definitely consider the loss of revenue during the winter."

"Excuse me," Sam spoke, "but if you were grading on the other side, would that count for mileage to the government?"

"Only if track is being laid," said Cole Price, looking at Sam with a hint of respect at his grasp of the facts.

"I'll go ahead and forward our opinion to continue through the winter to Mr. Crocker," Strobridge announced. As if some silent mutual agreement had been reached, he turned to Katy as he reached into his coat pocket and asked, "Miss Steele, do you mind?" Every man around the table except Sam had produced a cigar and was awaiting permission to light it.

"Of course not. Please, act as if I'm not even here."

"That would be quite impossible with a pretty woman around, but we'll carry on the best we can," Strobridge said with a smile. The sulfur fumes of matches filled the air for a moment as they lit their cigars and discussed other business.

When the meeting was over, Sam touched Katy's arm and said, "What about Chang?"

"Oh, I almost forgot!" She turned to Ringo Jukes and said, "Could we have a word with you?" Through the discussion they had found that Jukes was the rail boss immediately over the work gangs.

"Why, sure." They walked a few feet to the rail of the ship. After she had told him about Chang, he said, "How about letting him cook for one of the Chinese work crews? They're hard workers but very independent. Always divide themselves up into work gangs, each with their own cook."

"Sounds just right for Chang," Sam commented.

"I'll arrange it for you tomorrow."

"Thank you, Mr. Jukes," Katy said gratefully. He tipped his hat, still without a smile.

"Miss Steele?"

Katy turned to find Michael Yeats behind her. "Yes, Mr. Yeats?"

He smiled and said, "Please, call me Michael."

"Then I insist on you calling me Katy. After all, I'll be taking over your home," she said with a smile.

"Thank you—uh—Katy."

Sam, standing by and watching, rolled his eyes. *He'll start wagging his tail like a puppy in a minute.*

"I just wanted to tell you," Michael continued, "to be sure and look me up as soon as you get to the end of the rail, and I'll get you set up."

"Thank you. I'll be sure to do that."

"Yes, well—uh—good day to you, then," he said and turned back to the men.

"Good day to you, too, Michael," Sam called to his back, but he didn't hear. Sam turned to Katy and grinned despite her disgusted look.

———————

On the way home in the one-horse buggy that Sam had rented, Katy removed her bonnet and leaned her head back, drinking in the warm sunshine and crisp spring air. Unknowingly, a smile came to her full lips.

"'Young men's love then lies not truly in their hearts, but in their eyes,'" Sam quoted with a mischievous smile.

Katy looked at him strangely. "What?"

62

"Romeo and Juliet."

Katy sighed. "Oh, Sam, he's just a nice young man."

"I didn't see him catching any moonbeams to give to me."

"What he did is called being noble. Don't you have a noble bone in your body?"

"Of course I do. In the fifth grade I beat the stuffing out of a boy who had insulted Suzy Kenner's honor," Sam said, taking on an exaggerated Southern accent, making "honor" sound like "ahnah."

Lazily watching the boats on the river, Katy asked disinterestedly, "And how was Miss Suzy Kenner's *ahnah* tainted?"

"She had proclaimed me the best-looking boy in the school, and he had the nerve to question her judgment. What was I supposed to do, just let the affront pass?" he asked, flashing a brilliant smile.

Katy rolled her eyes. "You may have a creaky, misguided bone of nobility, but I'd swear there isn't a modest one to be found." Despite herself, she turned away from him and smiled. "What was your childhood really like?"

The playful look died in his eyes. He was caught unawares because no one had ever asked him that question before. All his adult life he had made sure that everyone he knew was kept at an arm's distance. His life had been one of wandering from town to town, either by himself or occasionally with a thespian group. He had had many romantic ties for he was rakishly handsome, and women were naturally drawn to his easy and fun-loving attitude. He had never felt the need to settle down into marriage and have children as most men do. He looked at Katy and saw that she had turned totally serious with her question.

"I'm sorry, I didn't mean to pry," she said. Katy was all at once embarrassed. She had never spent much time with a man her age and was afraid she had overstepped a boundary. *Maybe women are never supposed to ask a man something like that.*

"No, it's all right," he assured her but was still at a loss for words. He took a deep breath. "My childhood was . . . um . . . well, to tell you the truth, I don't remember many happy times. We were dirt-poor farmers, and my father was a fire-and-brimstone preacher. Whenever he wasn't trying to kill me with work, he was trying to beat a demon out of me."

"Sam, that's terrible!"

He shrugged his shoulders and flicked the reins at the horse a little harder than necessary. "I got out of there when I was fifteen."

He was quiet for a moment. Katy was getting ready to change the subject, thinking it was too painful for him, but he went on. "Ended up on a riverboat and learned how to gamble. I was running my own table at seventeen, but that's a dangerous way to make a living. I joined up with an acting troupe and went to New York, where I had some success. The war came along, and since it had nothing to do with me, I wanted no part of it. I came to California looking for my own personal pot o' gold, and here I am."

Katy absorbed the way this speech was delivered, in a flat monotone, and decided to press no more.

"What about you?" he asked.

She told him about her mother and Aunt Agnes, about her upbringing that was less than common and more than lonely because her father was away a lot. And, finally, about her fascination with Uncle Fred's scientific field and her frustration with not being able to work in a laboratory.

"Two birds of a feather, then," he remarked. "All this talent and no way to put it to use." He looked at her and grinned. "At least you were able to get this job—with my help, of course."

Katy sighed and shook her head. Turning to face him, she said, "Well, you may have charmed your way into Stanford's and Strobridge's graces, but you've shown me nothing to prove you can even find a mouse in a cheese factory." She turned until her back was to him, feigning interest in the shops of Sacramento they passed by.

"Pardon me, ma'am, but how many criminals have you chased down?"

"I'm just tired of everyone thinking I'm a bored little school-teacher who's not capable of crossing the street without a big, strong man to protect me."

When they arrived at Katy's house, Sam started to go around the buggy to help her down, but she managed to awkwardly step down by herself, skirts and all.

"What time do you want to leave in the morning?" he asked, amused at how quickly she had made her exit. They were going to the end of the rail line the next day, and Sam was to pick her up.

Katy straightened her hat, which had tilted in her scramble. "The train leaves at eight. Seven would be fine." She started for the front door.

"I'll be here!" he called to her back. With a last shake of his head, he clucked at the horse and left.

As Katy reached to open the door, the knob turned in her hand and the door was whisked open. Standing there with a surprised look on his face was a middle-aged man with heavy jowls and thick sideburns. He froze in the process of putting on his hat and said, "Why, hello! Uh—who are you?"

"I live here." Katy brushed past the boarder.

Katy entered the kitchen to hear: ". . . and you will treat anyone who walks through that door with respect!" Chang was preparing dinner on the stove with his back to Agnes's tirade and waved an arm at her impatiently, mumbling something in Chinese. "And stop speaking that dreadful, squeaky language at me like that!"

"Aunt Agnes?" Katy asked sharply.

Agnes turned and said, "Why, Katherine, I didn't hear you come in. I was just telling Chang that he has no right to—"

"He's doing his best, Aunt Agnes. He lives here because Papa wanted him to. Now, would you please tell me who that stranger was that surprised me at the door?"

"That was our first boarder, Mr. Phillips," Agnes said proudly.

"Weren't you even going to ask me about who moves in this house?"

Agnes put her hands on her hips and said, "No, I was not going to consult you, since you'll be prancing all around the countryside with this . . . person—" indicating Chang—"and a strange man."

"Did you ever stop to think that I'd be back?" Katy asked stiffly.

"Frankly, no. You go out in the world of men, and you pay the price," Agnes sniffed. "You'll probably end up a saloon girl."

Katy couldn't believe what she was hearing. Her aunt had let a bad marriage twist her into thinking that Katy wouldn't stand a chance away from her guidance. It was obvious that she resented Katy for even attempting it. Katy knew Agnes loved her in her own way, but now, looking at the small brown eyes defiantly awaiting a rebuttal, she heard the proverbial door slam shut on this part of her life. She could no longer live under the same roof with this poor, bitter woman who seemed destined for a life of loneliness and, eventually, despair.

Katy's shoulders sagged as the anger in her was replaced with sympathy. "Could we please talk after supper? I need to wash up."

Dinner was a dismal affair. Everyone carefully avoided eye contact and silence prevailed. Katy ended up pushing her chicken and vegetables around her plate, taking very few bites. When they had finished, Chang started gathering dishes, and Katy was about to speak when Agnes said, "Katherine, I'm sorry for the remark I made. It was uncalled for and mean. I'm just trying to come to terms with the fact that you may never come back."

Katy reached across the table and put her hand over her aunt's. "Of course I'll come back! Maybe not to live here, but I'll always visit you. You're the only family I've got left."

Agnes dabbed at her eyes with her napkin. "Yes, it's just the two of us now. I knew deep in my heart you would leave sometime soon. That's the reason I've pushed so hard for the boarders." She

looked Katy in the eye. "I just don't want to live alone. I thought I
did, but I now know I can't."

"It's all right. I'll feel much better knowing you won't be alone."
A thought came to her. "Please apologize to Mr. Phillips for me. I
was pretty rude."

Agnes smiled through her tears. "He's a nice man. Oh, I forgot
to tell you. Your replacement at the school will be staying here.
She's from San Francisco."

"That's wonderful, Aunt Agnes!"

"Yes, I thought so, too. Katherine, remember you're the only
family I've got left. So please be careful."

"I will. I promise." Just when Katy would give up on Aunt Agnes
as a mean-spirited woman, she would show a touching side that
demanded understanding, as if she knew when she had pushed
things too far. The conversation immensely eased Katy's anxiety
about leaving.

That night, she packed the rest of her things and took a long, hot
bath. She treasured her baths more than anything, often spending
as much as an hour in the hot, sudsy water. She suddenly remembered she would be living in a train caboose and hoped that
Michael Yeats had already installed a tub.

Returning to her room and brushing her hair thoroughly, she put
out her lamp and knelt beside her bed. "Lord, I'm starting a journey
tomorrow. I don't know where it will lead or how it will end up,
but please bless Chang and me with safety. Oh, and Sam, too.
Forgive me my anger today, and please help Aunt Agnes with
whatever she does in her life. Amen." She climbed into bed,
believing she would be awake for a long time, but she fell asleep
almost immediately.

Some time later she awoke. Looking out and seeing the stars
shining brightly, she turned over to go back to sleep when she heard
a noise downstairs. *Is Chang already up?* But it wasn't the clatter
of breakfast pans. It had been almost stealthy—a sudden noise cut

off by human hand, as if something had been stopped from bouncing on the floor in a room away from the kitchen.

Frightened, but determined to investigate, she put on a robe and started downstairs. On the way down, she winced right before she stepped on the fourth stair from the bottom, knowing it would creak even before it did. Stopping to listen closely, she heard no sound whatsoever, which seemed to make her more apprehensive than if she had heard a great deal of noise.

She reached the bottom of the stairs and was about to enter the living area when she heard a very soft, furtive rustle from her father's study. There was no doubt that someone was in the house. Fear leaped into the back of her throat with a sour taste. She realized she had no weapon of any kind and stepped into the parlor and grabbed a large silver candlestick. Brandishing it with both hands like a club, she moved to the office and stood outside the door a moment without looking in. Taking a deep breath, she whirled into the room, opening her mouth to shout. Feeble moonlight flowed through a window, and she saw that all of the books were laid on the floor and stacked on the desk, and papers were scattered all over. In the next second, she realized she had charged too far into the room and sensed movement behind her.

As she started to turn and scream, the dark room exploded with light; immediately after, she felt an excruciating pain in the side of her head. She felt another blow on the other side and groggily realized this was from her head hitting the floor. She was aware of heavy boots running away from her, the front door slamming, and then a black emptiness.

CHAPTER FIVE

End of Track

K aty awakened to find herself lying on the horsehair sofa in the sitting room with a cold cloth on her forehead. Agnes was sitting next to her on a chair, looking at her, brow creased with worry lines. "Well, it's about time!" she sighed with relief.

Katy gazed over Agnes's shoulder, lazily noticing the dust motes swirling in the rays of sunshine filtering through the window. She could smell fatback bacon frying in the kitchen. As if on cue, Chang entered carrying a breakfast tray, his small face lighting up immediately. "Ah, you awake! Chang very scared for while. You like something to eat?" he asked, setting the tray on a table.

Katy was becoming more disoriented by the second. "Why were you scared?" She started to sit up and regretted it immediately. A vicious bolt of pain shot through her head, making her gasp.

"No, Katherine, don't move!" Agnes took her by the shoulders and gently laid her back down.

"I was dreaming about my mother," Katy muttered groggily. In her dream they had been at some crowded hall, perhaps a town meeting, and her mother had been across the room watching her. When Katy felt the eerie sensation of eyes on her, she had turned, and her mother had smiled the sweetest smile Katy had ever seen. When she started toward her, her mother just vanished like smoke.

A knock sounded on the front door, and Chang went to see who it was, mumbling something about "Mistah Sam." Agnes eyed Katy with a guarded look. "What's wrong?" Katy asked.

Agnes looked down at her dress and smoothed it out, as if she couldn't meet Katy's eyes. "The doctor said you took quite a blow to the head, and he was worried about damage to the brain. And now you wake up talking about your mother, which you haven't done in years. That's what's wrong," she finished awkwardly, looking closely at Katy again.

"Doctor? What—why—"

"There was a break-in last night, Katherine. You interrupted him and got a nasty blow to the head for your troubles."

Katy's eyes locked on the far wall, but she didn't see it. Suddenly it all came back to her in a rush: the noises, the fear, the papers and books scattered everywhere, the sick feeling when she realized there was someone behind her.

Agnes's voice broke through her memories. "Why anyone would want to break in here is beyond me. There are much nicer houses with wealthier people living in them," she said, shaking her head.

Something was nagging at a part of Katy's mind that wasn't functioning yet. She knew there was a reason for the night visitor, but she couldn't put her finger on it yet. *He was searching for something specifically in Papa's study. There were books and papers. . . .*

At that moment Sam walked in quickly with a concerned look. "Are you all right, Katy?" He stopped suddenly when he saw her closely, his eyes widening with surprise.

"What's the matter?" she asked. "Do I have a bruise?" She inspected her face gingerly.

"No, no." He had never seen Katy without her hair pulled back in the painful-looking way she preferred to wear it. Now, seeing her there with thick, silky ash-blonde locks flowing around her face and on the pillow, he saw a woman he almost didn't know. "How are you?"

She gave him an uncertain look. "My head hurts."

"Let me see." Reaching down, he felt a huge knot behind her right ear. "Pretty nasty. I took a lump like that once. A man in Kansas accused me of dealing a stacked deck, hit me, and took my money. I think you'll live." He looked around the room. "What was taken here?"

All at once, Katy knew. "Sam, the papers!" He looked blank. "Papa's papers—the ones he was working on!" Her head started throbbing instantly in her excitement. "Quick, go check to see if the thief broke into the drawer!" He rushed off to the study.

Agnes had the stern look back on her face. "See what you've gotten by this silly job? You endangered the whole house and everybody in it with this nonsense! What are these papers?"

Katy ignored her sharp tone and explained the documents. "If this was really what the thief was looking for, they must be very important."

Sam hurried back in and nodded. "The drawer lock was scratched up by someone trying to force it, but it wasn't opened."

"Get out of this foolishness now, Katherine, and let the police and the railroad handle it," Agnes insisted.

"No, I won't, Aunt Agnes. I've made my decision, and that's that. Now, please give me a minute to think this out." She closed her eyes and tried to concentrate. All she wanted to do was go back to sleep so she could ignore the pounding in her skull.

Sam saw she was having a hard time and took over, turning to Agnes. "Have the police been here?"

"Yes, early this morning."

"What did you tell them?"

She glanced at him with ill-concealed dislike. "What could I tell them? I didn't see anything missing and didn't know anything about these mysterious papers."

"Good. If they come back, please don't say anything about them."

Agnes stared at him icily for a moment, then grudgingly half nodded.

He turned to Katy and said, "I'll go see that locksmith and get a key out of him today if I have to hold a gun on him. We need to see what's in those papers."

"All right." Katy was glad he was thinking clearly. She felt herself being drawn inevitably toward sleep. "But what about our trip?"

"That's definitely postponed until you get up and around. A train ride isn't exactly what the doctor would order for a busted head."

"But, I may feel better later—"

"No, Katy," he said with a stern look. "You never know how a blow to the head will affect someone. You ought to know that."

"All right," Katy sighed and almost immediately was asleep.

———⊷≺⊶———

As Katy stirred, the room was darker, the sun gone from the front window. Chang and Sam were sitting across the room speaking in quiet voices. Her mouth was completely dry, and she muttered, "Chang?"

He was on his feet instantly. "Yes, Miss Kahtee? You like tea? Watah?"

"Water, please." He poured some from a container and started to put it to her lips. "No, wait." She tentatively raised her head and, finding no searing pain, lifted herself onto her elbow to drink.

"Well, that looks like progress," Sam commented, looking pleased.

The cool water was soothing to her parched throat. She drained the glass without stopping. Setting the glass down, she gingerly pulled herself all the way into a sitting position, ignoring Chang's protests. Feeling slightly dizzy but without the agony of the headache she had had earlier, she gently explored her scalp. The injured area felt as if it had gone down from the plum-sized bump it was before.

"I guess you'll live," Sam said with relief.

She shot him an irritated glance. "Yes, I'll live. I'm glad you find this so entertaining."

"Sorry. I'm not much on pampering."

"So I see." She felt a sudden gnawing hunger. "Chang, I'm starved. Could you make me a sandwich, please?"

"Of course, Miss Kahtee," he said and started for the kitchen.

"Wait a minute, Chang," Sam called. "I thought I'd take Miss Katy out for dinner, if she feels up to it."

Katy glanced down at herself. "But I probably look a mess."

"Nonsense!" Sam exclaimed with a wave of his hand. "You women can fix that up in no time, right?" He didn't wait for an answer. "That's settled then." He picked up some papers he had been holding in his lap. "Guess what these are?" he asked.

"What?"

He looked exasperated. "Your father's papers, of course!"

"Already?" She hesitated, then asked, "Exactly how long was I out?"

"About seven hours."

"Seven hours!"

"You hardly moved the whole time. I used a little persuasion on our locksmith friend and got the key in record time. These papers were the only documents in the drawer, and I sure can't see anyone risking jail to try to steal them. Here, have a look."

What Katy saw were several baffling documents. Most of them were anywhere from a half page to a full page, but three of them were telegrams with only one simple line on each: "XUEA WH WBVXP," "CRKH ZPNIOJ," and finally, "BBDEQPX FWLJG."

She inspected the opposite sides of all of them and saw nothing.

Gazing at Sam with a bewildered expression, she murmured, "My father died for these?"

Sam moved over to sit beside her on the sofa. "Now, we don't exactly know that, Katy. Maybe they had nothing to do with his death at all."

"But we have to assume they do," she replied thoughtfully. "It's really all we have to go on right now."

"That's true," Sam conceded.

"But what does it mean? Is it a language?"

Chang had been standing by quietly but now spoke up. "Chang study ranguages in monastery for while." He shook his head. "Not see anything rike that before."

"A code, then," Sam offered. Chang shrugged his small shoulders.

"It doesn't spell anything backward," Katy commented, still scrutinizing. "And it sure doesn't mean something upside down. It *must* be a code."

"We have to find out for sure if it's a language or not," Sam said. "I was in a play with a man who was a language expert. I'll see if I can find him tonight or tomorrow morning and make sure about it. If anyone can tell us for sure, it's him." He slapped his hands on his knees and said, "Now, how about that dinner?"

Katy put her hands to her hair. "You'll have to give me a few minutes."

Sam looked into her hazel-green eyes and said quietly, seriously, "Just brush it out and leave it down."

Katy looked at him, lost for words. Sam said nothing, continuing to look at her soberly. *Is he teasing me?* The awkwardness she had felt at asking him personal questions in the buggy ride the day before came back to her in a rush. While growing up, boys had made fun of her. They called her "homely Katy" and, mistaking her aloofness for snobbishness, "prissy britches." The girls had even more cruel things to say. Now, looking into Sam's face, she realized he wasn't having fun with her. He really expected her to leave her hair down.

With a nervous laugh she said, "Oh, no, I couldn't do that." She started to stand, and he immediately rose to help her in case she took a fall, with Chang on her other side. The room swayed ever so slightly, and the extra blood pumping in her head at the exertion was alarming, but the feelings didn't last long.

"All right?" Chang asked.

"Yes, thank you."

Persistently, Sam asked, "Why not?"

Katy looked at him seriously but also sympathetically because he just didn't understand. "No, Sam. I just can't." She started toward the stairs carefully, still fearful of passing out. Except for a headache that she figured would be with her for a while, she felt fine. "I'll just be a little while."

Sam, hiding his disappointment, asked, "Are you sure you feel like dining out?"

"Yes, I'm fine. But I warn you, I'm famished!"

Sam found out she wasn't joking. The restaurant he had chosen specialized in seafood, and Katy ordered a baked salmon dish with shrimp cocktail as an appetizer. Sam, quickly calculating the result of the bill and the few dollars in his pocket, decided on coffee and the specialty of the day—with a special low price—broiled sea bass. The restaurant was fairly crowded, and the constant hum from many conversations filled the air. On the wall across from Sam was a huge mural of what seemed to be an artist's embellishment of tense moments from *Moby Dick*.

Katy had indeed pulled her hair back in the usual way and had chosen a pretty white dress with a red stripe around the hem and a high lace collar. Complimentary bread was brought, and he watched as she buttered a huge slice and took large bites. Noticing his amused expression, she quickly put down her bread and covered her mouth with her napkin as she finished chewing, her hazel eyes wide. He looked around at the diners casually so he would not embarrass her further.

When she could speak, she asked quietly, "Am I making a spectacle of myself?"

Sam had to laugh. "No." He scanned the crowd and said, "Well, just in front of me."

Katy rolled her eyes. "Do you ever stop teasing?"

The smile faded from his face. He looked down at the table as if contemplating something, then met her eyes. "Do you remember this morning when I first arrived and was so shocked?"

"Yes."

"Would you like to know why?"

She leaned forward and put her elbows on the table. "I knew there was something you didn't tell me. All right—why?"

"I almost asked your aunt where you were, because I sure didn't recognize you."

"What do you mean?" she asked, puzzled.

"Your hair, Katy." He unconsciously glanced at it. "I'd never seen you with it down, and you looked like a completely different woman. A very attractive woman."

Katy looked away quickly, her face warming. She had received few compliments before, except from her father and Uncle Fred. "No, that's not true," she murmured, trying to laugh. "Thank you, but that's not true."

"Don't you think I know a pretty woman when I see one?" he asked.

"No, no—it's just—I don't—"

"Katy, it's just a compliment, not a proposal of marriage." He leaned over and put his hand over hers briefly, his light blue eyes penetrating. "A compliment—you know what those are, don't you?"

"Yes." She looked him in the eye and said, "Thank you. Really."

"But you still don't believe me, do you?"

She nodded firmly. "Yes, I do believe you thought I was attractive for a moment today."

He shook his head slowly. "You really think you're unattractive, don't you? Why?"

The waitress came by to freshen their coffee, and Katy was afraid she had heard his question. As to the answer, she had no idea what to tell him. "I just never really think about it, that's all." She picked up another slice of bread and started buttering it so she didn't have to look him in the eye.

Sam wouldn't give up. "You look in a mirror every day, don't you?"

"Yes."

"And you somehow avoid seeing your face?"

"Can we please talk about something else?"

"I'm sorry, it's just that I've never noticed—really noticed—your face before because of the way you tie your hair in a knot. Why do you wear it like that?"

"Because Aunt Agnes—because I want to," she said softly with her head down.

"Ah, so that's it," Sam muttered, more to himself than to her. He slowly leaned back in his chair as he realized what she had been about to say.

"I'm not attractive," Katy went on, "and I don't want to be attractive. My nose is turned up—"

"I think it's sort of dainty."

"My chin sticks out—"

"Determined."

"My hair doesn't have any color—"

"Unusual, and some would say remarkable."

She threw her hands in the air. "You're impossible!"

"You're right," he agreed, grinning; then he turned serious again. "What was that you said about not wanting to be attractive?"

"I don't trust men," she said simply. "And I don't want to—complicate my life by having a beau or a husband."

77

"It sounds like that little speech was memorized a long time ago. Who taught it to you? Aunt Agnes? 'O tiger's heart wrapt in a woman's hide!'" he quoted. "That's from *The Third Part of Henry VI,* act one." He saw her starting to flare up again and patted her hand. "OK, enough for now."

"Thank you very much."

Their food was brought by a harried waiter. Katy sampled some of Sam's bass and found it tastier than her own salmon. Sam, realizing how hungry he was, merely grunted when she offered a portion of her dish, because he was so intent on attacking his own.

After a few bites, Katy had some questions of her own. "Why didn't you fight for Tennessee in the war?"

He slowly stopped chewing and pretended to consider his fork. He hadn't known Katy very long, but of one thing he was certain: She could sure ask probing questions. "That war had nothing to do with me. I didn't own slaves, and Tennessee wasn't my state anymore."

"Why, it'll always be your state, just like California will always be mine. Your soft Southern accent is—"

"No!" he cut her off. "It will not always be my state. I've tried to erase whatever memories I had from there, and I've been pretty successful." He took a sip of coffee. "My state is wherever my boots happen to be at the time."

"But you can't claim any roots, any past—sort of like a nomad."

"My roots are my experiences, and I've had plenty of those. Do you know how many knife fights I've seen over common saloon girls on riverboats? I even saw a slave shot in the head for spilling whiskey on a white man's trousers." He shook his head, staring over Katy's shoulder at the gargantuan whale in the mural. "I saw more killing before I was twenty than most people see in a lifetime. Then the war comes along, and they want me to go kill Yankee boys and be proud of it." His blue eyes came back into focus on her. "My state is myself, and my religion is to look out for Sam Bronte's skin. It's what I know, and it's what I'm good at."

Katy said nothing because there was really nothing to say. She had heard about men like Sam, but she couldn't understand how they got along in the lonely world they created for themselves. No family, no long-term friends, and always on the move looking for something to satisfy whatever needs they had at the time. Papa always said there were countless men like that working for the railroad, so she'd meet lots of them. That made her remember their plans for the next day. "We're still leaving in the morning, right?"

Sam looked at her closely. "Do you really feel up to making that trip? It won't be easy."

Katy smiled. "I'm feeling better by the minute."

He tilted his head to the side, as if gauging how truthful she was being. "OK, but if you feel worse in the morning . . ."

"Yes, Mother Bronte, I'll be sure and tell you."

The wood-burning train engine christened *Jupiter* spewed a thick cloud of black smoke almost a half mile long as it labored over the rolling plains east of Sacramento. The smoke billowed well beyond the four cars trailing the *Jupiter*. One was a passenger car with Katy, Sam, Chang, and eleven workers aboard. The other three were flatbed cars with various supplies for the railroad: the iron rails themselves, spikes for fastening them, and food for the workers.

The overcast day did not diminish the beauty of the countryside. Katy saw a combination of evergreen forests and tall grasslands pass by the window. She had seen herds of buffalo and cattle, a family of deer, and many prairie dogs. Occasionally Katy would notice the carcass of some animal lying beside the line.

"Why the dead animals?" she asked Sam as they passed by a particularly fresh body.

He smiled without humor. "These animals have no idea what a

79

train is and sure don't know it can kill them. So they get caught standing on the tracks thinking it'll veer away from them, but they get a big, sudden surprise."

Katy shuddered as the unwanted vision of the cattle-catcher plowing into a buffalo came to mind. She turned her thoughts to the beautiful Sierra Nevada Mountains looming in the short distance. Whenever the *Jupiter* veered north or south from its easterly travel, she caught a glimpse of them and tried to visualize how these majestic mountains could be such a problem to Huntington, Cole Price, and Michael Yeats. To her they were beautiful, not some monstrosity that had to be overcome by brute force and black powder.

They had been traveling all day and had just passed the small town of Cisco. It had had a main street—Katy had to stretch her imagination to call it a street since recent rains had turned the dirt into muck—with the usual businesses sprung up on either side: saloon, blacksmith shed, mercantile store, everything that was considered essential for a young boomtown. The area around the rails was littered with the debris of supplies that were being hurried to the end of the line to the east. A short man with gapped teeth removed his hat and waved at them as they went by, grinning from ear to ear.

Katy, Sam, and Chang all felt the urge to stretch their weary limbs before disembarking. Although the car's bench seats were padded, the passengers still felt stiff from the long ride. The calm landscape outside the window suddenly turned into a beehive of activity, with wagons moving to and from the end of the line and workers busily loading and unloading equipment.

The *Jupiter* jerked to a stop with a hiss of steam, and Katy saw Michael Yeats standing beside a pile of iron rails waving to them. He was wearing red suspenders with the sleeves of his white shirt rolled up to his elbows. Coming to meet them as they were stepping off the train, he called, "Good afternoon! I hope the ride wasn't too bad?"

"Quite an experience," Katy said. "I wouldn't want to do it every day, but the scenery was beautiful."

"Yes, it is. Sam, how are you?"

"Fine, Michael." He turned to Chang and introduced him. "Mr. Jukes said he'd find a job for him."

"Yes, Chang, I believe I saw Mr. Jukes a few minutes ago down by that work gang there." Michael pointed. "Just go introduce yourself, and he'll get you set up."

"Tank you, Mistah Yeats." Chang turned to Katy and Sam, saying, "Cook good suppah for you tonight, yes?"

After Sam and Katy exchanged glances with each other, Sam said, "That would be fine, Chang."

Michael removed his hat and wiped his forehead with a handkerchief. "Feel like seeing how this is done and stretching your legs?"

"I'm all for the stretching part!" Katy said.

"I'll have someone look after your bags. Johnson!" he called to a man close by taking a drink of water from a large barrel. "Take these bags to my caboose, will you?" They started walking beside the track, trying to stay out of the way of the wagons and workers. A large wagon went by on the track itself, and Sam inquired about it.

"Those are track trains," Michael said, obviously excited about getting to explain the operation to them. He removed a cigar from his trouser pocket, looked questioningly at Katy, and lit up. His movements hinted at clumsiness, and Katy didn't think he'd been smoking long. "They're loaded here at the supply dump with rails, fastening spikes, and ties, and then moved to the end of the line to be laid."

They had reached the actual laying of track and watched, fascinated. They could see men, almost all Chinese, in the immediate distance anchoring down ties. Directly in front of them, anywhere from eight to ten men would reach in the track train and haul out a rail, carrying it to the end to be spiked down by men with huge hammers. Katy was receiving many curious looks from the Chinese, and other kinds of inspections from the Irish workers.

Michael noticed and was slightly embarrassed. "Please excuse the men. I think this is the first time a lady has been out here."

"It's all right." Katy tried to ignore the stares by asking questions. "How much do the rails weigh?"

"They're sixty-six pounds to the yard and ten yards long. Six hundred and sixty pounds."

Sam whistled. "Now that's what I call a hard day's work!"

"Definitely," Michael agreed. "But don't let the size of those Chinamen fool you. They can outwork anyone."

An Irishman overheard Michael's remark and snorted loudly. Michael ignored him.

At that moment an explosion rocked the ground, startling both Katy and Sam. The loud noise echoed repeatedly off the near mountains. "Sorry," Michael remarked sheepishly. "I forgot to warn you about that. They're blasting a way for the tunnels in the mountains. They're using an explosive called nitroglycerine."

"Nitric and sulphuric acids?" Katy asked.

Surprised, Michael said, "Yes, they're used to treat the glycerine. How did you know?" He was obviously pleased at her knowledge.

"I've had some experience and schooling with chemicals."

"Have you now? Well, that could be helpful. I'll take you up there in a few days to see how the blasting works. The supply of nitro is very limited because it takes so long to get the materials we need. We can't ship it here in finished form, obviously, and we have to prepare it ourselves."

"I'd love to see how it works."

Michael scrutinized the work being done and nodded to himself with satisfaction. "Well, that's about it from here. After the track train is emptied, another is brought up, and the whole business just goes on and on until we reach the foot of the mountains. Once we get into the mountains, that's another matter entirely. The work gets much more dangerous and painstakingly slow."

"What shifts do they work?" Sam asked, nodding to the laborers.

"Sunup to sundown, with an hour break for lunch. In the tunnels we have three eight-hour shifts, twenty-four hours a day, since they work by torchlight. Want a job?" he finished with a smile.

"No, thanks!"

Michael turned to Katy. "Come on, I'll show you to your quarters—such as they are."

The caboose was sitting by itself on a sidetrack far enough away from the noise to be comfortable. It was painted red, but weather had dulled the finish on some parts of it. After entering the door to the rear, Katy found a small desk to the left, a couple of cozy-looking wing-back chairs, a small cot, and one corner curtained off. "What's behind that?" she asked.

"A little luxury," Michael said as he smiled, walked over, and pulled the curtain.

"A bathtub!" Katy squealed, extremely pleased.

"Just have a Chinese cook warm you up some water, and you can soak your cares away."

"Thank you, Michael. This is wonderful. I'll be very comfortable here."

Sam, who had stayed outside to talk to Ringo Jukes, stuck his head in the door, took a quick look around the cramped area, and said, "Dinner is served!"

Jukes had arranged for a table to be set up close by, and Chang had managed to buy a duck from one of the workers. Roasted quickly, but somehow not burned, he had treated it with his own special herbs and spices—"Chang's secret," he said—and they all agreed it was the best duck they had ever had. Along with potatoes and corn, the meal was consumed with many sounds of approval.

Afterward, Jukes excused himself, and Michael, Sam, and Katy moved their chairs away from the table. The sun was sinking into the west—a perfectly shaped, brilliant orange ball that turned the sky golden before dropping below the horizon. The four were content to merely observe the beauty of it without a word.

A group of Irishmen across the tracks broke the silence by starting to sing a soft, mournful tune. To their surprise, Michael began singing along with them in a beautiful, clear tenor voice. After the delicious meal, the stunning sunset, and the pleasant, peaceful singing in the cooling night air, Katy felt overwhelmingly content. *I could sit here all night listening to this,* she thought lazily.

When the singing subsided, Sam regarded Michael with pure admiration. "What I wouldn't give to have a voice like that!"

"It was really lovely, Michael," Katy said.

Michael tried to wave the compliments away, merely saying, "Thank you."

"Have you had lessons? It sure sounds like it," Sam asked.

"No, no training. I was just—born with it. Can you sing, Sam?"

Sam took his hat off, ran his fingers through his thick hair, and grinned. "Not a lick. I took up—other activities."

"Such as?"

"Acting, cards, and guns, not necessarily in that order."

Michael sat forward and said, "So, you're an actor."

"Well, there are some New York critics that would heartily disagree with that statement—but yes, I've done quite a bit."

"I've always admired the stage actors. It seems like such a free lifestyle," Michael said.

Sam said nothing. He had heard the same admiration from many people, but he knew they would probably be amazed if they knew the truth about the "free" lifestyle. With no place to call home, no steady income, and traveling that could be grueling at times, there were few individuals who found the career truly inviting after hearing the truth of the matter.

Michael went on, soberly this time: "I'd think the guns would do you better out here than singing." He nodded toward the Irish camp, which had turned to a rather bawdy tune. "Looks like trouble coming from that bunch."

"What do you mean?" Katy asked.

"The Irish don't appreciate the Chinese as much as we do. They see them as a threat because the Chinese work harder for less money. They feel their jobs are threatened."

Chang, who had been cleaning up the after-dinner mess, heard Michael's comment and broke in, "Bad feeling worse since Chang here before." He eyed the Irishmen warily, as if afraid they would hear him somehow. "Many Chinamen afraid of what Irish do."

"They won't do anything if Mr. Strobridge has a say in it. He was totally against hiring the Chinese at first, but after seeing their work habits and attitudes, he changed his mind pretty quick." He smiled at Chang. "Your people do have a weakness for their gambling games, but it's harmless." He turned back to Sam and Katy and said, "They learn very fast, they don't fight, and they're very clean in their habits."

Sam stood up and stretched. "Well, let's just hope there's no riot tonight. I'm bushed."

Katy sighed deeply and agreed, "Me, too."

"Fine," Michael said. "Let's turn in. I'll show you around some more tomorrow and introduce you to some people."

Chang and Sam went off to their tent after saying good night, and Michael said he was going to ride into Cisco to spend the night and pick up some personal things in the morning.

Later, Katy lay awake in the small bed listening to the sounds of workers bedding down for the night. The crickets were chirping enthusiastically, but instead of being bothered by the alien sounds of the new environment, she felt soothed. Her last thought before falling into a deep sleep was, *I forgot to ask Michael the name of that lovely tune!*

CHAPTER SIX

Coolies

Katy rose in the morning and dressed in her only riding skirt, a gift from her father on her last birthday. He had taken Katy seriously when she mentioned her yearning to learn how to ride. She had always lived in the city and had never had the opportunity to find out if she liked it or not. Most of her girlfriends had learned from beaux or their own fathers, but Katy never had the former and little time with the latter. The black loose-fitting, calf-length skirt was, in her opinion, more suitable to her upcoming activities than a dress. Besides, she felt she had stood out like an Indian at an officers' ball the day before when observing the work crews.

Stepping out of the caboose, Katy was surprised at the number of tents that had sprung up after nightfall. Gazing from the top step, she considered counting them but realized it would take much too long. *There must be a thousand of them! And that's only the ones I can see from here.* She inhaled the cool dawn air and stretched, aware of the soreness in her joints from the long train ride. But it was a good kind of soreness, as if her muscles were exhilarating from the use. *Stale,* she thought. *I was going stale back in Sacramento.*

Seeing Sam coming toward her through the maze of tents, she waved and noticed that he, too, seemed to have a bounce in his step that wasn't there the day before. Katy started toward him but stopped when she saw his head jerk to the right. Even from fifty feet away she saw the easiness go out of his gait, replaced with a tenseness that made his jaw clench. With a glance at Katy, he moved behind a tent to his right. His taut look told her that the perfect morning might be coming to an end.

Before she made it around the tent, Katy heard angry voices and a clanging sound.

"Back off, ye li'l slanty. I'll not be wahrnin' ye again," growled a compact little Irishman brandishing a skillet and soup ladle. He brought them together with a loud clang in the face of a coolie, creating the din Katy had heard. The coolie was boldly holding his ground, even though there were half a dozen Irish gathered around with more coming. The only other Oriental was a tiny, young, very pregnant woman standing beside the coolie. The Chinaman was speaking in his native language and gesturing at a large cooking pot that sat on the ground between the combatants.

Sam bent over and inspected the pot closely. He stood and said, "It's his. There's a Chinese character on this side."

"I bought that pot fair an' square in Cisco, lad," snapped the Irishman. "I don't care if it has a picture of Confucius 'imself on it." He gave the ladle and skillet another clang when he thought the coolie was getting too close.

"Stop that!" Sam raised his voice. "He's not some dog you can just scare away with a loud noise!"

"Yer right, he and his are lower than dogs! Maybe I should just take a switch to 'im!" He turned his burning gaze on the coolie.

Nu-Wen Chu glanced from her husband to the devil-man to the nice man. When she and Huan had found their cooking pot missing, they knew where they would probably find it. The devil-man had tried to buy it from Huan two days ago, offering only a few cents for a scarce commodity. The hateful glare Huan had received at the refusal had left them feeling that they had not seen the last of the devil-man.

Now Huan had no cooking pot for his work crew and would be

forced to join the coolies in their incredibly hard work. Nu-Wen could not allow her husband to be away from her until her baby was born, which she felt would be very soon. Seeing that the devil-man was paying no attention to her, she took her chance. She reached down for the pot and intended to run with it, pregnant or not.

When the Irishman saw Nu-Wen move, he swung the heavy soup ladle down onto her head as she bent over. Nu-Wen sprawled beside the pot. Huan stood frozen for a moment, too stunned to move. He couldn't believe that even the devil-man could be so cruel as to attack a small, defenseless pregnant woman, Chinese or not.

What Katy saw next happened so fast it took her mind a moment to translate it. She couldn't know it then, but the event would be the talk around every campfire that evening. She sensed a blur out of the corner of her eye where Sam had been standing, and the next thing she saw was Sam behind the Irishman, painfully twisting the arm that held the ladle behind the man's back. When the Irishman dropped the ladle, his hand was bent so far upward it was almost touching the back of his own neck. A gun had appeared in Sam's hand, and he held the muzzle against the Irishman's head.

"That's going too far, mick," Sam uttered, almost in a whisper. His face seemed calm except for a sneer that had turned up one corner of his mouth. The man was on his tiptoes, his twisted arm supporting most of his weight. A small moan escaped his lips.

"That'll be enough, Bronte!" a strong voice bellowed. Ringo Jukes moved into the small crowd, his spurs whispering their music softly but sounding like alarm bells in the stillness of the moment. "Put that gun away!"

Sam's face was only inches from the Irishman's, and he looked very closely at the frightened face before releasing his hold carefully and returning his gun to his holster. The Irishman, his face a mask of pain, gingerly moved his injured arm around, checking for damage.

Huan had moved to Nu-Wen and was holding her head in his lap.

She winced as her fingers came upon the spot where the ladle had struck. Almost immediately, her eyes opened wider, and her hands went to her ample belly. She looked at Huan and said something, and his own eyes went to her stomach.

Chang appeared at Katy's elbow with other coolies and, having heard what the girl had said, whispered, "Baby come. Very soon."

Ringo Jukes heard Chang and told three men to throw up a tent around Nu-Wen immediately. Then he pointed to the nearest man and demanded, "You—what happened here?" gesturing at the Irishman and Sam.

The man shifted on his feet, pulled an ear, and said, "These people here—" indicating Huan and Nu-Wen—"said that was their cooking pot, and Monte—" nodding at the Irishman—"said it weren't. Then this feller—" pointing at Sam—"looks at the pot and sees Chinese writin' on it. They argue, and the little lady tries to make off with the pot, and Monte swats her with the soup spoon." He regarded Sam with wonder and commented, "I never seen a man move so fast in all my born days!"

Jukes squatted down and peered at the pot in question. His grim scrutiny moved from the pot to Monte, who averted his gaze. Without taking his coal black eyes from the Irishman, Jukes stood and said, "Chang, take this pot back to where it came from."

"But Mr. Jukes, I—"

"Shut up, Monte! You're finished on this railroad. Get your gear and clear out."

All the bravado had left Monte. Of one thing he was certain: He didn't want to tangle with Ringo Jukes. The man had a reputation for making people see things his way, and he could be very rough at times. Monte shot a smoldering glance at Sam and walked away.

Jukes scanned the crowd. "You men get to work. We're burnin' daylight." With more than a few looks at Sam, the workers went about their business. The men had started putting up the tent around Nu-Wen, who was moaning in earnest now. Jukes motioned to Sam, and they moved away from the bustle of activity, with Katy following. As they were walking, Jukes said, "Be careful about pulling a gun in this camp. I won't have it, and Mr. Strobridge sure won't have it."

"Sorry, Ringo. I just couldn't let that idiot—"

Jukes stopped abruptly and faced Sam. "I understand that. I like to think I'd have done the same thing." He held up a finger. "Just don't pull a knife or a gun. We've got enough bad feelings around here without a weapon entering the picture. Got it?"

"Got it," Sam said, nodding. But he knew he would react the same way under similar circumstances. In Sam's book there was a line that could not be crossed under any condition. He realized Jukes had said something that might be important to their investigation. "These bad feelings—are you talking about the Irish and the Chinese?"

"There's more to it than that." Jukes looked over Sam's shoulder. "We'll talk after supper tonight. Here comes Michael." He moved off, exchanging greetings with Michael.

"Good morning!" Michael called to Sam and Katy in his usual cheerful way. "I trust you slept well in your lavish surroundings, Katy?"

"No complaints, Michael."

"Good, good." He noticed the tent with Chinese women scurrying in and out. "What's all the excitement? Did I miss something?"

Katy laughed, more from relief that the tense moment was over than from Michael's questions. "You'll need to get up earlier if you want to keep up with things around here!"

At that moment, a baby's shrill cry split the cool morning air.

———◦◦◦———

"When nitroglycerine explodes, it expands to form gases that take up more than one thousand times as much space as the liquid itself," Michael explained, his brown eyes shining with enthusiasm. Michael Yeats loved talking about anything, but his favorite subject was his job. Any aspect of it—from the lowliest coolie laying track to the science of engineering. When discussing and teaching, his movements became exaggerated, and Katy could not help but smile.

Katy, Sam, and Michael were in a buckboard wagon trekking to the nitroglycerine-production site. Due to the obvious danger associated with the highly volatile substance, the area was two miles from the rail line. The road they were traveling was extremely smooth—intentionally so because of the jeopardy involved with the transfer of the nitro to the sector chosen for detonation.

Michael continued. "The nitro's explosion is three times as powerful as an equal amount of gunpowder, and its speed is twenty-five times as fast." He glanced at Katy, and she nodded, very intrigued with the lesson. She had known the basic chemical aspects involved and was just as interested in the results of the deadly substance.

Sam had been listening in a distracted sort of way but now spoke up. "This is very fascinating, but if it's so dangerous, why are we going out here to stick our noses in it?"

Michael laughed and replied, "Don't worry, Sam. That's why I brought these three spyglasses." He reached behind the seat and opened a box that neither Katy nor Sam had noticed before. Inside were the glasses. "We're stopping at the top of the next hill to watch."

Sam was relieved to hear that. He had heard horror stories of the Civil War—men being literally torn to pieces by explosions—and wanted no part of dying in that way. He had even experienced dreams about charging into a battery of cannon loaded with grape-shot—grape-sized lead balls that essentially turned a cannon into a giant shotgun—and evaporating in a bloody red cloud. He had no idea why this particularly grisly form of dying had affected him so severely, but his palms broke out in a sweat just thinking about it.

They reached the crest of the hill, got out of the buckboard and considered the valley below. There was a large tent with a fire burning outside the flap and a rectangular table close by holding some utensils. Two men were sitting in fold-up chairs drinking coffee, and one of them stood and waved when he saw the three.

Michael handed Sam and Katy their glasses. "That's James Howden, our nitro preparer."

Katy raised the glass to her eye. She had never looked through one before and was startled to find the man seemingly only a few feet from her.

Sam was considering his surroundings and asked, "Are you sure we're far enough away, Yeats?" Katy rolled her eyes at him.

"I'm sure, Sam," Michael answered with a smile. "Now, do you see that large, deep pan sitting on the table?" All three of them were peering through their scopes at the sight below. "It holds concentrated nitric and sulfuric acids mixed together. Ah, James is ready. He knows why we're here and agreed to show us the process."

James Howden went over to the table and picked up a beaker of fluid. He held it up to the spectators before moving to the acids.

"That's glycerol, or some call it glycerine. He'll add this to the acids."

Howden very carefully poured a tiny stream of glycerol from the beaker into the pan. His helper came to stand behind him and started waving a homemade fan to keep the fog that had started rising from the mixture away from Howden's face. When he was through pouring, the aide kept fanning until the fog dissipated.

Michael went on. "If you were close enough, you'd see the chemical turning a golden color. That's nitroglycerine forming on the top, my friends."

Katy had expected to see a complex laboratory, a mindless maze of tubes and important-looking tools. "That's all there is to it?" she asked, taking her eye from the glass and regarding Michael wide eyed.

"That's all there is, Katy. The process is simple but time consuming because we're limited to a small amount at a time out here in the middle of nowhere. He'll wait about ten minutes and start scooping the nitro very carefully from the top of the solution. Then it's washed, first with water, then with sodium carbonate, a strong alkaline to neutralize the acids. It'll be put in thick glass containers and packed tightly for transport. In fact, Howden has some ready to go if you would like to take some back with us."

"No thanks," Sam replied instantly, jerking the spyglass from his eye. He considered Michael closely to make sure he wasn't serious, and his face relaxed when Yeats broke out laughing.

Katy asked, "Michael, the development process alone is so dangerous, I can't imagine how nerve-racking the detonation must be."

"Actually, that part is fairly simple, too. It's just a matter of placing the nitro in position, then exploding it by a long fuse. The whole situation is about to change, however, thanks to Alfred Nobel. He's come up with a safe detonating cap made of mercury fulminate. The nitro can be packed in a stick form, called dynamite. We should be getting some before too long. Much safer and more convenient."

They watched Howden as he completed the washing and storing of the nitro, and they started back to the camp as he began making the next batch.

Back at the rail line, Katy and Sam accompanied Michael to inspect the progress made during the day. The construction was almost completed on the west side of the mountains, so all the equipment would soon have to be moved to the eastern side to continue laying track. The magnitude of the operation continued to impress Katy, especially the tunneling through the tough Sierra Nevadas. The meeting of the railroads was, of course, the biggest news in the country now that the war was over. Katy doubted that many people across the nation had considered the painstaking planning and hard work that went into the project every day.

Katy and Sam returned to the caboose tired, dusty, and hungry.

Chang had prepared a large pot of beans and ham hocks. The smell was wonderful, even from twenty feet away. There were two young coolies with Chang looking so much alike that Katy knew they had to be related somehow. All three bowed when they approached.

"Miss Kahtee, Mistah Sam, I like you meet Key Sing and Lo Sing. They Chang's friends." The two bowed again. "They come over with Chang on same ship. Take care of Chang when very sick last wintah. Good friends, good friends."

"How nice to meet you both," Katy said. "Are you—related?"

Key and Lo appeared confused, but Chang offered, "They broth-ahs." Key was obviously the oldest, but by how many years Katy couldn't be sure. The Chinese she had seen were without exception smooth skinned and youthful looking. She assumed Key was about twenty and Lo fifteen.

Sam asked, speaking slowly so they could understand, "Do you have more family here?"

Key shook his head. "Fam'ly in China. Not want leave. Key and Lo want see America." His huge grin showed white, even teeth.

"How do you like it so far?"

The brothers shot each other a glance. Lo answered with a toothy grin of his own, "Very nice."

Sam noticed their hands. Both pairs were callus ridden and rough. Lo had his left hand bandaged with what looked like strips from one of the blue coolie outfits they all wore. He looked deep into their eyes. "How do you really like it here?"

They exchanged glances again, then looked inquisitively at Chang. They weren't sure whether they could speak freely about their feelings to Sam and Katy. Chang nodded encouragingly. His smile faltering a bit, Key said, "Much hahd wook. Miss famry." Lo nodded in agreement. There was an awkward silence.

"Must go cook foh wookahs," Chang interrupted, gathering cooking utensils. Key and Lo left after bows and started helping immediately.

"Can you imagine leaving your home to sail on a ship for a month to a place you had never seen before and you didn't speak the language?" Sam asked, watching them hurry away.

"I wouldn't have the courage, Sam," Katy stated simply.

An old memory flashed through Sam's mind. He thought of how scared he was when he had finally left his home in Tennessee. He had had no money, no job, and no prospects, but he couldn't stand another brutal beating from his father. Jacob Bronte had used an inch-thick rod of oak for his switch. He would make Sam grab his ankles, deliver a blow to the soft part of the upper thighs, and count to five. The pain from the first swat would just be starting to hurt in earnest when the second lick would come, invariably hitting the exact spot where the first one landed. Another five-second wait and so on. By the sixth or seventh blow, Sam's legs would be shaking, and involuntary tears would come to his eyes. On the day he left, his father had delivered nine strokes, and Sam had not waited around for the tenth. In fearful pain he had started running. He stopped when he saw Jacob was not chasing him and vented all of his hatred and fear at his father in one last tirade. Before he turned away he spotted his mother, who had come outside their small house to stare in awe at Sam's display of emotion. He was tempted to go to her, but he knew she would only talk him into staying. He was finished. Enough was enough.

". . . do now?"

Sam realized Katy was speaking and visibly shook off the reminiscence. "I'm sorry, what did you say?"

"I said, what do you want to do now?"

Sam pondered the question, still feeling the distant pain of a young boy. All of a sudden he remembered. "We're supposed to find Ringo Jukes. He had something to tell us." Katy noticed his distracted manner but said nothing.

They didn't know how to find him so they went to the camp where the workers were drifting back to their tents after the workday. Katy received more leering stares from the men despite, or maybe because of, her more sensible style of dress. She did her best to ignore them, but it was difficult. Jukes eventually came riding by on a horse. He declined their invitation for supper but accepted an offer of coffee.

Before sitting at the table, Jukes took off his hat, slapped it against his thigh, and generally tried to dust himself off. His forehead was very white, in contrast to the tan, leathery look of his face. Katy again noticed the compact way he had of carrying himself. Every move seemed deliberate and well thought out, yet natural. She could see how men would trust him and wondered idly what part he had played in the war. There was no doubt in her mind that he had been an officer of some sort.

They talked about the work done that day and of the nitroglycerine. Jukes was excited about getting some dynamite in the near future, knowing how much easier and safer the blasting would be. He was taking a sip of his second cup of coffee when Sam asked, "You were starting to say something this morning that you thought would help our investigation. What was it?"

A cigar appeared in Jukes's hand, and the light from a match lit up his eyes from dark brown to solid amber for a moment. He took a few puffs, the smoke drifting away lazily on the soft wind. "Whatever I have to say is only observation and hearsay. I'm in the position to hear a lot of talk—some of it reliable, some of it not worth a fence nail."

"We understand," Katy said.

Jukes thought a moment, then nodded as if coming to a decision. "First of all, I don't know anything at all about the death of your father, Miss Steele. I only knew him enough to nod when I passed by him. But some men you just get this feeling about, as if you're sure they can be counted on when the chips are down. I had that feeling about John Steele." He leaned back and propped his boots on the table. "What I'm trying to say in a long-winded way is, if I run across some information on your father's death, you'll be the first one I look up."

Katy inclined her head slightly and said in a low voice, "Thank you."

"That covers what I do know. What I don't know covers a larger area. If you want me to pick out a suspect for all the sabotages around here, I'll give you about five thousand of them within a mile of where we're sitting. Any one of them could have done it. But if you want me to pick out a man who loves trouble and has the means and opportunity to hire someone to cause it, that man would be Red Dancy."

"Who's he?" Sam asked after Jukes paused.

"He owns the Shamrock Saloon in Cisco. The man should have *trouble* stamped on his forehead. I don't know where he came from and don't particularly care, but if you want any dirty work done, they say he's the man to see. His name keeps popping up after bad incidents."

Sam turned to Katy and nodded. "We'll give him a visit tomorrow. Anything else?" he asked Jukes.

"Keep that gun of yours handy, and don't let Dancy's hired gorillas get behind you."

After Jukes left, Sam asked Katy, "What do you think? You've been awfully quiet."

Katy sighed and said, "I suppose I'm a little discouraged. Jukes was right. There are about five thousand suspects, and only two of us. It just seems so . . . difficult."

"Well, we've got someone to talk to tomorrow. Maybe we can stir things up a little with this Dancy character." He looked at her seriously. "I want you to do something for me, Katy."

"What?"

His chair creaked as he leaned forward. "I want you to carry this everywhere from now on." From behind his back he produced a small gun and set it carefully on the table between them. "It's a .32

Colt, specially made. It fires five shots—made for a woman or a man who wants to carry some extra insurance."

She picked it up and inspected it. It was about three inches long but surprisingly heavy for something so small. It was nickel plated and had a disturbing beauty.

"It's loaded, so treat it with care. I'll show you how to load and clean it later. For now, all you need to know about it is how to pull the hammer back and pull the trigger. I promise you, whoever's bothering you will go away."

Katy had not fired a pistol since her father had instructed her at fifteen, but she still remembered how to cock, aim, and shoot. She wondered if she could actually shoot another human being. Until just this moment she had not seriously considered it. But now she realized that this job wasn't a game—it was the real world with really dangerous people involved. People who had killed and maimed and destroyed. She practiced aiming at one of the windows of the caboose.

Sam noticed and commented, "Don't bother. If the man is as far away as that window, you don't have a chance of hitting him. This gun's range is short. Just stick it in the face of anyone giving you trouble and pull the trigger." He stood up and stretched. "Anyway, let's just hope you don't have to use it. But as Hamlet put it, 'Readiness is all.'"

After Sam left, Katy put the tiny gun on the table in front of her and stared at it for a long time.

CHAPTER SEVEN

A Visit to the Shamrock

The town of Cisco had just about everything a person would need—except a church. A place to worship God was not foremost on the founding fathers' minds. Making money off of the railroad was.

The Central Pacific Railroad was the master eating the gluttonous meal at his table; Cisco was the dog at his feet, patiently waiting for scraps to fall. And the scraps fell like manna from heaven. If a store owner needed a wagon wheel mended, the town blacksmith would charge a fair price. If the railroad was in need of the same thing, the cost would triple and sometimes multiply tenfold. The same went for supplies, equipment, telegraph service to Sacramento, and so on. The townsmen called the system "railroad cost" because "fraud" or "theft" just wouldn't do. Besides, the prevailing thought around town said, "Every other railroad depot practiced it, and Stanford and his cronies aren't going to miss a dollar or two here and there, are they?"

Katy ran right into railroad cost when she and Sam arrived the next morning. She wanted to send Aunt Agnes a short telegram telling her that she had arrived safely and that everything was fine. The Western Union teller had looked them over when they walked in, written down the message, and said, "That'll be five dollars, please."

Katy had been so shocked that no response came to mind.

"Five dollars for ten words?" Sam erupted. "That's highway robbery!"

"Nope," the clerk said matter-of-factly, taking off his spectacles to shine them on his shirt. "That there's railroad cost."

Katy found her voice. "Railroad cost? Do you mean people around here actually pay that kind of price?" The man nodded, not at all ashamed. "And you really get away with that?"

"What's Leland Stanford gonna do, build his own telegraph line? I don't think so," he chuckled, replacing his glasses. His face suddenly turned serious. "You people are with the CP, ain't ya?"

Sam caught on immediately. "No, we're not. We're here to visit a very sick friend who works for the railroad," he lied smoothly.

A handkerchief appeared seemingly from nowhere, and the clerk blew his nose mightily. Without missing a beat he said, "Then that'll be fifty cents, please."

"Can you believe that?" Katy asked Sam when they were outside. "He didn't bat an eye when he gave us the fair price."

"Yeah, he was really broken up about almost skinning two nonrailroad people, wasn't he?" He adjusted his hat to block the morning sun. "What's our plan, Katy?"

She started walking, and he followed. "I've got to get some suitable clothes. All I brought were dresses and one riding skirt, and it's going to be turning cold soon."

"All right, you go shopping, and I'll go get a shave and haircut. Then we'll go see Mr. Red Dancy."

Taking his time, he inspected both sides of the short street. He spotted the Shamrock at once, for it sported a gaudy sign out front with a badly painted picture of a dancing girl with a glass of spirits in her upraised hand. Right next to it was a mercantile store, with the barber shop beside that.

Sam entered the barber's and found that he was the only customer. The small room was cluttered with war memorabilia, and a picture of Robert E. Lee adorned the wall over the barber's chair. *No doubt about his loyalties,* he thought and hoped the man wasn't the sort that wanted to constantly rehash military strategies. To stay out of a conversation, he picked up a six-day-old San Francisco *Examiner* that the barber said was left by some drifter. An item on the front page caught his attention immediately, and he started reading while the man trimmed his hair.

NORTH PLATTE, NEBRASKA—Scouts for the Union Pacific railroad were attacked by a band of Indians on October 20, northwest of North Platte. Seven men were killed. There were no survivors.

Jack Casement, the superintendent of UP operations, told this reporter, "They were scouting the area ahead of the rail line to find the easiest possible route. All were well armed and supposed to be prepared for an Indian attack. Apparently, they were ambushed. My sympathies and those of the entire Union Pacific Railroad go out to their loved ones."

Indian aggression is not unknown to the UP. This is the fifth attack on railroad workers in the last month. A contingent of cavalry out of Fort Kearney was dispatched to attempt to find the marauding Indians, believed to be of the Sioux nation.

Besides Indian troubles, the railroad has reported a number of sabotages on the main rail line. Many local residents are beginning to wonder if the UP is simply jinxed.

Sam smiled at the last sentence. *It seems we're not the only ones with problems.* He tried to picture a map of the area in his mind. The UP was still laying track in Nebraska—they were only a little over halfway through the state, if Sam remembered where North Platte was. That means they still had the rest of Nebraska to go, with the Wyoming Territory ahead of them. No small feat. However, the

Central Pacific was still slugging it out in the Sierra Nevada Mountains, with the Nevada territory to cover. No one knew which railroad would make the most progress before they met.

After Sam's shave, the barber considered Sam for a moment, calculating his price. Sam took a deep breath and shook his head. "No, I don't work for the railroad." He flipped the man two bits.

Katy was just settling her bill when he walked into the clothing store. Once again, she had fought the railroad cost. The store owner also agreed to let her stow her packages behind the counter until their business was finished in town.

Sam put a hand on Katy's arm outside the store, stopping her. "Why don't you wait right here while I go in the Shamrock?"

"Why?"

"Why? Because it's a saloon, that's why. They've probably never had a real lady step foot in there, and I don't know why one would *want* to go in there if she didn't have to."

"But I have to," Katy said simply.

"Katy," he started, shifting his feet, "there's no telling what kind of riffraff are in there, not to mention . . ."

Katy waited patiently, secretly enjoying his discomfort. She had already anticipated that he would object to her going inside, but she was determined to go anyway. She really had no idea what to expect—saloon life had not exactly been considered a choice dinner conversation topic while she was growing up. But there was an adventurous spirit inside her that cried out to be obeyed. "Not to mention what, Sam?" she asked innocently.

"There are ladies—well, not really *ladies*—women that aren't very—just look at the sign, Katy!" he sputtered, pointing to the tawdry painting.

Katy had to laugh. "I know, Sam. But I'm going in, and you can't stop me."

He threw his hands in the air, saying, "'O most pernicious woman!' All right. Have it your way."

As they headed toward the saloon, Katy could feel butterflies begin to flutter in her stomach. She really wanted to go in, but the unknown was making her nervous. There were few people in town, so she hoped business was slow. She did not like being the center of attention but was sure to be when they walked through the bat-wing doors.

A disheveled bum stumbled out of the saloon, almost bowling them over. He was obviously drunk and stood gaping bleary eyed at Katy as they walked in, not sure he was actually seeing what he was seeing. They were all the way through the doors when Katy heard him slur, "Hey, wait a minute," suddenly aware that he was not hallucinating. The hinges squeaked as he marched right back in, sure that something exciting was about to take place.

There was nothing fancy about the saloon. No hanging chandeliers, velvet curtains, or professional gamblers looking for a game. There was only a bar to the left, ending next to some stairs and a piano, and fifteen tables with four chairs each. The walls were decorated with a huge set of longhorns on one side and a buffalo head above the bar, staring sightlessly over the room.

There was a bartender washing glasses and a saloon girl sitting at the piano carefully experimenting with "Dixie." A dusty drifter at the very far corner table nursed a glass of something dark, and two men were playing cards. One of them was average height but very slender with the palest blue eyes Katy had ever seen. The other was built like a bull, over six feet tall and muscle-bound. His clothes would obviously swallow an ordinary man's frame, but on him every seam was in danger of bursting.

All eyes were on Sam and Katy. The only sound was the piano because the girl continued to tap the keys while studying them. Sam could smell stale whiskey. Katy couldn't identify the scent—having never been around it—and struggled to keep from wrinkling her nose in distaste. She turned to see the drunk slouching just inside the doors, scratching at his armpits, his bloodshot eyes wide open. When she turned back to the room, she noticed the drifter was smiling now, as if happy for a reprieve from the boredom of the morning.

They strolled over to the bar as if in ignorance of being on stage, though Katy felt her face flush under the scrutiny and began to wonder if she had made the right decision to come in with Sam. She was trying to put him between herself and the spectators, walking so close to him her foot came down the side of his boot, making them both look down at their feet. "Sorry," she whispered with a sickly smile, knowing every pair of eyes took in the misstep and filed away the fact that she was nervous.

Sam grinned at her and turned to the bartender. "I'm looking for Red Dancy." Katy noticed he'd said "I'm" instead of "we're" and really felt like a fifth wheel now.

The barkeep shot a glance over Sam's shoulder to the card-players. Bringing his gaze back to Sam, he said, "Red ain't here."

Sam slowly turned his head to consider the two men. Katy heard his neck pop softly in the complete silence. "Anybody tell me where I can find him?" he asked while turning back to rest his eyes on the bartender.

"Who wants to know?" asked the blue-eyed cardplayer.

Sam faced him, rested his elbows on the bar, and said, "Who's asking?" A ghost of a smile crossed the man's lips, but instead of answering he picked up a toothpick from the table and parked it to the side of his mouth. The big man just stared, and Sam noticed his small, piglike eyes boldly looking Katy up and down.

Katy saw the examination and shifted her feet uncomfortably. She had tried on a new pair of riding breeches and cream-colored shirt at the clothing store and liked them so much she had decided to wear them all day. But now she felt as if she had nothing on at all.

Sam decided to give it one more try. "Let me ask an easy one. Would any of you talkative gents know when Mr. Dancy will be back to this fine establishment?"

After another lengthy silence, Blue Eyes slowly took out his pocket watch, made a great show of calculating the time, and put it back in his vest pocket. "Shortly," was all he said.

Sam looked at Katy and said, "We'll just wait." He had seen Blue Eyes's kind before. He had the look of a gunman—worse yet, a bored gunman yearning for something to do besides play cards. Sam knew he should steer clear of him, but his partner was another matter. Even though he and Katy were in a saloon, the brute was crossing the line of propriety with his unabashed examination of Katy. Sam had just taken Katy's arm and was ready to lead her to a table away from everyone when the big man spoke for the first time in a raspy voice.

"Maybe you and your lip should wait outside while the—" he paused and licked his lips—"lady and I have a little chat." The saloon girl abruptly stopped playing.

"Maybe you should go soak your head in the horse trough," Sam returned, then deliberately sniffed the air distastefully in the direction of the man. "Or are you allergic to water?"

The slitted eyes narrowed even more, and the man's face suffused with color. His meaty hands curled into fists and his whole body tensed. The bartender, sensing broken furniture and glass, called sharply, "Burl!" but it was too late.

Like a wounded moose, Burl gave a guttural cry and lunged at Sam. A thunderous right hand whistled over Sam's head as he ducked at the last moment. Sam threw a left-right combination to Burl's midsection. He heard a satisfying "Oof!" and moved to a clearer spot on the floor.

Katy backed away and found herself standing next to the drunk, who was watching the action with the same stupefied expression. She put her hands over her mouth in horror, realizing that this was the third act of violence she had witnessed in a week. Sam and Burl were the same height, but Sam appeared severely overmatched by the raw bulk of his opponent.

Burl continued his march toward Sam, trying to corner him between the bar and piano. Sam saw what was happening and tried to rush right by the brute, but Burl caught his coat sleeve. Sam was snapped back into a crashing right that landed solidly between his eyes. The blow was so hard it ripped the coat out of Burl's hand as Sam fell backward.

With lights flashing before his eyes, Sam shook his head vigorously, then managed to see that Burl was almost on him. He knew if the big man caught him again, he was finished. He kicked both legs with all his strength at the blurry figure and felt them meet flesh and bone solidly. Eyes clearer, Sam jumped to his feet as Burl fell against the piano. Sam followed and landed as hard a left hook as he could deliver. The punch jerked Burl's head and bloodied his lip, but his huge arms shot out and snagged Sam's coat lapels. Sam managed to land a right but did no damage in the close proximity. Sam felt himself being hurled completely over a table, landing on the hard floor. He made it to his hands and knees when he felt a tremendous kick to his ribs that sent him sprawling on his back. Before he could open his eyes, Burl delivered a kick to Sam's head, grazing his left cheek and leaving a nasty scrape.

Almost unconscious, Sam managed to open his right eye and watch helplessly as Burl raised his foot to smash it directly into his face. He turned his damaged cheek away from the impact and heard a thunderous explosion. He opened his eye and saw Katy standing five feet away, the .32 in her hand pointing to the ceiling. A small, thin curl of smoke filtered from the barrel.

"That's enough!" she shouted, bringing the small handgun down to level it at Burl's surprised face. His leg was hanging in the air, but he quickly put it down and turned to face her. Blue Eyes had let his hand slip to his side away from Katy, where he had his own gun. Katy saw the movement and transferred her aim from Burl to him. "Get your hands on the table, right now!" she spoke through clenched teeth. He hesitated, gauging her seriousness. She took a step toward him, brown eyes blazing. "I said, *now!*"

He relented, smiling the same faint smile.

Burl had been measuring the distance between Katy and himself. Since she had taken a step forward, he could . . . just . . . maybe . . . reach . . .

The gun swung around to his face again, and everyone in the room heard the sound of the hammer being drawn back into the cocked position. "Try me," Katy whispered.

Burl considered the hazel-green eyes opened wide with excitement and fear. He also noticed that the gun was held completely still and unwavering, the black hole of the barrel aimed directly at his nose. The chamber still leaked a minute amount of smoke, so faint he was sure he was the only one that could see it. He slowly raised his hands.

Sam pulled himself into a sitting position on the floor and stared at Katy in disbelief. He'd never expected her to actually pull the gun he'd given her, much less threaten someone with it—although he was very happy she had.

"I'd stand down, Burl, if I was you," a voice called from the entrance. Katy backed away so she could keep the gun trained on the two thugs and see the newcomer at the same time. He was of medium height, with a well-built frame and red hair. She noticed his eyes were almost identical to hers in color. Dressed in a black suit with a ribbon tie, he was smiling as if very amused and extremely glad he had entered the scene.

Katy took in the hair color and commented, "I don't suppose there's any chance you're Red Dancy?"

"In the flesh, ma'am," he replied, removing his hat. His eyes moved to Burl, who had not moved an inch but continued to watch Katy. "I said stand down, Burl," Red ordered, the smile leaving his face for the first time since he had entered. The transformation was remarkable to Katy. One moment he had seemed like a kindly uncle joining in the fun. The next moment his countenance was threatening, almost dangerous. Burl was obviously used to taking orders from him and dropped quickly into the nearest chair with a venomous glare at Katy.

"Rita!" Red called to the girl at the piano. "See to Mr. . . . ." He gestured at Sam and looked questioningly at Katy.

"Sam Bronte."

"See to Mr. Bronte's needs, if you will. And Miss . . . ?"

"Steele. Katy Steele."

"And a lovely name it is. Very strong name. Miss Steele, would you mind accompanying me to my office so we can work out whatever this trouble is all about?" he asked, his arm sweeping over Blue Eyes and Burl.

"You'll have apologies now from Burl Overmire and Grat Cummings," Red stated. Both men immediately mumbled, "Sorry, ma'am," and Cummings even touched his hat brim, but his deadly eyes registered the same detached amusement as he did so.

Rita came from around the bar where she had gone to get a bowl of water and some towels. Setting down the materials, she helped Sam into a chair. The left side of his face was swollen and bleeding, and he was inspecting his upper teeth on that side to make sure they were still intact. He shot a dark look at Burl, who merely watched with no expression. He showed no discomfort at the blow Sam had delivered with all his might, merely wiping his bloody lip every once in a while.

"Tick, don't you have something to do?" Red asked the drunk, who was standing in the same position as when he had come in. His mouth, which had been hanging open, snapped shut, and he seriously reflected on where he had been heading before Sam and Katy had shown up. "Never mind, Tick, just go sleep it off." Tick nodded dumbly and lurched out the doors.

With a look at Rita ministering to Sam, Katy felt a brief twinge of jealousy, but pushed it from her mind and followed Dancy to a door behind the piano that led to a small room. The office was plainly furnished—hat rack, desk, chairs, and a safe—but had a huge, attractive wooden carving of a shamrock hanging behind the desk.

After being seated, Katy explained what had happened at the bar. Dancy nodded occasionally, keeping his expression neutral. When she was finished, she asked, "Do those men work for you?"

Dancy took a cigar and match out of a drawer in the desk. "Do you mind?" Katy shook her head. "They keep the peace around here on Saturday nights when the rail workers come in here to howl at the moon. The rest of the time they do some buffalo hunting. Where they're from and where they're going from here's none of my affair." He lit the end of the cigar, and Katy watched the tip glow white-hot as he inhaled. As his eyes slitted to keep the smoke out, he said, "I'll iron out Burl and Grat. You said you came here to see me about . . . ?"

Katy took a deep breath and let it out slowly. The adrenaline she had felt pumping through her during the altercation was gone, and she was beginning to realize that she had almost shot a man. She had felt no hesitation when she saw what Burl was intending to do to Sam—reflexes had told her to put a stop to it any way she could. But while Dancy had been talking, a little voice in the back of her mind had told her of the seriousness of her actions. She had drawn a gun on a dangerous man and had, in essence, stared him down. She never wanted to be in that position again. Forcing the thought away, she answered, "There's been some trouble on the railroad, Mr. Dancy, and Sam and I've been hired to find out who and why."

"Congratulations on your new employment." He puffed his cigar again, showing no surprise that a woman had been hired to accomplish what was normally considered a man's job. "I'll ask once more—why are you here to see me?"

"Your name keeps popping up after these incidents." Katy watched his reaction carefully. She saw, for just a split second, surprise.

"Oh?" he asked with raised eyebrows. "In what way?"

He's very good, Katy thought. He had covered up so fast she was starting to doubt that she had even seen the look. "Do you know anything about the sabotages, Mr. Dancy?"

"Are you accusing me of something, Miss Steele?"

"Why are you answering a question with a question?"

Red Dancy's face turned red. He was not used to being spoken to so bluntly. Suddenly he laughed—a good, long belly laugh. "Miss Steele," he managed finally, "my hat's off to the Central Pacific on their hiring the best detective available. You almost had me thinking I *did* have something to do with this business!"

Katy started to think she would never get anywhere by being tough with Dancy. He was probably used to that from men and well defensed against it. She smiled sweetly. "I only asked if you had any knowledge, Mr. Dancy. Not 'where were you at such and such a time.'" She forced a how-could-we-have-such-a-misunderstanding laugh.

Dancy recognized that he really was sounding guilty. He had been talking to Katy for less than a minute, and she had him dancing to her puppet strings. He was a shrewd man and prided himself on his ability to skip around the edges of the truth when he had to. *I'll have to keep a close eye on this one. She's trouble with a capital* T. A lawyer in Dodge City had once cornered him on the witness stand in a murder trial. Red was merely reporting what he had seen at the crime, but by the time the lawyer was through with him, everyone in the courtroom knew he was lying. Red Dancy did not like to look bad in front of anyone. He had had Burl Overmire break one of the lawyer's legs.

"Miss Steele, I'm a businessman. I own this saloon and have a ranch outside of town where I raise horses. Being in the position I am, I hear a lot of drunks talk. And that's just what it is, drunk talk. From that unreliable information, my opinion is that the incidents are sparked by someone inside the CP." He held up his hands as she started to comment. "That's just my opinion from the gossip I've heard. You came here on information from someone else, and I could send you to other men I suspect, but that wouldn't make them guilty—just as I'm not guilty. Do you understand?"

"Of course. Do you understand that my father was probably murdered by the same people who are doing these things, and I'll stop at nothing to bring them to justice?" She leaned toward him. "Nothing."

"Your father?"

"John Steele, the detective before Sam and me. You didn't know him or hear of him?"

Dancy stubbed out his cigar. "No, I didn't. But please accept my sympathies. I assure you I'll cooperate in any way I can."

Katy was at a total loss, not knowing whether he was telling the truth about her father.

———

In the saloon, Sam flinched, saying "Ouch!" and jerking his head back.

"I'm sorry!" Rita said quickly, grimacing as if she were the one who had gotten hurt. She was carefully applying a wet cloth to his cheek, wiping the drying blood from the nasty scrape Burl's boot had caused. The area was swollen almost to his eye, but Rita was still taken with his handsome face. She had noticed him as soon as he and Katy had entered and had liked watching him—the smooth way he carried himself and his overall manner of being in control of the situation. But being close to him, she couldn't help but be attracted to his freshly cut mane of thick black hair, darkly tanned skin, and light blue eyes.

"It's all right. I feel better when I think about how his foot must hurt," Sam said, trying to grin but succeeding only at wincing as she applied the cloth again. As she tended to him, he was holding his ribs where the vicious kick had landed.

"Here comes the really painful part," Rita warned, taking a fresh towel and dousing it with whiskey.

"Well, let's get it over with fast." Sam gripped the arms of the chair firmly, determined not to flinch. His breath whistled through his teeth as the burning alcohol stung his skin.

"All done. Here, take this wet cloth with you in case it keeps bleeding."

She started to get up to put the pot of water and towels back, but he put a hand on her arm. He considered her closely for the first time, since his face had been turned away from her as she mended him. She had dark hair like his, but it fell almost to her waist. She had dark eyes, high cheekbones, and a small, dimpled chin. Despite her obvious beauty, there was a hardness about the eyes—a palpable fatigue that suggested more than a lack of sleep. He couldn't help but think she looked world weary. He smiled and said, "Thanks, Rita."

"You're welcome." Very uncomfortable at his close inspection and direct gaze, Rita stood quickly and started for the bar.

"Maybe I'll see you again sometime—under better circumstances."

Setting the items on the bar, she turned and smiled the saddest smile he had ever seen. "I'm here every night."

Katy and Dancy emerged from the office with Dancy remarking, "Please feel free to visit again, Miss Steele. There's a bad shortage of pretty ladies in this town." Despite his anger at the way she had seen right through him, he couldn't help liking her and admiring the way she carried herself.

Sam looked at Katy questioningly. After receiving an almost imperceptible nod, they started for the doors. Sam glanced at Rita one last time, and she smiled her sad smile at him.

"Did we learn anything?" he asked when they were out in the bright sunshine.

"We learned that Red Dancy has a guilty look about him, and I'm sure he's involved somehow—maybe even behind the whole thing." Katy watched Sam put the cloth to his face, checking for blood. "I'm so sorry, Sam. You were hurt, and I didn't react fast enough."

"Thanks, but it's my own fault. Someday I'll learn not to get cheeky—no pun intended—with men twice my size." He laughed. "You know, that's the first time I've ever been rescued by a woman. Maybe I should hire you as my bodyguard."

"Oh, stop it. Just don't ever get in that situation again, and you won't need rescuing."

"I sure got some good nursing out of it," he said with a smile.

"But, Sam . . . she's a bad woman, isn't she?"

He gave her a surprised look. "I don't really know what 'bad' means. She's a mighty pretty one, though."

Katy said nothing but was disturbed. *How could a woman work in a saloon and not be immoral?* Possessing a scientific mind as Katy did meant everything was categorized into what it was. Oxygen was oxygen, and hydrogen was hydrogen. There was no way to get around that. A person was either good or bad, in an overall sense. She considered Sam and herself in the "good" area, because they had a definite sense of caring for other people, upholding the law, and a general knowledge of what was right and what was wrong. There was no conceit in Katy—only black-and-white ideas. She couldn't think of anyone associated with a saloon as anything but a "bad" person. A saloon meant gambling, drunkenness, debauchery, and corruption—everything against God's law. And if Sam was thinking of getting closer to someone like that, wouldn't that put him in moral danger?

She mentally washed her hands of the dilemma. It was none of her business anyway.

Back inside the Shamrock, Dancy said to Rita, "Make him fall in love with you, Rita. I want to know everything they find out as soon as they find it out."

"But, Red, I can't just magically wave a wand and make him fall for me!"

"Maybe not, but you can sure keep him coming back if you want to," Dancy sneered with a quick scrutiny of her body.

"No," Rita stated firmly. "He seems like such a nice—"

Her words were cut off with a cry of pain as Dancy grabbed her arm and twisted cruelly. "You will do it," he snapped, "or your face'll look worse than his!" He held her gaze for a moment, his eyes full of anger. Then he released her and moved back into his office.

Rita slumped into a chair, tears forming from pain and frustration. Red never hesitated to hurt her to get what he wanted, and she wondered, like so many times before, why she stayed at the Shamrock.

CHAPTER EIGHT

Meetings

Red Dancy had always started his day off with a cup of coffee spiked with Irish whiskey, whether he woke up at his ranch or the Shamrock. "One without t'other is like a babe without 'is mother," his dad used to say in his heavy Irish brogue. Red involuntarily began the ritual at eight years old when his dad had told him he was "man enough." He had sputtered and coughed when the burning liquid reached his young throat, much to his father's delight. Red had had no choice but to get used to the concoction since it was placed before him at every breakfast.

He smiled and shook his head. "Here's to you, Da," he toasted to the saloon ceiling. "Too bad you couldn't stay a step ahead of that jealous husband."

Turning his attention back to his business ledgers, Red made a tally of his profits for the last thirty days. The figure made his eyebrows rise. He knew he had been prospering, but the last month had been one of his best. The Shamrock always showed a minor profit—nothing to crow about but sufficient to keep the doors open. His ranch was showing a generous income, mostly from the sale of workhorses and mules to the railroad.

But the real money came from another expertise Red provided. The documents and figures from that enterprise were kept in his office safe, the combination of which was known only to himself.

And the money will always be coming in. The need for what I supply has been around a mighty long time—maybe forever.

Red's musings were interrupted by a small boy bursting through the bat-wing doors. He was out of breath, and his eyes grew wide as he spotted Red sitting at a table with a gun pointed directly at the boy.

"Don't barge in on a man like that, kid! You could make a man nervous." Red smoothly replaced the Colt in its holster with a whisper of leather. "Well, come on in, don't just stand there with your eyes hanging out."

The boy went over to him with trepidation and held out a note. Red took it and studied him for a moment, taking in the hesitation and fear—relishing it. "Get out!" he snapped. Instantly the boy was on the run again, losing his hat in his mad scramble to get out. He stopped and picked it up with one last terrified glance at Red, then was gone. Red laughed delightedly. *There are few greater joys in the world than scaring someone!*

He opened the small sheet of paper, and his merriment quickly faded. "Meet me in the stable" was all the note said, but Red was very certain of the sender's identity. *Funny,* he thought without humor, *I was just thinking of you.*

Putting on his hat and coat, Red stepped out into the sunshine of another picture-perfect fall day and started toward the stables. He had been wondering when Booth would contact him again. About three weeks had passed since Red had done the last job for him.

The huge front door to the stable was ajar. Red passed through, quickly latching the door when he heard a wagon approaching town. He didn't want to be seen here, and he was sure Booth didn't either. The interior was murky with the windows boarded up, the only light coming from the sunshine through the cracks in the boards. There was a thick silence inside, since the stable was empty at that time of day. Letting his eyes adjust to the gloom, he called, "I'm here!" to the emptiness. There was no answer.

After a moment, Red spotted cigar smoke drifting from the very last stall. With a shake of his head, he thought, *The man sure has a taste for drama.* The meeting places were always of his choice and never failed to have the touch of the theatrical in them. Booth had surprised Red in his own office one night. Another time, Red had been saddling his horse at his ranch before daylight for a trip to town, and the man had called out to him from the deep recesses of the barn, startling Red and his horse. The last meeting had been in a dark railroad car after midnight. At no time had Red ever seen the stranger's face. He had mentally started calling him Booth, for the famous—or infamous—actor.

"That'll be far enough," Booth declared when Red had almost reached the stall.

Red had been hoping Booth would show his face today, since this was the first meeting in the daytime. He even considered ignoring the order and meeting Booth face-to-face, but he quickly put the temptation out his mind. The man paid much too well. *Someday,* he thought. *Someday.*

"I have another job for you," Booth said. The voice was cultured and authoritative. Red guessed he was not used to having his requests ignored.

"Why are you afraid to show your face? I can tell from your voice I don't know you."

The question was ignored. "There's a load of nitroglycerine going up the mountain road tomorrow. Put a bullet in it. The whole ledge will probably collapse with the blast, and it'll take a month to repair it." Red saw more smoke waft into the air.

Red had always done the jobs without question, but this time he couldn't resist. "Why are you trying to stop the railroad?"

"You're paid to complete jobs, not ask questions. And paid very well, I might add." A thick envelope was pushed through a crack in the stall and fell in the straw with a soft rustle. Red retrieved it and thumbed through the cash quickly, grunting with satisfaction.

"Well, let me ask you one more. What about these two detectives—Steele and Bronte? I haven't talked with him, but she sure is a sharp one."

"Let me worry about them. Miss Steele has something of mine that—"

"What?" Red exploded. "She's onto us?"

There was a long pause. Then Red heard a low, menacing laugh. "I see you've figured out that if *I'm* caught, you're going down with me. Whereas if *you're* found out, it's 'Bye-bye, Red,' and I'll just find another man for the jobs." His tone became even more sinister. "Don't let your idiot henchmen botch this up like the last one, or I'll have your liver for breakfast."

Red didn't mention that the plans for John Steele's murder had been his own. "How did they find out it wasn't just a heart attack?"

Booth snorted contemptuously. "She's a detective—she detected. Why didn't you just set his house on fire or throw him off the mountain? There's no need to be so fancy with your 'accidents.'" He paused, considering. "Ah, never mind. It's done, and we can't change it." Red sensed another pull on the cigar. "Is there a problem with today's instructions?"

"No."

"No, *sir.*"

Red hated this part. Booth always insisted on trying to show who was top dog in their dealings. *Watch the dog behind you, Mr. Booth. He might bite.* "Yes, sir."

"Good. Stay in here for five minutes."

Red heard the squeaky hinges of a door and then a slam. Moving quickly to the nearest wall, he put his eye to a crack and searched frantically for the running figure. Seeing no one, he raced to the other side of the stable and tried another crack. Nothing. He ran to the back door and, taking a deep breath, opened it enough to push his head out. The closest building was almost a hundred feet away. The man had vanished.

Sam and Katy had worked all morning on the codes her father had found. Sam's friend in Sacramento had definitely ruled out a language, so they were left with trying to solve a code of some sort. They'd tried for hours to solve it, substituting every combination of letters they could think of, but their troubles had gotten them exactly nowhere. It was exhausting, tedious work, and both were discouraged from the hours spent with no progress.

"You know what we have here, don't you?" Katy asked, not even wanting to say it.

"Yeah—a man going cross-eyed." Sam put his head back, rubbing his eyes gently.

"Besides that. We've been trying to substitute letter for letter, and it obviously doesn't work. I'm afraid there's a book somewhere with the only solution."

"What do you mean?"

Katy picked up one of the telegrams. "For instance, the x in this word probably has a wholly different meaning from the x in this word. We need the book to solve this."

The magnitude of what she was saying dawned on him. "A code book. Do you realize it could be anywhere?" He shook his head and donned his hat. "I need a break. Think I'll go for a ride—you want to come?"

"No, I think I'll go nosing around and see what I can find out."

Michael Yeats managed to find Sam a horse that was available— a spirited bay colt with a long tan mane. Michael had told him of a nice creek that was a couple of miles toward town off the road. Sam thanked him and allowed the colt to run off the morning's staleness since he had been in a fenced area.

Sam felt better immediately, feeling the fresh air rush past him, the smooth efficiency of the horse's flanks working beneath his thighs and the sun shining on his face. He had not gone for a ride while in Sacramento, merely walking or taking a carriage for his errands. Every time he got on a horse after a long interval, he promised himself to never let the layoffs happen again because he enjoyed riding so much.

When he felt the colt tiring, he eased him down slowly to a trot. The horse resisted walking, as if he were anxious to get to their destination. Sam turned off the road at the landmark Michael had told him about and spotted the creek after topping a small hill. He was surprised and disappointed to see a wagon parked in the small clearing next to the water, and he decided to look for another place to sit on the bank.

He had turned to ride farther down the creek when he heard a shout from below. A woman was sitting on the other side of the wagon, waving at him with urgency. He rode toward her, scanning the area for movement. He had heard of highwaymen setting traps in just this way, but then he realized that even a stupid thief would have set his ambush beside the road, not out of sight of it.

As he neared the wagon, he was startled. "Rita?" he called out in surprise.

"Sam! I was so afraid of who might find me, but I need help."

He dismounted and let the horse go to the nearby creek to drink. Rita had not moved, and the skirts from her dress sprawled around her. Other than her worried look, she appeared as if she were merely whiling the time away, relaxing by the water. "What's the matter?"

"I stepped in a hole and twisted my ankle—maybe sprained it." Sam saw that her foot was uncovered, and she was tenderly kneading the area.

"Let me have a look," he said while squatting down. He gingerly inspected the ankle, noticing she was wearing brown hose to match her skirt. "It doesn't seem to be broken."

Rita made a disgusted sound from deep in her throat and explained, "I tried to get in the wagon, but my ankle just wouldn't support me. I kept falling and just decided to wait until someone came along. Luckily you came to my rescue before I had to wait too long." She smiled at him.

"It's starting to swell. Take off that stocking." Sam soaked his bandanna in the cold stream, carefully keeping his eyes averted while she removed her stocking. Sam returned to her, and her breath drew in sharply as the ice-cold cloth touched her ankle and then again as Sam lifted her leg to wrap it around.

"I get to be *your* nurse today," he observed with a crooked grin.

"Yes, and quite a nurse you are. You've been here five minutes, and I'm already short one stocking." She winked playfully. "That's a pretty impressive bruise you have there."

"Thank you." His cheek was still swollen a bit and had turned a sickly shade of yellow. He had a darker discoloration starting under his eye.

"Don't worry, Sam. It doesn't take away from your dazzling good looks."

He laughed and said, "Thanks." He was silent for a few moments, then said, "You know, I don't even know your last name."

"Devoss."

"Devoss. Devoss," he repeated, as if testing it on his tongue. He went to the horse and tied him to a tree branch. "I like that. It's very exotic." He returned to sit beside her. "By the way, why were you out here in the first place?"

"I just like to get away from that nasty saloon every once in a while. And it's so beautiful here." Sam watched her look around and noticed her nose was slightly hooked but not unattractive.

He could smell the scent of perfume on the soft breeze and breathed in deeply. "So, where do you come from, Rita Devoss?"

"Originally? Pennsylvania."

Sam waited for more, but she just reached down and adjusted the neckerchief on her ankle. "Pennsylvania's a long way from Cisco, California."

"Yes, it is." Another pause.

"I'm sorry, I don't mean to pry. I'm just naturally curious—bad habit."

Rita watched him as he picked up a small rock and threw it in the creek. She hated talking about herself. Most of her liaisons were with men who didn't care a bit about her past. There was very little small talk in her line of work, and when there was, it usually consisted of her listening instead of talking. Men loved to talk about themselves, but Sam seemed genuinely interested in her, and her reluctance melted away. She sensed that he was not like the typical man that came along in her life. *Besides, he has trusting eyes,* she thought.

"My father was a coal miner, but he was killed in a mining accident when I was very young. My mother remarried, but—I didn't like the man very much. I ran away when I was fourteen, with a fast-talking salesman." She smiled sadly and shook her hair out of her eyes. "He was the answer to a little girl's dream of getting out of a mining town and seeing the world. He abandoned me in St. Louis."

"You were in St. Louis?"

"Yes."

"So was I! I worked on a riverboat that was moored there—*The Jolly Molly.*"

"I know that boat! A gentleman took me to dinner there once."

"Did you try the gaming tables after dinner?"

She nodded. "He played poker, and I played roulette."

Sam laughed and said, "Then maybe I took some of his money. I ran a table for a while."

They decided that maybe they had seen each other before. Sam liked her laugh and her openness, and they ended up talking of many things. Her relationships had been much the same as his—fleeting, passionate, and fun, but with a little something missing that made separating from the various people easy.

He told her how he and Katy had met and what they were working on. Rita listened carefully, not because Red had told her to, but because she found herself liking everything about him—his voice, his knowledge, and his interesting experiences in the theater. At one point he became animated in telling a story, and she found herself staring at his hands.

Noticing, Sam asked, "What is it?"

Rita took one of his hands in both of hers and turned it over and over. "You have nice hands."

"I do?"

"Yes. Strong, but, well, like a musician or an artist." She raised her dark eyes to meet his.

Sam became very aware of her closeness and her soft touch on his skin. With his free hand he cupped her dimpled chin and brought her lips to his in a kiss—slow and delicate. The smell of her perfume was intoxicating him, and it was with regret that he slowly pulled back.

She liked Sam all the more for his consideration, for she knew that most men wouldn't have stopped with just a kiss. They simply sat beside each other, neither talking—and not needing to talk— holding hands and watching the creek flow by them.

After a while they agreed it was getting late, and he picked her up, wincing from his bruised ribs but managing to cover a groan. He carried her to the wagon, kissing her gently before releasing her. Neither of them wanted to leave.

"I'll see you soon," Sam said softly.

"Wait—your neckerchief," she said, starting to take it off.

"Keep it," he urged, "and remember today."

Rita smiled. "All right." She watched him as he mounted and rode away, stopping at the top of the hill to wave. She returned the wave and thought, *Red doesn't have to worry about Sam falling in love with me. He has to worry about me falling in love with Sam.*

The next day was Sunday, and although the railroad didn't allow the day off, the workers didn't have to start until midmorning.

Katy and Sam had breakfast with Chang's work gang, and after they were through eating, Chang came up to them, smiling broadly. "Come—" he motioned to them—"have surprise for you." They followed him to another area where twenty or thirty coolies were gathered, sitting on the grass. Katy saw Key and Lo Sing, who waved enthusiastically at her.

"Like you meet James Chan," Chang announced as a smiling Oriental walked up to them. "He speak very good English."

"Miss Steele, Mr. Bronte, how are you?" James said with no accent whatsoever.

Katy and Sam exchanged surprised glances. Katy stuttered, "How—what?"

James laughed and said, "My father was a whaler from China, and he decided to relocate here when he retired. I was born in San Francisco, and my mother taught me English as well as Chinese. I bring supplies to the Chinese every Sunday since the Central Pacific doesn't bother getting them the food they're used to eating."

"How nice," Katy said. "What do you do in San Francisco?"

"I have a shrimp boat, and my wife grows vegetables like those in the Shandong province, where Chang and many others come from."

Chang broke in. "Come, come, must get started," and off he went to the front of the crowd.

"Chang preaches a small sermon every Sunday," James explained as they made their way, "and he asked me to translate for you today."

"Great!" Sam said with pleasure. He was feeling very cheerful after his encounter with Rita the day before. He hadn't mentioned it to Katy when he'd returned, preferring to savor the meeting rather than explain it. Besides that, he really didn't know *how* to explain it and had carefully avoided trying to evaluate his feelings for Rita, choosing to remember the afternoon with fondness rather than confusion.

Sam couldn't remember the last time he had heard a sermon. His father had beaten any desire to learn more of the gospel right out of him. But that was deep in the past. He didn't want to think about those memories today.

They seated themselves, with James slightly in front of them so they could hear his translation. Katy looked around the small crowd and saw no Irish faces. She supposed that even if some of them wanted to attend, the peer pressure would be too great if they associated with the Orientals.

Chang cleared his throat and said something. Immediately James started translating. "Let us pray. Dear Father in heaven, we seek your Holy Spirit and your blessings today. Bless this gathering and reward them for their hard work they do today. We pray for our loved ones across the ocean, that you may keep your merciful eye upon them. In Jesus' name we pray. Amen."

Chang held up a small Bible and continued, with James translating for the Americans. "This is God's Holy Word. I had never seen a Bible until I came to this country. When my wife and daughter were killed in the accident earlier this year, I was heartbroken and had no will to live. I prayed and prayed to the Buddha to relieve my pain, but my prayers were never answered.

"One day, a white man came to me and handed me this Bible. His name was John Steele." Chang turned to look at Katy and smiled.

Katy had been listening to James's translation with one ear when she suddenly heard her father's name. When James was through translating, tears stung her eyes, for Chang hadn't mentioned to her how instrumental her father had been in his conversion. She realized there was so much she just didn't know about her father, and the regret she felt was a very real and sudden pain in her heart. The tears she'd been trying to hold back suddenly broke free and trailed warm tracks down her cheeks. A handkerchief appeared before her blurry vision, and she gave Sam a grateful look as she took it from him.

Chang continued, "He told me to read about a man in this book that bore a burden unequaled in anyone's memory, before or since. So I read about him. Then one day I prayed to him, for he is the Son of God. And my own burden was taken from me, and he put it upon his shoulders. Since that day, I have known peace like never before in my life.

"Some of you here do not know my God. You ask, 'Who is this God that we cannot see?' I tell you that this God has walked the earth, some eighteen hundred years ago, in the form of Jesus Christ.

"Let me read from a book called Colossians about this man called Jesus: 'He is the image of the invisible God, the firstborn of every creature: For by him were all things created, that are in heaven, and that are in earth, visible and invisible, whether they be thrones, or dominions, or principalities, or powers: all things were created by him, and for him: And he is before all things, and by him all things consist.'

"My friends, it is simple. Jesus said, 'Come unto me all ye that labour and are heavy laden, and I will give you rest.' Nothing could be easier than that. Believe me—I know." Chang smiled radiantly.

"Today I publicly praise the name of Jesus for giving me peace," Chang continued, "and for giving my soul rest."

Katy scanned the coolies sitting quietly and listening intently. She had seen one man get up and leave when Chang had mentioned his disappointment in Buddha, but the rest of the people remained rooted to their spots, definitely intrigued.

"If any of you have more questions, please come see me or Key

Sing, and we will be happy to try to help you. Thank you for coming, and God bless you."

Katy managed to control her tears. She still missed her father, but she thought that these tears were for herself now. At this moment, she wanted nothing more than to sit down with John Steele and talk to him about God. She wanted to question him about his quiet faith.

Likewise, Sam was touched, not moving through the whole sermon. He had never heard of a forgiving and nourishing God— only one that punished severely for wrongdoings. His father never even preached about Jesus, only about the wars and tribulations of the people of Abraham, Moses, and David. He had been vaguely aware of Jesus' life, but Chang's obvious personal relationship with him made Sam want to learn more.

Key Sing appeared and asked, "How you like?" with a toothy grin.

Both Katy and Sam assured him they were impressed, with Katy saying, "It's been a long time since I've been as moved as I was during the sermon. I'd like to talk to you and Chang more in the future if I can."

"Oh, Key like that very much, Miss Kahtee. Key look forward to telling wife back home about Jesus, too, when she get heah."

When Chang came by, Katy said, "Thank you, Chang. That meant so much to me."

"Is nothing, Miss Kahtee," he said with a wave of his hand. "Without Mr. John, Chang not know where I be today."

"I wish I'd known him," Sam said softly.

Katy put her arm through his as they walked back to camp. "Me, too, Sam. Me, too."

From her wistful tone, Sam wasn't sure if she was speaking for him or for herself.

CHAPTER NINE

Nitro

Katy slammed her pen down on the wooden desk in frustration when she saw what she had done. Despite the fact that she was almost sure there was a code book somewhere, she couldn't leave the puzzle alone. Whenever she passed the locked drawer in which she kept the papers, her eyes invariably strayed to the half-moon iron handle that mocked her in its resemblance to a huge grin. Before she knew it, she would have the codes spread over the desk, stubbornly attempting to solve them by sheer willpower. Whenever working for an extended period, she would sometimes find small doodles on her paper that she didn't even remember drawing. Today, there was a large capital *E* with a line drawn down the right side of it, enclosing it, and small flowers drawn inside. A *W* was done the same way. There were sketched clouds all around, some with lightning bolts shooting through them, straight at some terrorized stick people on a hill. She had to laugh at the mindlessness of this last one. Cocking her head, she considered it for a moment. *Hmm, maybe not so mindless after all,* she thought, as she drew a sign pointing to one of the men that said "Sam." And she also noticed one figure had long hair. *I've got to stop being so negative,* she told herself. *We're going to catch the killer before anything strikes us.*

Several days had passed since the Sunday sermon, and Katy

felt they were no closer to the criminals than when they had arrived. She had talked to dozens of workers, and the only information they could give was to show her the tent where her father was found. The space where it had stood was starkly vacant in the sea of tents. No one chose to sleep there, whether out of respect, which everyone claimed to have for John, or from superstition. The men that saw him on his last night on earth claimed he was feeling fine, was in good spirits, and had acted perfectly normal in manner. In other words, Katy had nothing—except the codes, which she and Sam hated with a passion because they were so confounding.

Sam's contribution had dropped to almost nil. He had gone to the Shamrock every day, leaving Katy with most of the interviewing. Chang had helped her with the coolies, translating when she needed it, but the Orientals knew even less than the Irish. Katy doubted that the Chinese would share any information they did have, preferring to let the white man sort out his own problems. Sam had helped her occasionally, but his attentions were mainly spent courting Rita. He would inevitably make some excuse, and off to the saloon he would go, leaving Katy to handle the lion's share of the work.

Katy was tired of it.

When Sam returned for lunch, she asked to speak to him in the caboose. "Did you have a good time today?"

"Sure," Sam replied, not sensing the dangerous tone Katy had used. "I'm teaching Rita how to play chess, and today she almost—"

"I don't care how Rita's chess game is going!" Katy stated crossly. She had intended to have a calm conversation with him but didn't realize until then how moody she was feeling. "We have a job, Sam. We're employed, and we're getting nowhere!" She found herself pacing around the small area, needing to burn off angry energy. Sam was watching her cautiously, much like he would watch a mountain lion that was irritated at his presence. "We have a responsibility here, an obligation to find some very bad men and put them away and prevent them from destroying something or someone else. Do you remember, Sam? Do you?"

"Of course, I—"

"Well, I'm almost positive that we can rule out Rita as a suspect, aren't you? She just doesn't seem like the type of girl that would blow up a railroad or murder somebody, does she?"

"What are you getting at, Katy?" Sam asked, feeling anger build up inside himself, too.

"I'm saying that out of five thousand people in a ten-mile area, I'm fairly certain four are not suspects: Chang, you, me, and that—that—"

"Be very careful, Katy."

"—that dance-hall girl-for-hire that you have no business with—"

"Enough!" Sam erupted, slapping his hat against his thigh. "You have no right to tell me my business! And who are you to judge anyone else? You don't even know Rita."

"I know she's a saloon girl, Sam. She doesn't sit around playing checkers with the boys every Saturday night."

They were standing face-to-face now, both wide eyed with excitement and anger. Sam said, "Her business is none of your affair, either."

"It's wrong, Sam. What she does is wrong, and you know it."

"I do what I want, when I want, Katy," he pronounced, jamming his hat on his head. "I told you that when we first met. Kindly keep your nose out of my business, and we'll get along better." He turned and left, slamming the door so hard the caboose rattled.

Katy stood with her fists clenched, then became aware of her fingernails digging into her palms. She put both hands on the desk and leaned over with her head bowed, willing herself to calm down. Her eyes went to the coded messages involuntarily. *I've got to get out of here! I can't look at those things again today.*

Deciding to go find Michael Yeats, Katy asked around the work crews and was told he was at the foot of the mountain. She arranged for a horse and wagon from Ringo Jukes, since the mountain was miles away.

Katy wished her confrontation with Sam had been calmer, but the damage had already been done. She couldn't understand why he hadn't seen her point about Rita being the wrong kind of girl. The relationship was taking Sam away from their investigation, but that wasn't the only thing that bothered her. She had nothing against Rita, but Katy cared about Sam and didn't want him to be hurt. That seemed to be the only way an association with a saloon girl could end up. *Why can't he see that?* she wondered.

Then again, maybe Sam was right in telling her to mind her own business. He was a big boy and had gotten along fine without her so far. Being a gambler and thespian was not the most prestigious choice of careers, so surely he had been around that kind of woman before. With a silent nod she decided to apologize to him for overstepping the lines of friendship. But she wouldn't go back on her insistence of his spending less time at the Shamrock and more time on the job.

As Katy neared the mountain she saw a narrow road carved into the side, ending at the mouth of a tunnel about halfway to the top. She could see a wagon going up the incline carrying supplies to the workers in the tunnel. She hoped Michael was at the foot of the mountain like she had been told.

A coolie informed her that Michael was in the tunnels for the day, supervising the workers. Then he pointed to Cole Price, who was directing the loading of some rails and ties into a wagon with two tired-looking mules. Katy had seen glimpses of him around the construction before, but they hadn't had a chance to speak. He cut an authoritative figure with his height and strangely white, but beautiful, flowing mane of hair. *I need to talk to him anyway,* Katy thought and picked her way to the work gang through fallen branches and twigs scattered about the site.

Price happened to glance up and see her approaching, and his eyebrows raised in surprise. "Good morning, Miss Steele! Or should I say afternoon?" He pulled a pocket watch from his black vest and peered at it. "Well, it's almost lunchtime." He turned to the coolies and announced, "We'll break for something to eat as soon as this is loaded."

"You mean you actually take a break every now and then?" Katy asked.

He grinned slightly and answered, "The men do. I've just got too much to do."

"The railroad just won't be finished without you?" Katy teased.

"I like to think so," he said with a smile. "So, what brings you out here?"

"I just wanted to see how things were going and decided to come out to see how this end of the operation works."

He waved expansively. "Here it is. Loading is about the only thing done down here. I just stopped off before going up into the tunnel." He removed his hat and wiped the sweat from his brow. "So, how's the investigation going?"

Katy didn't meet his eyes. "Slowly."

Price didn't miss the discouraged undertone of the one word. "That bad?"

"It could be better," she sighed.

Katy heard her name being shouted, and she turned to see Key Sing and two other coolies waving at her from a wagon slowly heading up the mountain road. She waved back and watched until it was out of sight.

Price gave a small chuckle. "There's a job that makes me glad ranking has its privileges."

"What do you mean?"

"That's the nitro wagon."

"Really?"

"Yep. A brand-new batch for the tunnels. It'll be coming into sight again in a moment. Come over to this clearing, and I'll show you the extra springs under the wagon to keep from jarring the cargo." They walked to a spot that had been freed of trees and brush in order to drop supplies that were to go into the tunnels.

Stopping beside a pile of railroad ties, Katy shaded her eyes and searched the mountainside. About a quarter of the way up, she saw that a short stretch of the road was visible from where they were standing. A thought occurred to her. "There are only coolies on the wagon? No Irishmen?"

"The Irish won't have anything to do with nitro. They leave all of that to the coolies."

"And you let them get away with that?"

Price looked at her in surprise. "It has nothing to do with me, Miss Steele, I assure you. The orders come from the very top. The Big Four figure there were enough American lives lost in the war, so the coolies are more—" He paused, searching for a word.

"Expendable?" Katy finished for him.

"Well, that's not the word I was going to use, but—"

"That's *despicable,* Mr. Price. Who do they think they are—gods?"

Price suddenly pointed, very glad to be able to change the subject. "There it is." The wagon had come into sight, still moving very slowly. The two mules' heads were bobbing up and down with the strain of pulling a heavy load. Despite the distance, Katy could see quite clearly. "Do you see underneath? Those huge springs? They were invented by James Howden, the man who mixes the nitro. With those springs, the cargo barely moves when either hitting a bump in the road, or swaying from side to side. And, of course, the nitro's securely packed inside."

Katy saw that the wagon was indeed moving very smoothly, and she started to ask, "Have you had any accidents so far, Mr.—"

The wagon suddenly became engulfed in a tremendous ball of

flame, growing so quickly that wagon and mules disappeared instantly in its expansion. The noise of the explosion came an instant later, along with an invisible tidal wave of concussion that took Katy and Price to their knees to steady themselves, hands locked to their ears against the earsplitting roar.

Katy was sitting on her feet in a kneeling position, face almost to the ground. With her breathing magnified tenfold because of the sudden adrenaline rush, Katy realized she was hyperventilating and willed herself to slow down her panting. She became aware that she was praying in a rush of feeling—out loud or in her head, she didn't know. *Please, God, don't let it be true. Please, God, tell me I didn't see that. Please, God . . .*

When she felt Price's hand on her arm, she forced herself to open her eyes and look at the destruction.

A gigantic hole had been blasted out of the side of the mountain, fire licking around the edges. Of wagon, man, or mule there was no sign.

———※————

Katy felt a definite sense of déjà vu as she glanced around the table.

Strobridge's office was a hastily built affair, with only a desk, chairs, and a wood-burning stove to occupy it. The meeting consisted of the same people who were on the paddleboat in Sacramento, minus the personal secretaries.

"A horrible accident," remarked Price, Strobridge's assistant engineer. His handsome face was scored with worry lines as he rubbed a hand over his chin. He was sitting beside a window, and the sun shining directly on his curly white hair was almost too bright to look at. "Not to mention we'll lose a good two weeks constructing a new ledge."

"That long?" asked Ringo Jukes. As he spoke he pulled out a couple of cigars from his shirt pocket. He stuck one in his mouth and offered the other to Price.

Cole took the cigar and nodded his thanks. "If not that long, only a day or two short of it."

James Strobridge, always the pragmatist, waved his hand impatiently and said, "We'll deal with that however long it takes. I want to know how this happened and a way to prevent something like it ever happening again."

Price glanced at Katy as if confirming what he was about to say. "I was staring right at the wagon. There wasn't any sort of jostling or sudden movement that I could see. None of the coolies on the wagon were moving around—"

"*Men,*" Katy interrupted curtly. "They were *men,* the same as all of you. Why does everyone have to make a point to differentiate between the Chinese and everyone else?" All heads turned to her, and she defiantly met every gaze. She hated to seem quarrelsome, but she had had enough of the prejudice surrounding every aspect of the railroad operation. Besides, her heart still sank every time she thought of Key Sing and the other two men. She could not think of a time that she saw Key when he wasn't smiling. Chang had wept openly when he learned of his death, and Katy had felt that very real pain, too.

"I'm sorry, Miss Steele," Price said, inclining his head. "I didn't mean—"

"Old habits die hard, Miss Steele," Jukes commented in his quiet but strong voice. "We've always referred to the Orientals in that way. I believe even they call themselves that."

"Yes, they do," Price said. "But we'll try to watch ourselves in the future," he added sincerely. Katy gave him a look of appreciation but said nothing.

After an awkward silence, Strobridge continued, "No bumping around, no sense of alarm from the drivers—what could have set it off, then?" he asked of no one in particular.

"Nitro is very volatile, as I'm sure you're all aware," reasoned Michael. "Maybe one of the jars just tipped over. Or one of them developed some sort of leak. Who knows?"

"What if it wasn't an accident?" Sam asked quietly. He had pushed his chair back away from the table, and Katy had almost forgotten he was there. "Anybody think about that?"

Katy smiled for the first time since the explosion the day before. "I did," she said in a low voice, only to Sam. She was pleased that he had brought the opinion to view.

Sam continued, "Whoever's trying to destroy this railroad—and let's face it, gentlemen, someone definitely is—they won't stop at murder. We've already seen that. We could reason that the deaths from the derailments and supply-dump explosion were a matter of people being in the wrong place at the wrong time. But John Steele's death was no accident. And if this wagon was detonated on purpose, the scum that did this knew there would be drivers and that they wouldn't have a chance." His blue eyes burned with a cold fire, and Katy realized that Sam was really angry—as angry as she had ever seen him. "And the area where it happened certainly delays your work. It could be by design."

Strobridge and the others all exchanged glances in the quiet that followed. After some sort of silent agreement, Price cleared his throat and said, "The possibility had occurred to us, Mr. Bronte. But we were hoping to be able to confirm this as an accident, as morbid as that sounds, because the possibility of something other than that is even more serious."

Strobridge exhaled loudly, as if he had been holding his breath, and said, "This simply has to stop!" He pointed a finger at Sam and Katy. "Question everyone that was even near that place yesterday. *Somebody* had to have seen something."

"I don't think we'll find out anything that way, Mr. Strobridge," Sam said. "There's only one way that cargo could have been detonated if we rule out wagon trouble."

"How's that?" Strobridge asked.

"A clean rifle shot."

From a distance, the site of the explosion seemed to Sam as if a giant with a huge gun had decided to shoot into the side of the mountain, corrupting the beauty of it. The hardwoods were showing off their fall colors, much like a peacock fanning his tail feathers for a mate. But in the center of the view, an obscene hole showed through. Earth and rock were exposed in the middle, with the surrounding trees charred black from fire.

Just like a bullet hole, he thought and immediately hoped the idea wasn't some kind of horrible premonition for him or Katy. The ones who sabotaged the railroad obviously didn't put much stock in human lives. They had killed John Steele as surely as if they had put a bullet in him, and it was no secret that Katy and Sam had stepped into his investigative shoes for the railroad, which put them in the line of fire.

Sam, easygoing by nature, felt himself growing more paranoid by the minute. The death of Katy's father had been tragic, but Sam had never met the man. Key Sing was someone he had talked with, gotten to know—he had liked the cheerful little Chinaman. The killer had snuffed out his life as if stepping on a bug. This unfortunate development had sent home, for the first time, the very real degree of danger he and Katy faced—which reminded him of something else.

"Katy, I'm sorry for blowing up like I did yesterday—was it only yesterday?—about spending too much time away from the job."

"It's all right, Sam. I came on a little strong and said some things I shouldn't have. I should probably apologize, too."

Their wagon passed the spot where Katy and Price had been the day before. Workers were collecting fill dirt for the huge crater in the side of the mountain. Three wagons were almost full. Sam and Katy had discussed whether the rifle shot could have come from that area, but Katy was sure she had heard no noise before the explosion. If the gunman had been in the area, she would have surely heard the gunshot. They had decided to scout the area around the crater.

The road up the mountain quickly turned steep, and the horses began to labor at the climb. When they reached the hole, Sam stopped the horses, and they dismounted. The sheer magnitude of the blast was almost overwhelming for both of them. They struggled to keep visions of broken body parts out of their minds as they started up the mountain, circumnavigating the crater.

The climb was difficult. They were both wearing boots and kept slipping on the damp pine twigs that carpeted the ground, having to grab trees to support themselves. When they reached the highest point of the opening, Sam considered their position for a moment and observed, "This is too close to the blast. He wouldn't have endangered himself by firing from this range. Let's try looking a little higher."

They worked their way up and away from the place they'd left their wagon. They didn't bother with the area below the crater because they knew the gunman would have to shoot down instead of up to avoid the raining fallout. They both cast glances back to the void as they walked, hoping to find a clear line of fire in the dense forest.

After a while they both stopped, winded. Katy asked between gasps, "You don't think he shot from the road, do you?"

Sam took a few more deep breaths before answering. "I doubt it. The men in the wagon might have seen him and had warning of the shot." He gulped more air and put his hands on his knees.

Katy, who had been looking around, suddenly started off in a direction perpendicular to their previous course. "Sam, this way," she called without turning, and the excitement in her voice made him follow her immediately, winded or not. Then he saw where she was heading—a large, flat rock jutting out from the natural slope of the mountain, directly overlooking the crater.

They approached the rock from above, not wanting to disturb

any evidence should this be the place. They stopped about ten feet above it, and Sam breathed, "This is it! Look at that line of fire." He pointed, and Katy didn't bother telling him that her eyes were already locked on the clear path that ended right at the center of the huge blast-hole about fifty yards away. "Perfect angle," Sam continued, more to himself than to Katy.

Both of their gazes moved from the line of fire down to the rock ledge. It formed a natural platform, almost the size of a small room. Moss and earth layered the top to the very edge. There was one very clear boot print in the dirt.

Sam and Katy exchanged cautious smiles. The sun, which had been behind a cloud, broke through and fell full on Sam's face. She saw fine whiskers shining on his cheeks and started to playfully tell him he needed a shave, but he didn't give her the chance as his gaze shifted to the ledge and he squinted fully alert. "Look, Katy! Is that what I think it is?" he asked excitedly, shading his eyes now.

Katy turned and saw the sunlight glinting off an object close to the edge. She was almost afraid to say the words, as if by uttering them the shiny metal would miraculously vanish. "If you think that's a cartridge shell, you're right."

Examining every spot before putting a foot down, they moved to the ledge. Sam picked up the brass shell casing and inspected it closely. After a moment, he grunted in surprise.

"What is it?" Katy asked.

"It's from a rifle that's very rare around these parts—as a matter of fact, in the whole country."

"It's foreign?"

Sam nodded and said, "An Austrian rifle called the Wänzl. I saw a demonstration in Washington not too long ago. The Austrians were trying to convince Congress to adopt them for the military right after the war. Look, the name's right on the cartridge." Katy studied the brass casing and saw *Wänzl* and *Aus* stamped into the brass before Sam slipped the cartridge in his pocket.

After carefully going over the area for more clues and finding none, they turned their attention to the boot print. There was a logo on the heel—a capital *G* inside a circle. The impression was of a left boot, and the top corner where the big toe would be had a deep gash through the sole. Sam placed his own boot next to the print and calculated that it was about two sizes smaller than Sam's size ten.

"I'll go get some tar from the work train, Sam. You look around and see if you can find any other clues."

"Right."

Katy made a quick trip to the work train and found the tar that was used to treat the hooves of the riding stock. She returned with a small pot half filled with the black substance. Sam built a small fire, and when the tar was melted into an ebony liquid, Katy carefully poured it into the cavity. They sat down, looking over the wreckage below, saddened by the loss. Finally the tar was cool, and Katy carefully removed the cast and held it up, smiling. "We have two clues, Sam."

He returned her smile, but his was listless. "Sure—now we only have to inspect ten thousand feet and an arsenal of rifles."

CHAPTER TEN

Always a Fresh Deck

In November the railroad engineers ran into a problem. The survey conducted in 1863 for the area between Sacramento and the mountains wasn't as complete as they thought. In order to maintain grade, the Central would have to make a cut through the remaining rolling hills to hook up with the mountain tunnel. To their consternation, Strobridge, Cole Price, and Michael Yeats found that the dense granite from the Sierra Nevada Mountains extended out much farther than the mountains. In order to blast a deep cut, black powder would have to be used. Every ounce of nitroglycerine was needed for the Summit Tunnel—the main route through the mountains. The Summit work was much slower and needed the nitro because of the efficiency of the liquid, and it was much cleaner than black powder smoke in an enclosed area.

To make matters worse, the Chinese had organized a strike among themselves after the nitro explosion. They had tried striking three times before, Katy and Sam learned to their surprise, and this one ended up much the same as the others.

James Strobridge, everybody knew, was boss of the railroad. He was a hard worker, stern but fair. But hundreds had witnessed his violent temper when an obstacle to the construction raised its head. His favorite ban was on alcohol in camp. Many a sad Irishman found his whiskey stores burned on the spot and considered himself lucky to escape without personal injury.

Upon hearing of the planned shutdown—Strobridge refused to use the word *strike* and wouldn't tolerate his subordinates saying it either—he found the closest pick handle and headed off to the Chinese camp to find the ringleaders. The Orientals, who considered Strobridge one step above any other man, held their own with him for a grand total of ten minutes. Strobridge stood before them in wrathful silence, pick handle gripped in both hands, seeking Chinese leadership with one blazing eye. He spotted the instigators by some sixth sense and brought his wooden persuader into action, not very particular about where it landed. The strike ended very soon afterward.

The short work stoppage, coupled with the new development of building a cut through the hills, had put Strobridge in a foul mood, which was the dread of all involved.

Cole Price passed along all this information to Katy one day when he stopped by the caboose on his way to the construction site. Katy was surprised to find him at her door and, after establishing a first-name basis, made them some tea she had borrowed from Chang. She found herself liking the green concoction and offered Cole his first taste. He took a tentative sip and struggled mightily to keep from spitting it out.

When he saw Katy attempting to keep from laughing, he said, "I guess you have to develop a taste for it."

"I guess you do," Katy said, laughing out loud. "Sam's reaction was the same as yours, but he did spit his out!"

"I'll just stick to coffee, if you don't mind." He smiled, showing small dimples at the corners of his mouth that Katy hadn't noticed before. His teeth looked very white against his tanned face—almost as white as his hair.

"I'll make some coffee, then?" Katy asked as she started for her small cupboard.

"No, no, Katy—"

"It's no problem."

"I won't put you to the trouble—today, anyway."

Katy caught the implication in his phrase but ignored it. "What area do you supervise, Cole? I haven't seen you as much as I've seen Michael."

"I'm mostly in the east tunnels. Did you know there were four other tunnels being built besides this monster?" he asked, gesturing with his head at the mountain looming in the distance.

"No, I didn't."

"Now with the new problem, Stro wanted me here. So here I am." He leaned forward and put his elbows on the table. "Listen, Katy. There's going to be a big dance in Alta. Have you heard about it?"

Katy nodded and said vaguely, "I heard some talk about a dance the other day but not the details."

"The details are that it's Saturday night and I'd like to escort you."

"Oh, no, Cole, I couldn't," Katy answered, flustered.

"Why not? If you don't mind my asking, of course."

"It's just—I'm not—I'm too busy, Cole. Our investigation—"

"Will wait." After a moment, he smiled and leaned back. "That sounded pushy, didn't it? I don't mean to seem that way, Katy." He rose and put on his black hat. "I've got to get to work. Maybe some other time?"

Katy, confused at what her mind was telling her and what she really wanted to say, stood and said, "Of course, Cole. I'm sorry, but—short notice and all . . ."

"I understand, believe me." He stepped out the door, turned back, and said, "Have a good day," and touched his hat brim.

Katy sat back down immediately after closing the door. *Why did I do that? He's charming and so handsome!*

At that moment there was a knock at the door. *He's decided to*

147

give me one more chance! she thought as she opened the door to find Sam.

"What was Price doing here?" he asked as he climbed the stairs and closed the door.

"Oh, just passing along some information," Katy said, trying to hide her disappointment. She mentally pushed Price to the back of her mind and told Sam everything about the new construction and the strike.

Sam had some news about the tar imprint. "One of the Irish workers happened to be a shoemaker when he lived in Great Britain. He was surprised to see the logo and told me that the boot was a Gaylord, handcrafted in England. An expensive boot, he said, and he's sure he's never seen any over here. They are two-tone, black and brown, with a high heel and pointed toes."

"Well, it's encouraging that it's rare," Katy commented, "but we can't very well search every tent in the camp."

"I know—we'll just have to find a suspect and hope he has a pair of them." Sam picked up a cup, saw the green tea, and put it back down with a look of distaste. Before Katy could ask him if he wanted coffee, he continued, "We have the same problem with the rifle. It's Austrian and rare in these parts, but with every man in the area carrying a weapon, we can't inspect them all."

Katy sighed and planted her chin in her palm, looking gloomy.

"I know you were expecting more from what we found, but every piece of evidence we get will link together like a puzzle."

"I know—I was just hoping for some miracle, I guess."

"We do know one thing, though," Sam said after some thought. "Our man isn't one of the Chinese because of the English boots and Austrian gun."

"But they could have bought them, Sam," Katy pointed out.

"Not likely. These people don't have the money to buy those items, and they probably wouldn't have heard of either since they all came here directly from China."

"So are you thinking that one of the Irish is responsible? They would be familiar with both the boots and gun and could have brought them to the States with them."

"That would seem to be the logical direction to look." Sam thought for a moment and then said, "And what's more Irish than the Shamrock? Maybe Rita could help with some information on Dancy."

The mention of Rita's name sent off a red caution flag in Katy's head. Sam had kept his promise to spend more time investigating than romancing, and Katy was silently thankful. She just hoped his comment didn't mean spending more time at the Shamrock, but she didn't want to mention it, afraid to broach the subject again.

Sam was staring out the small window of the caboose when he suddenly asked, "Have you heard about the dance Saturday night?"

Katy looked up sharply—a bit too sharply, Sam noticed—and said, "Mmm—yes, I have." She saw that Sam noticed her reaction and tried to steer his attention away with a question of her own. "Are you going?"

"Sure." Before she could ask, he added, "I'm taking Rita."

She nodded and returned to her papers, not really seeing them.

"You still don't approve, do you?" he asked, trying to sound merely curious.

"It doesn't matter whether I approve or not, Sam," Katy replied without looking up.

Sam continued to watch her. She seemed distracted, maybe a bit confused about something. And now after mentioning the dance she . . . "Did Price ask you to the dance?" When he saw her reaction, he grinned and said, "Aha!"

Katy was not in the mood to be teased. "I told him no, Sam."

"No! Why? He's so handsome *I'd* probably go with him!" he laughed.

"Because I have too much to do."

"On a Saturday night?" As he said it an unwelcome thought

popped into his head, and his smile vanished. "Does that mean that I have too much to do, too?"

Katy put down her pen and sighed. "Sam, we're friends, aren't we? I mean, I think we are." He nodded. "Well, please allow me my opinion. I care for you as I'd care for any friend, and I don't want you hurt." She held up a hand when he started to protest. "Wait! Let me finish. I was raised to think of people in an overall good-or-bad way, and what Rita does—it just doesn't sit right with me, and I hate to see you get involved with her. That's all. Do you understand?"

Sam had almost voiced an objection when he thought she was about to give him another speech about Rita. But after hearing what she had to say, he began to understand. *Katy really can't see gray areas in situations. She's always had a home, unlike me, with people there to tell her right from wrong, black from white.*

"All right, Katy," he answered, his eyes softening. "I understand. But let me sink or swim on my own. I'm sorry you disapprove, but let me sort out things for myself and decide what's right for me. Deal?"

"Deal," she said, glad to finally have the subject closed.

"Now, it's my turn to be nosy. Why did you say no to Price?"

"I hardly know him! And besides, we've got all this—" she gestured out the window expansively—"to work on."

"Katy, can you dance?"

"What? Well, of course I can dance!" Sam looked sideways at her and her shoulders sagged. "A little," she finished, holding her thumb and forefinger a fraction of an inch apart and looking sheepish.

Sam stood up and held out his hand. "Come, m'lady. Your first lesson," he pronounced grandly in a British accent.

"Here? No, Sam, I can't," Katy hesitated.

"Why not? Don't you want to learn?"

"I've always wanted to learn, but—"

"Then come on! There's no time like the present." When she still hesitated, Sam leaned closer, his hand still outstretched to her. "Katy, you *are* allowed to have fun every once in a while, you know."

She considered his laughing eyes for a moment; then, giggling like a schoolgirl, she took his hand, and he began showing her the waltz steps. They swept around the small room for thirty minutes while Sam taught her a few ballroom dances. They laughed when she stepped on his toes, and Sam praised her as she improved. When Katy stumbled badly once, he circled his arms around her waist to steady her balance, and she found her face nestled against his neck, her hands gripping his broad shoulders. Fleetingly, she smelled the faint scent of shaving lotion, a trace of cigar smoke, and an aura of what could only be his own skin, clean and masculine. His hands on her back held her firmly, and she could detect no sign of his letting go. Slowly she brought her head back and looked in his eyes, seeing the same sort of confusion that she felt, but neither made an attempt break the embrace. Feeling one of his hands shift, she thought he was about to back away, but instead she felt his soft touch at the tortoiseshell comb in her hair. There was no sensation of the comb leaving, but the release of her thick hair from the severe bun gave her a strangely liberating satisfaction.

Sam ran his fingers through her hair, considering the uniqueness of it. Bringing his face close to hers, he hesitated the instant before their lips met, but Katy could control herself no longer. She closed the gap by raising slightly onto her tiptoes, and she found his mouth warm, yet laced with hesitation.

His reluctance served to bring her back to who she was and what she was doing, and the boldness in her vanished. As if sensing she was about to break away, Sam's hold on her tightened, and she found his gaze searching her features carefully, as a man does when he finds a treasure in barren sand.

"I like your hair this way, Katy," he breathed softly.

All of Katy's self-confidence had left her, and this time his hands didn't prevent her from taking a step back from him. Nervous and embarrassed to the point of bolting, her hands unconsciously went to her freed hair, and she said the first thing that came to her mind. "Do you think I've got the waltz down well enough?"

Disappointment flashed across his face, just for an instant, before he answered, "I think you'll do fine." The moment was over, and Sam reached for his hat. "Maybe you'll even teach Cole a step or two."

Katy smiled, or thought she did. She felt the corners of her mouth turn up like they were supposed to, but the action was fueled from discomfort rather than emotion. She watched him leave, *willing* herself to say something, but no words came.

Sam didn't look back.

The town of Alta was twenty miles west of Cisco. It had been the official railroad depot before the line had extended far enough toward the Sierras to warrant a new one. The distance was discouraging, but the dearth of social activities in the area around the railroad made the trip worth the trouble.

Katy, Sam, Rita, and Cole decided to take a stagecoach to the dance. A regular run was made from Sacramento and San Francisco, and since the driver would not be returning to those cities until Sunday, Cole hired him for the short run to Alta and back.

After debating with herself until she felt she would go insane, Katy decided to wear her hair down. She knew she would be self-conscious about it for the whole evening, but she had felt increasingly free since the day she'd arrived at the end of the line. The episode with Sam had released something inside her that had frightened her at first. But after further contemplation she realized that Aunt Agnes's strict instructions to avoid drawing attention to herself were melting away layer by layer. Katy felt like a teenager, discovering herself and the world in general for the first time, and she was aware of the defensive plates of armor falling away plate by plate.

Rita's reaction to her long, flowing locks was the strongest. When she saw Katy, her eyes widened noticeably, and her mouth all but dropped open in surprise, but she said nothing. Cole recovered quickly from his shock, and an admiring look came into his eyes as he took her arm. "You look wonderful, Katy," he said with a smile. Sam had shown no surprise at all; his face held a knowing look, and with a small nod he turned to Rita and started a conversation.

At the beginning of the ride everyone was slightly uncomfortable. Polite conversation soon ran out, leaving awkward silences. Sam and Katy had carefully avoided any mention of their moment in the caboose. They'd kept their conversations limited to business and found themselves behaving with more courtesy than they'd exhibited before, as if the moment was forever lost and impossible to discuss with each other. Katy felt the need to discuss what had happened, but she didn't know what to say and sensed that Sam wanted to avoid the issue.

Sam, ever the spotlight seeker, couldn't stand the quiet moments in the coach and ended up talking of his thespian career and some of his more humorous adventures. By the time they reached the city, he had produced a pack of cards from his coat pocket and was showing them card tricks. All three onlookers were amazed at Sam's talented, quick, and nimble fingers. When the stage pulled up to the town hall, all four passengers were ready for a good time at the dance.

Katy felt self-conscious in her dress. She had been wearing split skirts for so long that the elegant black-and-green gown made her feel overdressed. Glancing at Rita in her simple blue outfit, Katy guessed the same thoughts were going through her mind. The one time Katy had seen Rita, she had been wearing the traditional saloon girl attire of off-the-shoulder, short-cut dress with tassels.

Rita noticed Katy watching her, and Katy looked away quickly. The two women had not spoken directly to each other except for exchanging greetings.

The hall was crowded with about fifty or sixty people, Katy supposed. Cole had told her there could be a crowd with the combination of local people, settlers, and railroad employees. There was a small band consisting of piano, guitar, banjo, and fiddle with a sign draped above them, proclaiming Alta Glee Club. Few couples were dancing, Katy was glad to see. She would prefer to watch for a moment before trying it in public.

Sam and Cole went to get refreshments, leaving Katy and Rita in the uncomfortable position of having to make small talk. "Nice crowd, isn't it?" Katy asked, trying to break the ice.

Rita attempted to smile, but the result was a failure. "Yes, it is."

"Have you ever been to Alta before?"

"A few times."

Katy gave up and watched the dancers, wondering idly if she would step on Cole's feet. Sam had reassured her again before they left Cisco that she would do fine, but Katy still felt that she was clumsy.

She spotted Sam and Cole returning and was struck by how handsome the two of them were. She noticed many female heads turning to watch them cross the room. Katy's eyes went to the holstered .44 Sam was carrying. Most men looked uncomfortable carrying a weapon while wearing a suit, but Sam and Cole wore them with easy grace, as if the massive guns were part of them. Every other man in the room was armed, too.

They brought cake and lime punch, and Sam suggested, "Let's find a table, if there's still one left." He craned his head and spotted a vacant one against a far wall, and they started making their way through the crowd, trying not to spill their drinks. A commotion behind them caught their attention.

Red Dancy had apparently run into a lady, spilling her punch, and her escort called to his back something about being rude, but Red either didn't hear or ignored it. He was noticeably weaving and appeared to be making a headlong dash directly to the refreshments. Katy thought he would barrel right through her, but he stopped abruptly when he saw Rita.

"Ah, Rita. I din't know you were here!" he slurred, and from four feet away Katy could smell the whiskey fumes. Red turned to Katy and tipped his hat. "Miss Steele," he said, exaggeratedly formal. He glanced behind himself as if searching for someone, then turned back to Rita. "I seem to have lost my escort for the evening. Rita, I'll pay you double Bronte's fee for the evening if you'll—"

"Back off, Dancy!" Sam stepped between Red and Rita. "This is a social event, not your trashy saloon."

Red laughed loudly, glad to have gotten a reaction out of Sam. He brushed past Sam rudely and headed toward the bar.

Before Katy could sit down at the table, Cole asked, "Would you like to dance, Katy, before we get settled in?"

"All right," she replied, glancing at Sam, who gave her an encouraging nod. Butterflies fluttered in her stomach as she took Cole's offered arm. The dancers had multiplied when the band started to play a waltz, and Katy was surprised to pass by Michael Yeats, who was dancing with a pretty blonde woman.

"Katy! You look wonderful!" he greeted and quickly introduced his partner as Marcy before whirling her off in a different direction.

Cole commented, "I believe Michael's stricken—he's spent every spare minute with her lately," speaking louder than usual to be heard over the music. He took Katy in his arms, proving to be a graceful dancer and easy to follow. After a few minutes Katy felt as though she had been dancing for years, the steps becoming almost second nature.

Sam and Rita appeared at their side as the waltz ended, and partners were good-naturedly switched as a new one began. Sam merely smiled at Katy without a word, but she could sense his approval. Katy suddenly wanted very badly for the strain between them to vanish and said with feeling, "Thank you, Sam." She saw that he understood that her gratitude included the incident of a few days before, not just the dance lessons. The moment was perfect until Red Dancy stepped in.

He appeared out of nowhere, slid between Sam and Katy smoothly despite his obvious drunkenness, and whisked her away with his hands locked around her waist. Katy tried to push him away with both hands, but he laughed, saying, "You've some fight in you, lass!" The stale alcohol smell made Katy's stomach turn over as he pulled her closer and attempted to kiss her. Redoubling her efforts, she hit him in the chest as hard as she could. She was surprised when he suddenly lurched backward.

Sam had seized the back of Dancy's coat and with a massive effort threw him across the dance floor. When Dancy stopped rolling, he was almost fifteen feet away. Had the circumstances been different, the startled expression on his face would have been comical. The look quickly vanished and was abruptly replaced by a dark, murderous glare as he scrambled to his feet. Dancers scurried to get out of the way, leaving Sam and Dancy standing alone on the dance floor.

Dancy's fingers moved to his gun, his once-blurry eyes clearing somewhat. "Don't do it, Dancy," Sam warned in a calm voice. "You're drunk and probably can't tell which of me to aim at. Don't do it." Not really believing his order would be heeded, Sam slowly put his left hand behind his back and pulled his coattail away from the .44 on his right hip. Sam watched Dancy's eyes and saw them squint ever so slightly.

Dancy went for his gun. Before it was even clear of the holster the sharp metallic click of Sam's .44 being cocked rent the still air. There was a multiplied gasp from the spectators—from the tenseness of the moment and the way the .44 seemed to leap into Sam's hand.

Dancy stood frozen, the muscles in his face giving way all at once, as if his puppet master had put down his strings. His pallor changed from a flushed red to ashen white, and he swallowed hard. When he spoke, his voice was a croak. "Don't shoot, Bronte!" He brought his hand up slowly in a supplicating gesture.

Sam didn't answer. His arm outstretched, aiming the gun directly at Dancy's face, he advanced slowly. His head was slightly down, blue eyes burning, and his mouth was drawn in a tight line. When he reached Dancy, he planted the barrel of the pistol directly under his nose, pushing slightly so that Dancy's head tilted backward, the whites of his wide-open eyes glowing from the overhead chandelier.

Sam carefully removed Dancy's gun from his limp fingers and threw it behind him. Bringing his hand back to grasp Dancy's shirt under the collar, he lifted him to his tiptoes and started walking him slowly toward the door. The spectators divided as he went, all eyes locked on the pair.

Cole appeared at Katy's side, his hand covering his own gun. He took her arm, and with Rita they followed Sam and Dancy out the door, as people crowded around trying to witness the outcome.

With a mighty heave, Sam tossed Dancy again, this time out into the dirt street. "Get out of here, Dancy! And the next time I see you, I'll take it for granted you'll try to pull that gun again!"

"You can count on it, Bronte!" Dancy yelled, his bravado restored now that the gun wasn't jammed under his nose. He stormed to his horse and mounted. Jerking the reins savagely, he fixed Sam with another fiery glare and repeated, "Count on it!" as he rode into the night.

When Sam faced them, breathing deeply from pent-up anger and exertion, his gaze fell on Katy first, and she was frightened by the deadly look on his face. For a moment she was very glad the look wasn't meant for her. His eyes were totally without feeling or emotion—unsympathetic, cold, and most of all, dangerous. She realized that Sam had been very close to pulling the trigger.

"I swear, Sam," Cole remarked, shaking his head in disbelief, "I've seen a few shoot-outs—even been in a couple myself—but I've never seen a gun clear a holster that fast!"

Sam didn't answer but looked at Rita instead. She went to him and put a hand on his arm. "Are you all right, Sam?" He nodded without speaking.

Katy felt a swift stab of jealousy and wanted to get away immediately. Rita was Sam's date, and there was nothing she could do about that. She glanced at Cole and nodded toward the door. He understood and said, "Come on, Katy, let's go have some of those refreshments."

Sam thought of saying something to Katy, but his mind was swollen with anger, and nothing came to his lips. After watching them return inside, Sam suggested to Rita, "Let's go for a walk." They started down the sidewalk with their arms around each other. He heard Rita sniffle and looked down to see that she was crying. He looked around, saw a few people on the street, and pulled her into a doorway for privacy. Holding her at arm's length, he asked, "Rita, what's wrong?"

"You just don't get it, do you?"

"Get what?"

"He'll kill you, Sam!" she blurted, tear-filled eyes boring into his. "Somewhere, sometime, you'll be alone. That's all he'll need. He'll either ambush you himself or hire it done. He won't ever meet you face-to-face—not after tonight."

Rita fell back into his arms, and Sam softly stroked her hair. As before, no words came to mind.

They stood as they were, the sounds of the music drifting through the open door down the street as if nothing had happened. Rita sighed contentedly and nestled closer to him. After a while, she whispered, "I wish I'd met a good man before—before I became what I am."

Sam felt himself smiling. "Always a fresh deck, Rita."

"What do you mean?"

"Just something gamblers say. It means you can always start over."

"Could a man forget? About—you know—"

"Some men could."

Rita pulled back from his embrace and announced, "I'm not a bad person, Sam. Despite everything that's happened to me, there's still something in me that's good."

He grasped her upper arms, looked deep in her eyes, and said, "I know that, Rita." She drew close and kissed him. He knew she was begging him to take her out of the life she knew. He also knew that the only one who could do that was Rita herself.

CHAPTER ELEVEN

Trouble at Camp Six

Katy couldn't take her eyes off of the sky as Cole drove them to the caboose in his wagon. The full moon in the eastern sky guided them as a lighthouse beckons a ship, while the stars proudly twinkled their eternal brilliance. The midnight air was pleasantly cool, but Katy had remembered to bring a light cloak with her. It would have been the perfect ending for a pleasant evening out except for the trouble with Dancy.

Sam had been unusually subdued on the trip back to Cisco, in stark contrast to his outgoing manner on the way to the dance. After thinking about it, Katy reasoned that a live-or-die situation such as a gunfight would have to be a delayed traumatic event. Sam's excellent reflexes had kicked in to save his life, but the thought of having been inches away from dying, much less killing another man, would probably have sent shock waves to his brain. That's probably why he was so quiet. Unless Rita and he had had words about something. But they held hands most of the way.

Katy was so deep in her musings that she was startled when Cole spoke up beside her in the buckboard. "How about letting me sample that Chinese tea again tonight?" he asked with a smile.

Katy was taken by surprise, and her first inclination was to say no. She didn't know what most women her age did when confronted with the question. *Is inviting a man in for refreshments*

161

after the first date, with no chaperone, considered acceptable? I'm the only woman around for miles. Who would know if I committed a faux pas? Besides, I like him and was going to fix myself a cup of tea anyway.

"I'll give you one more chance," she teased, holding up her forefinger.

"Great!" Cole replied, genuinely pleased.

The tent village was mostly quiet at the late hour, but Katy could hear a few rambunctious late revelers from the Irish camp. She heard a wolf's lonesome howl somewhere deep in the mountains, and she glanced once more at the lovely sky before entering the caboose.

Stoking the small stove and putting water on to boil, she said, "Cole, we've never gotten around to your background, and you've heard all about me tonight. Where do you come from? I can tell from your accent it's the South."

Cole had seated himself at Katy's desk after hanging his hat on the back of the chair. "Yes, I'm a Texan through and through. There's not much to tell up until the war. A normal childhood, good parents. My father was an engineer, and he apprenticed me. Eighteen sixty proved to be a bad year. My father died, and then my mother four months afterward. They were very close, so I guess you could say she died of a broken heart."

"That's so sad!"

"Yes, it was. When the war broke out right after that, I enlisted in the Army of Tennessee. I built bridges and railroads, then would watch through spyglasses as the Yankees tore them up." He was quiet for a moment, and his eyes became foggy with private memories. "So much destruction," he murmured, as if to himself. Then he said simply, "A very bad business, that war."

"I can't imagine the death and waste—don't even want to try."

"No, you don't, Katy." His face brightened a bit and he contin-

162

ued, "So, I took an oath to myself that I would only build things I could be proud of—and structures that wouldn't be destroyed."

"I don't blame you for that." Katy mixed the tea and brought the steaming cups to the desk, sitting opposite Cole. "What will you do after the railroad is completed?"

"Rise to the top of my profession." The statement was made as if there were no doubt that it would happen. "All I need is the right connections and a suitable wife at my side, and I'm on my way." His eyes showed nothing as he took a sip of tea, then regarded her over the rim of the cup, but to Katy the word *wife* seemed to hang in the air after he'd finished.

Wanting to make the word disappear quickly, she asked, "So, you've got it all planned out?"

"All except the wife part. And I'm working on that."

This is ridiculous—he doesn't even know me! Katy looked down at the desktop and nervously took a sip of her own tea, searching desperately for a way to change the subject, when Cole himself did it for her.

"How's your investigation coming?"

"We have a few leads," Katy answered carefully. After they'd gathered the evidence at the explosion site, Sam had suggested that they keep their information strictly between themselves and the Big Four, to whom they wrote a biweekly report. His reasoning was that her father, who was a careful man, apparently had been murdered for information he had unknowingly told to the wrong party, and the fewer people who knew about their inquiries the better.

"Keeping it close to the vest, eh?" Cole asked with a small grin.

"It seems better that way."

They discussed the new cut being constructed for the rail line and a few inconsequential subjects. When Cole spotted Katy trying to stifle a yawn, he drained the rest of his second cup of tea, remarking, "I guess this tea really does grow on you. I didn't choke on that cup at all." He grinned broadly, and Katy again noticed the small dimples appear at the corners of his mouth. "I've got to go." He put on his hat as Katy walked him to the door.

Before opening it, he turned and leaned down to kiss her. Katy's heart leaped in her throat—from discomfort rather than surprise. "I'm not ready for this, Cole," she said, taking a step back.

His smile didn't falter as he nodded an assent. "We've got plenty of time, Katy. Just give me a chance."

Katy smiled hesitantly, saying simply, "Good night."

"Good night, Katy."

Katy poured herself another cup of tea and sat down. The small room seemed somehow larger without Cole's indomitable presence. *Charming, good looking, and affable. I should be turning cartwheels over the prospect of Cole Price courting me! But then again, I'm the only woman around to court. That has to be why he's so interested in me. What else could it be?*

<hr />

In the days following the dance, the Central Pacific made very slow but steady progress through the Sierra Nevadas. Katy and Sam had gone out and watched the Chinese crews planting the black powder to blast through the granite hills. A coolie would get into the cut with his powder and charges, set them, then climb out to safety before the explosion. Their extreme nimbleness at scrambling out of the blast site had earned them the nickname "powder monkeys." After the cut became too deep, they were lowered down in wicker baskets to place charges with longer fuses that would give them time to be hoisted back up. Or that was the plan, anyway. With such a chancy operation there were some casualties. It was dirty, dangerous work, but the Orientals were well suited to the job because of their small statures and seemingly endless amounts of energy.

The general superintendent of the railroad paid a visit. Charles Crocker was a huge man of almost two hundred and fifty pounds.

However, because of his six-foot-four-inch height, he didn't seem fat to Katy, only big. Crocker was full of energy. He traveled from site to site bellowing orders, visiting with engineer and laborer alike, and sometimes good-naturedly joining in the work. He was very encouraging to Sam and Katy, promising to check in with them the next time he was in the area.

Cole continued to see Katy often. He stopped by almost every day after work for tea or coffee. His offer to take her to Cisco at the last minute one evening was politely refused. Katy insisted on holding Cole at arm's length, not confident enough to take his advances seriously—but most of all trying to avoid getting hurt.

Red Dancy received another note ordering him to meet Booth in the stable again. Red smiled with satisfaction on his way to the meeting. He enjoyed steady and generous income, no matter how he had to earn it.

Booth was in the very same stall as before, smoking the ever-present cigar. "Stir the Irish up," he ordered without preamble. "I want chaos between them and the Chinese. Have them break a few heads—or at least go on strike until Strobridge agrees to get rid of the Chinks."

"How do I do that?" Dancy demanded.

A thick packet of money slipped through a crack in the side of the stall. "You'll find a way. Do it today."

Dancy, once again, never caught a glimpse of Booth leaving.

———

The very next day, Strobridge sent for Katy and Sam. They knew something was wrong when they walked through his office door. Pacing back and forth in an agitated state, he glared at them with his one good eye, his face red and stormy.

Brushing their good-mornings aside, he told them grimly, "Two Chinese were killed last night, and some others were hurt."

Alarmed, Katy asked, "How?"

Strobridge waved his hand in a gesture of pure impatience. "The Irish, that's how! Some coolie supposedly stole some food, or something idiotic like that. How do these things ever get started?" he asked the air in general. "Now I hear the Irish are striking until the railroad gets rid of the Chinese. That's eighty percent of the workforce they think we can release! Ridiculous!"

"I didn't hear any commotion last night," Sam observed.

"That's because it happened seven miles away at Camp Number Six. It's another tunnel camp farther east." Strobridge plopped himself down in his chair while he talked, rearranged some papers on his desk, then immediately stood and started pacing again. "I just don't have time to go see what happened. We're at a very critical point in this construction, and I can't—" He stopped and seemed to become even more intense. "I need you two to go see what all the ruckus is about. Can you go? Today? Right now?"

Katy and Sam exchanged glances quickly. Then Sam replied, "Yes, sir."

Camp Six was due east, but they soon found that getting there wasn't as easy as following a straight line. Michael Yeats gave them directions to use a crude road carved through a mountain pass. The camp was only seven miles away, but it took most of the day to get there because they had to travel slowly on the rough road to keep from breaking an axle on the wagon. Huge holes appeared every hundred feet or so, all of them forming natural craters to hold rainwater. By the time they reached their destination, they were both tired and sore from the bumpy ride.

The camp looked much the same as their own, with tents dotting the land like big white kernels of popcorn. They happened to enter on the Irish side of the encampment, where a group of men materialized, and Sam stopped the wagon.

"G'day, gents," Sam called, but he received nothing but stares for an answer. Sam introduced Katy and himself and said, "Hear you had a little trouble here last night?"

"Ha!" one of them barked. "T'weren't us what had the trouble. The Chinks did!" This was met with lively laughter from the group, as they turned and left without another word to Sam or Katy.

They rode farther into the camp, eventually coming to the Chinese area a good distance from the Irish, as if battle lines had been drawn. They saw more than a few Orientals nursing various injuries. "This really irks my hide," Sam muttered. He raised his voice and called to a gang gathered around a cook fire, "Any of you speak English?" This was met with sullen, distrustful stares. Sam didn't blame them. For all they knew, he could be Irish.

Sam picked up the reins to move off when one of them spoke up. "English?"

"Yes, English. You speak?" Katy asked. He nodded, glanced at his companions, and walked over to the wagon. He looked about forty years old, with salt-and-pepper hair cut close to the scalp. "What happened here last night?"

"Very bad. Mickey say we steal food. We not. Mickey come back with many friends, and they very mad. Beat Chinese. Kill Chinese. But Chinese beat some mickeys, too." He seemed extremely pleased that they had defended themselves to a certain degree. His smile died instantly when he saw something over Sam's shoulder.

Sam turned to see Burl Overmire and Grat Cummings walking toward them from the Irish camp. Overmire's face held his usual permanent scowl while Cummings had a slightly amused look about him. Cummings's light blue eyes held no humor, though. *He has corpse eyes,* Sam thought. *Deader than dead.* He started to turn and tell the coolie to get back, but he had already disappeared into the group around the fire.

"You people lost?" Cummings asked sarcastically. "This ain't your camp." They stopped about thirty feet away. Cummings rested his hands on hip and gun, seemingly relaxed, but Sam knew a skilled gunfighter would be constantly on guard despite his appearance. Overmire merely stood with his hands in his pockets, his hard eyes locked on Sam.

"You know, it's funny," Sam said, resting his own hand close to his pistol. "Trouble just seems to follow you two fellas around." His tone was easy, but Katy sensed how taut his frame had become. An almost palpable danger hovered over the whole camp. Katy had noticed it when they arrived. There were no rowdy voices or normal sounds of suppertime that pervaded her own camp. It was as if the area were a powder keg waiting for its fuse to be lit. With the entrance of Overmire and Cummings, the chances of a spark going off had probably doubled.

"Yeah, I guess we're just lucky," Cummings replied, never losing his eerie smile. "What brings you around?"

"Not that it's any of your business, but we were sent to try to stop whatever's going on around here. I guess it'd be a waste of my time to ask what hand you had in this mob."

"Me? Why, none at all. Burl and me was just passing through, and see what happened! A gen-u-ine incident, right under our innocent noses." He shook his head sadly. "Shame what a man can do to his Chinese brothers, ain't it?"

Sam shook his head, too, as if commiserating. "Yeah, it's a real shame. Why don't you and the gorilla there clear out of here right now, and maybe things won't be so bad around here. What do you say?"

Overmire took a step forward but was halted as Cummings put a hand on his chest. Cummings clicked his tongue as if sorely offended. "Now, Bronte, if I was the sensitive type, I'd be mighty shamed by that remark. But seeing as how I like to get along with most everybody, I'll just chalk that comment up to you having a bad day and not really meaning what you just said." His dead smile had left his face for good as he drawled, "You didn't mean to insult me and my friend here, did you?"

Sam's playful tone vanished, too. "With all my heart." His hand moved slightly closer to his .44 as he said, "'Stand not upon the order of your going'—that means git!"

Katy found herself trying to melt into the buckboard seat to make as small a target as possible if shooting started.

After a moment, Cummings snarled, "I'd watch myself if I was you, Bronte. Keep your back to a wall at all times 'cause the next time I see you I won't be so nice." They started back to the Irish side, both of them with their heads twisted around, not taking their eyes off of Sam until they were out of sight.

"Well, that was extremely pleasant," Sam said grimly.

"Sam," Katy said quietly, as if the two ruffians were standing next to them instead of one hundred yards off, "did you see Cummings's boots?"

"No, I was watching his eyes. Why?"

"They were Gaylords. Two-tone black and brown, with high heel and pointed toe. Not like any boots I've ever seen."

"Are you sure, Katy?" Sam asked, excited and surprised at the same time. He really hadn't expected to find the boots and had mostly forgotten about them for that reason.

"I'm positive. I was staring at them all the time—I hope he didn't notice." Katy's forehead wrinkled with thought. "We need a way to get one of them so we can have a look."

"Why don't we just ask him?"

"But, Sam, that would be too dangerous! What if he tries to put up a fight—or worse yet, draws on you?"

Sam took off his hat and ran his fingers through his long, wavy hair. "That would be better than sneaking around trying to steal one and getting a bullet in the back. At least I'd have a fighting chance."

"I don't like it," Katy debated, gnawing on a thumbnail. Her eyes unconsciously fell to her bag with the tar imprint wrapped in cloth. Katy knew Sam was fast on the draw, but gunfighting was Cummings's way of life, his profession. *What if Sam were wounded, or even killed?* The thought was unbearable.

Sam put his hand on hers and gazed into her eyes intently. "Katy, I know it's scary. But it's the first break we've had on this case, and we can't just ignore it. If we can arrest him, we might find the people behind all this. I can't picture Cummings being the mastermind of all this destruction. His gun is for hire. He's a lackey that's told what to do by someone else. Besides, what reason would he have for destroying the CP?"

"Let's sleep on it, Sam." She glanced at the sky turning dark with thunderheads and said, "It looks like rain pretty soon, so let's get our tents set up and decide in the morning."

Sam flicked the reins at the horses and said matter-of-factly, "I don't think there's any other way, Katy."

The thunderstorm wasn't as bad as the forewarning had seemed. The heaviest rain skipped to the south of their camp, but the ground was still damp from a few showers.

Katy had slept poorly. This was her first time sleeping in a tent, and she was doubly thankful to Michael Yeats for the use of his caboose. The fear that things could get out of control the next morning and the unfamiliar sounds and surroundings had combined to create shadows underneath her eyes from lack of sleep.

Sam had taken down their tents, then gone searching for the construction boss, but the man had gone to another camp to get reinforcements to help stop the trouble. Sam and Katy were the only ones in authority to stop a riot. Katy suggested they wait for the extra men before trying to arrest Cummings, but Sam was afraid he might leave first—if he hadn't already.

Katy offered to fix breakfast, but after Sam told her he wasn't hungry, she found that her nervous stomach would probably rebel at food being forced down. She couldn't imagine how Sam's stomach must have felt.

He hitched up the wagon, and they started toward the Irish camp, not really knowing how to find Cummings but determined to try. It turned out they had no need to search—Cummings and Overmire were having coffee with a crew of Irishmen at the edge of a wooded area, and they stood up when Sam and Katy approached.

Sam muttered, "'Time to let slip the dogs of war,'" as they dismounted and moved to within about twenty feet of the crowd. Sam gently guided Katy a safe distance away from himself in case bullets started to fly. Cummings wore his usual half smile as he watched them. The workers sensed trouble looming—or were informed by Cummings of the bad feelings he had with Sam—and moved to the side to see how the tide turned.

Sam glanced down at Cummings's boots and saw they were exactly as the Irish boot maker had described them. He took a deep breath, hoping that there wouldn't be a showdown.

"Bronte, you're like a case of poison ivy—hard to get rid of," Cummings said, and there was nervous laughter from the onlookers. His face fell into the gunfighter's glare Sam had seen the night before. "I told you I wouldn't be so nice the next time we met, so that was my joke for the day. What d'ya want?"

"Your boots," Sam replied simply.

For just an instant, uncertainty passed across Cummings's face, and he almost looked down at his boots. Sam had been hoping he would look down. The chance of bloodshed would have been cut to almost nil if Sam had gotten his gun trained on him before he knew what was happening.

"Is that your idea of a joke, Bronte? Because it wasn't very funny."

"No joke, Cummings. I just want to see one of your boots. After you drop your gun."

Cummings waited for Sam to go on, extremely curious about where this was leading, and after a moment demanded, "Why?"

"To see if it matches this boot print of the man who exploded that nitro wagon and killed three men," Sam said, inclining his head at Katy. She held up the tar imprint very slowly. Her heart beating very fast, Katy was as scared as she had ever been in her life. She could tell by looking at Cummings that he wasn't one to just give up his gun without a confrontation.

Cummings glanced at the tar very quickly, not wanting to take his eyes from Sam. "What makes you think that's my print? It could be anyb—"

"It's yours, Cummings. Boots made by Gaylord of England. And I'll bet my hat your left boot has a gash in the sole, under the big toe." Cummings couldn't stop the shocked expression that widened his eyes. Sam saw Overmire give a small surprised jerk and ordered without looking at him, "Stay out of this, Overmire." Sam wanted Burl to be aware that his movements were noticed, too. Overmire became very still, but didn't move away.

"You ain't looking at my boots, Bronte!" Cummings snapped, showing alarm for the first time.

"Yes," Sam said calmly, moving his right leg forward, "I am."

Cummings drew his pistol in the blink of an eye and fired. Sam had anticipated the draw and plunged to the ground at his left, thrusting with his extended right leg. He felt Cummings's bullet tear through his right sleeve as he drew his own gun and fired. Sam's lightning-quick movement had thrown Cummings's timing off for a fraction of a second, and as he was aiming to fire a second time, a blossom of bright red blood appeared in the direct center of Cummings's chest. He took a full step backward and managed to look down with confusion at his bloodied shirt before he collapsed in a heap.

"Stop, Overmire!" Katy shouted as she aimed the small gun that had been hidden in her left hand. Overmire's pistol was clear of his holster, but he stopped when he saw the gun aimed at his head. "Drop it!" Katy yelled, adrenaline rushing through her from witnessing the shooting. Overmire dropped the gun with a resigned look, as if he couldn't believe this woman had bested him a second time.

Sam picked himself up, holstered his pistol, and went to the unmoving form of Grat Cummings. When he reached Cummings's pistol, he kicked it into the woods. After checking for a pulse and finding none, he sighed deeply and shook his head. Picking up Cummings's left boot, he saw the circled *G* on the heel with the telltale gash in the toe. He let the dead man's foot drop without an attempt to lay it down gently. The boot thudded softly on the damp ground.

Sam fixed Overmire with an intense glare. "Take him back to Cisco with you. Tell Dancy I'm onto him, and he's finished. Do you understand?"

Overmire's mouth worked, but no sound came out because of his surprise at the sudden vehemence in Sam's tone.

"Do you understand?" Sam shouted, moving right in his face. Overmire flinched, then nodded and lifted Cummings's body easily. With one last look back, he started walking toward the tent city with Cummings draped over his shoulder like a sack of grain. Katy went to stand beside Sam as Overmire walked off.

"Are you all right, Sam?" Katy asked softly.

Sam was watching Overmire disappear around a tent. "No, Katy, I'm not." Katy panicked and started probing his sleeve gently where the bullet had passed through, searching for a wound. "That's not what I meant, Katy," he said quietly, as if very tired. "I'm just . . ." He shook his head when he couldn't find any words.

Katy remembered how out of sorts Sam had been after the gunfight at the dance. She squeezed his arm and tried to smile. "He drew first, Sam. It's OK." He had no reaction to her words.

Suddenly realizing that the crowd of Irishmen was gathered around, she faced them and decided to try a bluff. "Nobody came here to force you to work. Mr. Strobridge says to either stop this foolishness and go to work—or leave the camp. There'll be no negotiations." Katy met each and every gaze without blinking. Eventually their attention centered on a burly man standing in the midst of them who continued staring at Katy. He regarded Katy for a long time, as if evaluating her seriousness and authority. Katy had no doubt that the workers for miles around were aware of her story. The swift verbal grapevine of the railroad was legendary. Finally, a ghost of a smile passed across his face, and he said to the others, "Come on, lads. Let's go lay some track." They drifted away with him, with a few sullen glances thrown back at Katy.

Relieved that something had been accomplished without a fight, Katy turned back to Sam and saw that he hadn't moved. He was sightlessly watching the area of Overmire's disappearance, and his face still held the haggard look. Another crowd was gathering, curious to see what the shooting was about. Taking his hand, Katy led him behind one of the nearby tents where they sat down at a table. "Sam?" she asked uncertainly.

After a moment, Sam mumbled dreamily, "I've never killed a man before, Katy. I've never—"

"He didn't give you a choice, Sam." Reaching up and gently bringing his face to hers, she said, "There was nothing else you could do."

Sam shook his head. "I rode two thousand miles to get away from killing—saw it more times than I can count—and now it's caught up with me. Only this time, it's me that—that—"

Katy put her arm through his and leaned her head on his shoulder, noticing that he was trembling. "You have to go on, Sam. Put it behind you. There was nothing you could do."

"Makes me think life's pretty hopeless."

"Don't say that!" Katy exclaimed, tightening her hold on his arm. "There's more to life than this. We're not puppets being manipulated into situations by some mad puppeteer. There's a reason this happened—maybe it was God's will."

Sam was silent for a moment, as if letting her remark sink in. "For a human being to die by my hand today? I wish I could believe that. . . ."

CHAPTER TWELVE

A Note for Sam

When Burl Overmire told Red Dancy the news of Cummings's death, Red's brain could barely absorb the facts. He stared at Overmire with unbelieving eyes. Cummings had worked for Red for ten years, carrying out many orders thoroughly and efficiently. No one had even come close to beating Cummings in a draw, and now Red was hearing that some two-bit railroad detective had killed him with one shot.

Overmire stopped rambling about the incident when he saw Red's face begin to turn a deep red. With trembling hands and a look of pure hatred, Red picked up the closest object to him, which happened to be a lead paperweight, and with a vile curse threw it against his office wall as hard as he could. The weight struck forcefully and dislodged a hanging picture of President Andrew Johnson, which crashed to the floor, breaking the wooden frame.

Red stalked over to the one window in the room and clasped his shaking hands together, trying to stop them from quivering. Muttering to himself, he turned his burning gaze to Overmire and growled, "I'll kill that . . ." Red's lips tightened into white slits as he struggled to bring himself under control. *That little tramp Katy Steele got the best of me again! Tar imprint my foot! Booth said he'd take care of her, but since he hasn't gotten around to it, it's my*

175

turn. Suddenly, an idea began forming. *Got to check with Booth first, I suppose. Don't want to make him mad.*

"Burl, go put the Help Wanted sign in the front window."

"You wanna hire somebody to take Grat's place with a Help Wanted sign?" Overmire asked, dumbfounded.

Red sighed raggedly. "I've got my reasons—just go do it!"

Overmire nodded and left. Red shook his head and rubbed his chin, deep in thought. *It might work. In fact, it will work.* He would have to explain his plan to Booth when he saw him, but Red knew he would approve. Booth had told Red to place the sign in the window of his saloon if he needed to meet, emphasizing that it had better be important if he ever did. Red had no doubt Booth would consider this important.

That night, as Red was restocking his supplies for the bar, he walked into his storage shed behind the saloon and was startled to hear, "Red, I'm over here in the corner."

Red nearly dropped the box of rotgut whiskey he was carrying. He stifled a curse when he realized who was there and demanded, "Why do you have to sneak up on a man like that?"

A thick silence ensued, and Red was starting to wonder if he had imagined the voice until he heard, "Maybe I should take my business elsewhere."

"Now don't start that again! I'm just nervous about walking into dark places for some reason." He set the carton of bottles down and peered through the gloom of the shed for a glimpse of his visitor, but the darkness was too intense. "You've heard the news, I guess?"

Disdainfully Booth said, "About your puny strike and riot falling apart? Yes, and I must say I'm not too surprised that you failed again. Incompetence seems to be the rule around here."

"I sent my best man! How was I supposed to know Bronte was that good? Where did he come from?" Red didn't like the whine that entered his voice but could do nothing to stop it.

"He's a nobody, Dancy. Maybe Cummings wasn't as good as you thought he was. It doesn't matter anyway—just another gunman gone to his just reward." The way Booth managed to so easily write off human lives spooked even Dancy. His voice became more menacing. "After a lot of thought, I've decided to give you one more chance to set things right instead of shooting your eyes out, which was my first inclination. Are you up to it, Red?"

"I'll take care of this one personally."

"That's what I like to hear! Never give another man a job if your own life hangs in the balance. And your life would come to an abrupt halt, my friend, let me assure you. I'm an excellent shot. Don't make me prove it to you."

Normally Red would count this sort of talk as bluster, but he had no doubt that Booth would follow through on his promise. Red hated dealing with the man without seeing his face, but Booth paid too well to make a problem out of it. "What do you want done?" Red asked, though he thought he already knew.

"Bronte and Steele were amusing for a while—stumbling around and not knowing where to turn. But they've proven to be more resourceful than I thought." Booth paused, and Red just knew it was for dramatic effect. "Get rid of them both. I don't care how you kill Bronte—a shoot-out, a bomb—whatever. But listen to this very carefully. Are you listening, Dancy?"

The smug, arrogant tone made Red want to curse him unmercifully, but he merely answered tightly, "I'm listening."

"The girl's murder *has* to look like an accident. No excuses. I don't want more detectives being sent to investigate the railroad. If people think she was murdered the same as her father, we could have U.S. marshals in here. *I do not want that.* Do you understand?"

"I understand."

"Good. Don't fail me this time, Dancy. Now get out of here, and don't pull that stupid stunt like you did at the stable, trying to see me when I leave."

Red knew better than to even try. *The man's a ghost! He's mysterious enough as it is without pulling a disappearing act on me every time he leaves. The very fact that I haven't been able to catch a glimpse of him in the two times I've tried doesn't make me want to attempt a third one.*

Red angrily stalked back into the saloon. He was tired of his plans going wrong and hated feeling like an amateur in front of Booth when they did. *I know who to take it out on, too.*

Rita was sitting at one of the tables filing her nails and relaxing when she heard the unmistakable sound of a pistol hammer cocked in her ear. She froze, afraid to turn around.

"I need you to do me a favor, Rita," Dancy whispered.

"S-sure, Red." He had never treated her kindly, but aiming a gun at her head went beyond everything else he'd ever done.

A pad and pencil were thrown onto the table in front of her, the pad landing with a slap that made her jump. "Write a note to Bronte. Tell him you're in danger and to meet you immediately at the deserted grain mill outside of town." When Rita hesitated, Red jammed the barrel of the gun into her neck. "Go on, girl! Write!"

Rita picked up the pencil and began to write.

———

"Sam! I've got one!"

Grinning at her girlish excitement, Sam put down his fishing pole and walked to Katy, who was standing a few yards away.

"What do I do?" she shouted.

"Stop yelling for one thing—then pull him in." Katy's pole was bent at a sharp angle and jerking around so hard it was clearly difficult for her to hang on. *Must be a monster!* he thought. "Pull, Katy! Don't let go!" The temptation to snatch the pole from her hands was great, but he held back, wanting Katy to catch her first fish all by herself.

Starting to back up the bank, Katy said, "I can't—he won't—*unnnggh!*" she grunted, tugging as hard as she could in one massive effort to bring the fish to ground. Suddenly clearing the water, the fish sailed right toward her. Katy sidestepped, and it landed softly in the grass behind her, flopping desperately.

"A bass!" Sam exclaimed, very pleased for her. "Looks like about two pounds!" He went to the fish and placed his foot on it so he could grasp its mouth.

Katy clapped her hands excitedly as he held it up. "Did I do good?" she asked excitedly. "Is he a big one?"

"It's a great size. Easy to fillet and delicious to eat."

"Can I touch him?"

"Sure."

Katy reached out with two fingers extended and tentatively ran them down the sleek side. "Eeww, it's slimy," she pronounced with wrinkled nose, wiping her fingers on her pants.

The second morning after the gunfight, Katy had decided enough was enough. Sam couldn't shake his deep depression. He rarely talked, never ate, and couldn't sleep. Katy felt she had to do something to bring him out of it, so she had suggested they go fishing in a pond Cole had told her about. Sam refused at first, but after Katy hounded him unmercifully he gave in.

The night before, Sam had cut some sturdy branches from a tree for their poles, and Chang had gotten them some fishing line from a coolie. They'd left at dawn, huddled in coats because of the fall weather that had arrived overnight, but had been able to shed them when the sun rose higher.

Katy had been fishing no more than five minutes when she caught the fish, and the smile on Sam's face while she was struggling with the bass pleased her. They fished through midmorning until their hunger took over. Katy counted twenty-one fish in their catch, and Sam seemed to be in much better spirits.

Chang had fixed sandwiches for them, and Sam used the empty picnic basket for the fish. They sat down under a tree to eat, and Sam unfolded his long frame and rested on an elbow. Katy heard him sigh deeply and hoped it was from contentment rather than lack of sleep.

Silence prevailed while they ate—mainly because they were both so hungry they didn't take time to talk. Instead they watched a duck family fishing for themselves across the large pond. They even spotted condors in flight overhead.

It was Sam who broke the tranquillity. "My father used to take my brother and me fishing a lot." He paused, but Katy said nothing, wanting to hear his thoughts. After a moment he went on, "I remember once—I must have been about seven or eight years old—I ran across a water moccasin one day, and he bit me. I got very sick and was sure I would die. My father told me that the snake bit me because I had spoken against God, just as the Israelites did in the book of Numbers."

Katy was watching his face as he talked and saw in Sam's eyes the fear and hurt of a little boy who thought he was going to die.

"Instead of taking me to a doctor, Pa took me home and put me in the woodshed, alone. Before long, I was so sick I *wished* I would die. My leg had swollen to twice its size, and I had a deadly fever. Even now, I'm not sure if what happened next was real or a fevered hallucination.

"Pa came in with what looked like a broken hoe handle. At the end was a crude snake carved from wood, tied to the handle with hay wire. He said that God had told him, just like he'd told Moses, that if I 'looked upon the serpent I would live.'" Sam chuckled without humor. "I didn't have much choice—he was waving the thing around in my face—but the next day my fever broke and I was fine." He looked at Katy when he finished and saw her staring at him with a look of disbelief and horror, her half-eaten sandwich still clutched in one hand.

"That's the saddest story I've ever heard in my life," Katy breathed, realizing she was no longer hungry.

Sam didn't comment. Turning his gaze away, he continued slowly, "I guess that old moccasin had bitten something before me and used up most of his venom. That's the only explanation I can think of for not dying that day." He paused and said quietly, as if to himself, "I think that's the day I started hating my pa."

Katy couldn't imagine the pain Sam felt from that experience. *And that's just one example. What else had that man done to a small, innocent boy? No wonder Sam is so hard and afraid to trust anyone.*

Without looking at her, Sam said, "I shouldn't have told you that—don't know why I did." Embarrassed, he looked down and considered his fingernails.

"I'm glad you told me, Sam. I—I understand you better because of it."

"Really?" he asked, raising his eyes to hers.

"Really."

He considered her for a moment. "Not many people understand us, do they? As the bard says, 'He jests at scars that never felt a wound.' This was a good idea, Katy. Thanks."

"I'm glad you enjoyed it—even though I caught more fish than you did!"

When they returned to the camp, a man neither Katy nor Sam had seen before was waiting for them at the caboose. As soon as they'd gotten out of the wagon, he approached Sam and asked, "Are you Bronte?"

"Yes."

"Then this is for you." He held out a slip of paper, but as Sam reached for it, he pulled it back and held out his other hand, palm up. Sam sighed and searched his pocket for money and gave the man a quarter. He peered at the coin, bit it, and gave Sam the note. Without another word, he mounted and rode off toward Cisco.

Sam opened the crumpled paper, and Katy saw his eyes go wide. Stuffing the note in his pocket and saying to Katy shortly, "Got an errand," he dashed for the wagon and turned the horses the same way the messenger had gone.

"Sam, wait! What is it? Where are you going?" Katy called, but he either didn't hear or chose not to answer as he whipped the horses into a run. *Now, what in the world was that all about?*

Sam used the whip unmercifully on the horses, forcing them to run all the way to Cisco. The note said to come to the grain mill just north of town, and as he neared the city he veered off the road in that direction. *What could have happened? It must have something to do with that rat Dancy. If he's hurt her, I'll . . .* The horses were tiring badly, but Sam couldn't worry about that. He saw the grain silo in the distance and spurred the tired horses, thinking crazily that he could crawl faster than the horses were running.

When he reached the site, he pulled the horses to a stop and looked around frantically for a sign of Rita but was disappointed to find no one. A movement in the corner of his eye turned his head, and he saw Rita walk from the doorway of the run-down grain office twenty yards away. She had a wild look on her face and, after a harried glance behind her, screamed, "It's a trap, Sam! Run!"

No sooner had the words reached his ears than a volley of gunshots erupted from the building, bullets slapping into the buckboard seat beside him. Sam reached down, slid his rifle out of its sheath, and jumped down behind the wagon. Jacking a round into the rifle chamber, he shot at the blue smoke in front of a window, hearing a satisfying grunt of pain. Only then did he notice that Rita lay sprawled on the ground fifteen feet away, unmoving. "Rita!" he shouted, but she didn't stir, and a ricochet sent his head back behind the safety of the wagon.

A growl escaped his throat as he raised up and rapidly emptied the Henry rifle at the building, aiming at all three windows with his five shots. Reloading while he waited for answering fire that didn't come, he brought his rifle above the buckboard for another volley when he heard a shout from behind the granary. With a careful glance at the office windows, Sam pushed to his feet and ran to the silo and around it. Two horsemen were just topping a hill behind the structure and disappeared as Sam watched. He wanted badly to follow them, but he had to help Rita. *If she's still alive,* a small voice spoke in his head.

She was alive but had been shot in the back. Sam gently took her into his arms and saw that the bullet had not gone through. *It's still inside her. Got to get help—fast!* Carrying her to the horse, he whispered in her ear, "Rita, it's Sam. I don't know if you can hear me, but we're going to get help. Hang on for me!"

Rita moaned and mumbled something unintelligible.

———

Katy paced like a tiger in a cage.

Her nervousness multiplied in direct proportion to the coming of night. The last glimmer of light was fading from the western sky as she said for the third time, "Where is he?"

"Katy, you've walked around this table forty times," Michael Yeats noted, "and it won't bring him here any quicker."

"Why don't you sit down and rest?" asked Cole. The men were seated at a table outside the caboose, their eyes following Katy as she circled them time after time.

"We've got to go look for him," she stated, stopping to glare at them both. "He could be hurt, lost, or—or—anything!"

Cole's face revealed exaggerated patience. "For the tenth time, Katy, we don't have any idea where to start looking! He could be anywhere."

"He's right, Katy," Michael agreed. "Besides, if we left now he could come back while we're out there and—"

All three heads turned at the sound of a wagon rumbling down the road at a very fast pace. "Sam!" Katy cried, rushing to meet him and noting the heavily lathered horses. She stopped abruptly when she saw Rita bundled in his arms.

"She's been shot," Sam said breathlessly, "and I couldn't find the doctor in town. Is there anybody—?"

"I don't know of—," Michael started.

"I had some medical training years ago," Cole said. "Is the bullet still inside?"

"I think so."

"Then get her inside," Cole said, removing his coat and starting there himself. He rattled off to Katy a half dozen items he would need, and she set off immediately to find them.

Sam carried Rita inside and gently laid her on the bed. Breathlessly he asked Cole, "What can I do?"

"I need you to wait outside, Sam." Sam started to protest, but Cole looked him in the eye. "Do you want her to have a chance?"

Sam nodded.

"Then wait outside, and let Michael and Katy help me. You're too tired and keyed up." Cole went about preparing to dig the bullet out as Sam dejectedly made his way outside. Michael appeared carrying bandages and patted Sam on the shoulder as he passed him.

Sam's weariness hit him full force when he collapsed in one of the chairs. He felt a thousand years old. Katy passed by and asked him something. He answered her but then couldn't remember what they had talked about. Letting his head drop until his chin touched his chest, he thought, *Just sit here a minute to get my breath. Then I'll help whether Cole wants me to or not. . . .*

His next sensation was of someone shaking his shoulder.

"Sam? Sam, wake up!" He opened his eyes and saw Katy standing over him, her brow creased in worry.

"What—what is it?" He stood up and tried desperately to clear his sleepy brain. The whole day came back to him in a rush, and he said, "Rita—how's Rita?" He looked from Katy to the caboose, seeing Cole's and Michael's shadows on the window blinds.

"Cole says she'll be all right. The bullet wasn't very deep—he thinks it ricocheted off of something before it hit her."

Sam's shoulders slumped with relief. "Thank you, God!" he breathed. He didn't know how Rita could live with all the loss of blood, not to mention being bumped around in a wagon.

"She's a strong girl, Sam," Katy said, as if reading his mind.

"Must be."

"Who shot her?"

Sam shook his head. "I'll have to tell you all about it later. For now, Rita has to have a place to stay—someone to look after her. There's no way she can go back to Dancy. Could you possibly . . . ?"

Without hesitation, Katy said, "Of course I can, Sam—on one condition."

Surprised, Sam asked, "What's that?"

"That you go get some rest. You haven't slept in two nights, and you look like you're about to fall down."

Sam gave her a tired smile. "You've got a deal."

CHAPTER THIRTEEN

Discovery

A week passed, with Rita steadily getting stronger. The wound was indeed shallow, and she was already going for short walks with Sam. Katy had had to use every ounce of her persuasion to keep him from going after Red Dancy.

"We need solid evidence, Sam," she'd told him one day.

"Rita admits he made her write the note! What else do we need?"

"To wait until she's strong enough to testify. Come on, Sam, you know the procedure. We can't just go into the Shamrock with guns blazing."

He'd calmed down after that, but inside he still seethed.

Katy had been sleeping on a small cot beside the bed and woke up one morning after sleeping through the whole night. It was the first time Rita hadn't awakened and needed something. Feeling shabby from sleeping in her clothes, Katy changed into one of the riding skirts she'd purchased in Cisco the day she and Sam had gone to visit the Shamrock for the first time. The heavy material had proven too stiff to wear without two washings, but now the dark blue garment was soft and formfitting. She discovered a small hole in the sleeve of her black cotton blouse and quickly mended it. She'd no sooner put it on than a knock sounded at her door.

With a glance at Rita, Katy opened the door and found Cole smiling up at her. Katy put a finger to her lips and went outside, closing the door softly. The cold air hit her with a jolt, and she wished she'd remembered to bring her coat.

"How's our patient?" Cole asked when they'd walked a few yards away from the caboose.

"She slept all night." Katy watched the work crews preparing to go to the end of the line. Men were cramming themselves into wagons while some chose to walk the mile and a half instead of waiting for a seat. "Chang's going to stay with her today while I take care of some things."

"Good. I've really got to go. We've got a few problems with— hey, Michael!" He'd spotted Michael driving by in a wagon filled with Irishmen. Michael didn't hear over the din of the activity and was out of hearing distance almost immediately. "Confound it! I need the elevation plans, and I'll bet he doesn't have them with him."

"Can I help?" Katy asked.

"Come on, Price!" Ringo Jukes called from a passing wagon. "We're late!"

"I'm coming!" Cole put a harried hand to his mouth, looked after Jukes's wagon, and seemed to come to a decision. "Katy, I really need those plans—could you go get them from Michael's tent and have them sent out to the site? Would it be too much—"

"No trouble at all, Cole. I'll even bring them out myself."

He took her hand and squeezed it gently. "Thank you. I've *got* to go." He started off at a run, stopped abruptly, and called, "I think he keeps them in the left drawer of his desk—or is it the right?" he finished to himself.

"Go, Cole! I'll find them."

With a grateful grin, he took off at a run.

Katy went back inside and got her coat. When she came back out, she saw Chang making his way toward her, his slightly bent figure bundled in a worn black cloak. She explained where she was going, then debated to herself on whether to find Sam. She ruled out the idea. He'd been exhausted the night before, and she knew she shouldn't wake him.

She passed a few straggling workers as she made her way to Michael's tent, every one of them sporting a fearful look in his eyes. Strobridge was not a man that easily forgave tardiness.

The engineers' tents were set off from the general population, close to Strobridge's one-room wooden office. Michael had pointed his new home out to Katy when she'd expressed misgivings about taking over his caboose. He'd assured her that he was comfortable, but Katy still felt a twinge of guilt over his having to leave the comparatively lush accommodations for a simple canvas tent. Feeling as if she were intruding, she nevertheless went inside the open flap.

The tent was surprisingly spacious, whether from the size of it or Michael's spartan furnishings she didn't know. A small cot, washstand, and miniature oak desk with a chair were the only items, and she went immediately to the desk with the intention of getting out as soon as possible. The only articles on the desktop were a few stacked papers, a geometric compass, and a faded, framed photograph of a plain woman sitting in front of a stern-looking man with heavy sideburns. *Must be his parents,* she thought absently as she tried to remember which drawer Cole had said held the plans. Her mind was a blank, and she didn't want to open the wrong one for fear of *really* invading Michael's privacy.

She decided on the left one, for no particular reason except that she had to choose one. The drawer slid out with a scraping of wood on wood, and the first thing she saw was a large black pistol resting on a brown cloth. Underneath was a letter that began, "Dear Marcy," and Katy closed the drawer with a sharp slam. *I do not want to be here!* she thought, extremely uncomfortable.

Relief passed through her as she opened the right drawer, finding a folder marked "Elevations," and she snatched up the booklet, closed the drawer hastily, and froze.

Her mind belatedly registered what she'd seen beneath the elevations folder, and she felt her throat close convulsively. With a trembling hand she slowly reached down and eased the drawer open again, praying fervently that her eyes were playing tricks on her—but they weren't.

A code book!

Letters thrown together, seemingly at random, stared up at her, mocking. Beneath the alien language were penciled notations in English written with a precise, careful hand. Phrases such as "Delay shipment of rail ties in Sac.," "Change manifest orders on . . . ," and "Stir up the Irish" assaulted Katy's brain like a lightning storm. Mechanically, her hand placed the elevations folder on top of the desk, and she reached inside for the code file. A shudder ran through her as her fingers came into contact with the papers, and the image of touching the cold, rough scales of a snake leaped into her mind. Turning the pages with trepidation building to numbing proportions, her wide eyes locked on two familiar notations. Despite the letters having no business being side by side, she had stared at them so many times that recognition came to her at once.

XUEA WH WBVXP
BBDEQPX FWLJG

Beneath was written

BLOW UP DEPOT
EXPLODE NITRO

Katy became aware that she was holding her breath, and the air hissed from her open mouth as she let it out. *The depot explosion that killed Chang's wife and daughter. The nitro detonation that killed Key Sing and two others.* The thoughts rang flatly through her dizzy mind with a sickening surety. Turning more pages, her heart seemed to stop when she saw

CRKH ZPNIOJ
KILL STEELE

The document fell from lifeless fingers to land with a slap on the floor.

Oh, Michael—how could you? The words repeated themselves over and over in her battered mind like some sort of mad litany. She stared at the folder sprawled on the grass floor and saw evidence of at least six murders. Six! And those were only the ones she was aware of. The document held more coded letters and telegrams that hadn't been explored yet.

Slowly Katy reached down and picked up the pages, making her way on wooden feet to the caboose. At one point her vision blurred from tears—hot tears of anguish, frustration, disappointment, confusion, and anger. By accident she had found the one thing she'd come to the railroad for, the one victory she'd been dead set on claiming, but no feelings of satisfaction filled her.

All that was left was a somber curtain of gloom and sadness.

———⊷◉⊶———

"What did you say, Sam?" Michael Yeats asked, his dark eyebrows arched into half-moons.

"He said you're under arrest," Katy replied. "Get your hands up."

Michael was squatted beside a cook fire outside Strobridge's office, his coffee cup frozen halfway to his mouth. With him were Strobridge, Cole Price, and Ringo Jukes. All had returned from the construction site at the urgent request of Katy and Sam. Katy had wanted to go to the site and arrest him there, but Sam wanted privacy from the eyes and ears of the rail grapevine.

Strobridge, Price, and Jukes were staring dumbfounded, their

191

gazes shifting from Sam and Katy to Michael. "You're not serious—are you?" Strobridge asked in complete surprise.

Katy held up the code book, a grim look on her face. "It's all here. All the evidence needed to convict him."

"Of what?"

"At the very least, conspiracy to commit murder."

"What?" Michael almost shouted as he came to his feet instantly.

"Easy, Yeats," Sam warned, drawing his gun and pointing it at Michael's chest.

"Are you out of your minds?" Michael asked in a voice filled with disbelief. "What *is* that book—and how is it connected to me? I've never seen it before!"

Sam threw Ringo Jukes a length of rope. "Jukes, would you do me the honor, please?" Jukes glanced at Strobridge questioningly. Strobridge didn't move.

"If there's a question of authority here, Mr. Strobridge," Katy stated, "we could take it up with Mr. Stanford. He hired us to arrest a killer and stop the sabotages, and that's what we plan to do, with or without your help."

"I can't believe this," Cole said, shaking his head.

"Answer me!" Michael pleaded to Sam and Katy. "What is that book?"

"You know what it is, Michael," Katy said bitterly. "I found it in your desk."

"I—I've never seen it before!"

Sam handed Katy his gun. "If he moves, shoot him." He took the rope from Jukes's hand, moved behind Michael, and started to pull his hands behind his back.

"Let go of me!" Michael shouted, jerking his arms.

Instantly Katy covered the few feet to him and pointed the gun to his head. "Don't you move, Michael! You had my father killed, and if you move again, I'll kill *you,* so help me!"

Michael froze, his face a mask of confusion and surprise. Slowly he raised a hand in supplication. "Katy, I don't know what you're talking about." He didn't resist as Sam took his arms and began tying him up.

"Save it for the jury, Michael," Katy snapped. Her eyes burned into his, and before she knew it, she found herself stepping up to him and slapping him across the face as hard as she could. "I trusted you!" she screamed, only inches from his flaming cheek. Hating herself for it, she felt tears well in her eyes and repeated softly, "I trusted you." She felt hands tentatively grasp her trembling shoulders and then heard Cole speaking softly to her.

"Come on, Katy. It's all right. Give me the gun."

She felt the .44 being taken from her while her attention never left Michael. His mouth worked, but no sound came out, and he still wore the same confused expression when Sam spun him around. "I'm making your toolshed into a temporary jail, Mr. Strobridge. Could I have the key, please?"

Without a word Strobridge nodded to Jukes, who said, "This way. I'll unlock it for you." The three men left, and Michael looked over his shoulder briefly at Katy.

"I'm innocent, Katy," he announced briefly before they rounded a tent.

Katy shrugged herself out from under Cole's hand on her shoulder and went to stand a few steps away from him. On top of everything else, Michael was apparently a very good actor. For an instant, she'd been sure she'd slapped an innocent man—but there was no doubting the truth of the evidence.

"What will you do with him?" Strobridge asked quietly. Michael was one of his favorite employees, and his arrest had shaken him to the core.

"Take him back to Sacramento and turn him over to the law there. When does the next train go back?"

"Day after tomorrow."

193

"This is just—I still can't believe this!" Cole repeated. "What *is* that book, anyway?"

Katy explained briefly, and both men were left speechless by the implications.

Sam and Jukes returned, with Jukes assuring Sam, "I'll post a guard and see he gets fed. Gonna get cold in that shed at night, though."

"I couldn't care less," Sam said grimly. "And post *two* guards— dependable men."

"All right."

"Let's go, Katy."

"Katy?" Cole asked, "Is there anything I can do?"

"No, thank you, Cole," she said in a monotone. "There's nothing left to be done."

Sam and Katy walked in silence most of the way back to the caboose, until Sam said, "There *is* still one thing to be done." He caught her eye. "Dancy."

"It won't be long now, Sam. Michael will have to confess, and I'll bet Dancy's the one he hired for the dirty work."

Chang was outside cooking some egg-drop soup for Rita, and Sam lingered to talk to him while Katy went inside.

"How did it go?" Rita asked carefully. She was sitting up on the bed with pillows against her back.

Katy sighed as she put some water on the stove to boil. "We arrested Michael, and he denied knowing anything."

"I'm really sorry, Katy—I mean, I'm glad you caught him, but I'm sorry it was Michael."

"Me, too."

Rita paused, as if deciding whether to speak her thoughts, then said, "I was watching you and Sam as you walked up. Are you in love with him?"

Katy almost dropped the teakettle. "What? Why do you ask that?"

Shrugging, Rita replied, "I don't know. Just the way you two are together—sort of like you're in tune, like a piano. All the keys adjusted to make beautiful music." She was staring out the small window at Sam and Chang, a dreamy look on her face.

"Rita, is your fever back?" The joke fell flat, and Katy said softly, "I don't think I'm in love. I don't even know how it feels." She sat at the desk facing Rita, her chin propped on her fist. "Sam and I have been through a lot in a short amount of time. It's . . . bonded us in a special way, I guess."

"It shows. More than you know."

Katy found herself struggling to put her thoughts into words, much the same as Rita had earlier. It had been on her mind for a few days, and she decided the best way to say it was from the heart. "Rita, I've gotten to know you in the past week, and I've got a confession to make. I need you to forgive me."

Rita faced her, surprised. "What for?"

"When Sam first started seeing you, I told him you were a bad person because of . . . what you do for a living. I judged you, and that was wrong. I think you're a good person in a bad situation, and I apologize."

After staring at her a moment, Rita put her head down and whispered, "Thank you, Katy. But you didn't have to tell me that."

"Yes, I did. You see, I've found new strength through God, and it's a sin to judge someone. Only he can do that."

"I've had regular customers who were preachers. If you're talking about *that* God, I'll pass."

"Those men are the worst sort of hustlers. They only use God to get what they want, and I think you're smart enough to figure that out for yourself. I'm talking about a loving, forgiving God who only wants love and respect in return." Katy waited for her to reply and, when she was silent, went on. "I think you're doing some soul-searching, and I'm just saying that it always helps *me* to pray. Maybe it would help you, too."

195

Rita stared at her hands for a long time before answering. "I'll think about it, Katy. Really I will."

"Good for you, Rita," Katy said, smiling. "And I'll keep praying for you."

———⋙◆⋘———

Late that night, Katy felt herself being shaken awake. She had been sleeping soundly and groggily opened her eyes to find Rita leaning over the bed with her hand clinched tightly on Katy's arm. "What—what is it?"

Through the gloom, Rita's face clearly showed fear. "There's someone knocking on the door!" she whispered.

As if on cue, Katy heard a firm rapping. Putting on a robe, she shivered as she walked across the cold floor to the desk and retrieved the small gun Sam had given her. Grasping it firmly in hand, she went to the door and asked, "Who is it?"

"It's Sam."

Opening the door, she started, "Sam, what's the matter? Do you know what time—"

"Michael's escaped, Katy," he said curtly.

CHAPTER FOURTEEN

Rita

W hat in heaven's name are you doing here?" Theodore
Sedgewick demanded in a tight, gravelly voice. "I've
told you never to contact me—I always contact *you!*"
He nevertheless opened his door to the man Red Dancy called
"Booth."

"I rode all night to get here, and I don't need your lip!" Booth
removed his hat and went to the fire Sedgewick had started. The
sun had not broken the horizon, and the night air whisking past
Booth on the running horse had chilled him.

"What's happened? Why are you here?" Sedgewick asked as he
pulled his silk robe more snugly around his lanky frame.

"Things are heating up. Somehow, they've gotten ahead of
schedule and plan on being through the Sierras by spring instead
of late summer or fall."

"What! How did *that* happen?"

"It doesn't matter *how* it happened—what are you going to do
about it?"

Sedgewick sat heavily on his huge, thickly padded sofa. He
hated the thing, but he'd agreed on taking it when he'd hastily
purchased the house in Alta. He also hated the hick town, but he
couldn't resist being near the mayhem that he caused on the Central
Pacific Railroad. He scratched his head, thinking furiously, when

197

the idea dawned on him. It was so simple! He stood and crossed the room to stand by his employee near the fire. "You just received a shipment of that new dynamite, didn't you?"

"Yes."

"Well, let's see how good that explosive is, shall we? Blow the big tunnel."

Instead of the surprise Sedgewick had expected, the man stared into the fire for a moment before nodding slowly. "That would sure set them back a ways." He chuckled. "You sure have a devious mind, Sedgewick. Why don't you tell me, once and for all, why you are so interested in destroying this railroad?" Booth avoided facing the man, thinking he would be more willing to answer if the question seemed spontaneous, which it wasn't. Booth really wanted to know and had for a while.

"For the same reason as you, mostly—greed. But I must admit, I do have a small ax to grind with Mr. Leland Stanford."

Booth waited for him to go on, covering his surprise. He didn't even know that Sedgewick knew Stanford.

"You see," Sedgewick started, beginning to pace, "I was once an employee of Stanford when he was governor, a minor campaign manager. He probably doesn't even know my name or face, but that's all right. My father was a large contributor of his through his organization. He put a large sum of cash in Stanford's pocket to run again in '64, but Stanford chose to lead this railroad instead of the people of California. His motives were purely greed, too, you see. You and he have a lot in common." Sedgewick smiled when the man looked sharply at him, then went on: "Anyway, Stanford didn't pay my father back—he invested it in his new business interest—and Father lost his entire savings. Except for one important document."

"What was that?" Booth asked when he paused.

"A very generous life-insurance policy, of which I was the sole benefactor since my mother's passing in '62."

A thick silence filled the room, with the only sounds being the crackle of the fire and the soft ticking of a grandfather clock. Booth found himself frozen as he searched Sedgewick's face.

"Father didn't have the guts to demand his money back, and I'll be horsewhipped if I'm going to live in poverty because of my father's gutless nature." Sedgewick sighed and shook his head in genuine regret. "So, I had to take matters into my own hands. And now, through my design, Leland Stanford will pay with his own poverty, and my plentiful stock in the *Union* Pacific will go into orbit."

Booth hated to ask, didn't *want* to ask, but he had to know who he was dealing with. "You killed your father?"

"He had an unfortunate heart attack." The statement was made flatly, as if Sedgewick were reading a newspaper item out loud.

Booth immediately thought about John Steele's "heart attack" but made no comment. Instead, he said curtly, moving to the door, "I've got to get back. The sooner this is taken care of, the better."

"Agreed. By the way, you *have* been disposing of those letters and telegrams, haven't you? We can't be too careful."

"Do you think I'm a fool? My neck is on the line more than yours."

Sedgewick went to the door and opened it for him, putting a hand on his shoulder. "Good. Then I'll expect to read about a serious setback for the CP in the paper tomorrow. The Union Pacific will have to win the race after this, and we'll be rich men!"

After Booth climbed onto his tired horse, his shoulder still tingled unpleasantly where Sedgewick had touched him.

———

". . . and he just—vanished," Sam told Rita as they took their afternoon walk after Michael's escape. "We searched all night, but he must have cleared out of the whole area."

The day was very windy, giving the trees a voice of their own as branches scraped together and long, solid trunks groaned while leaning. For the third time, Sam reached up and grabbed his hat before a particularly strong gust could carry it off. Tired of the ritual, he finally sighed heavily, removed it, and carried it.

To Rita, his exasperated sigh spoke volumes. He'd been fidgety and withdrawn for the past two days, and she was afraid he was growing tired of her. *After all, what sort of man wanted to play nursemaid to a woman?* she thought for what seemed the tenth time that morning. There could be many things bothering him, but she needed to know where she stood with him—needed to know very badly. Taking a deep breath, she asked, "What's really bothering you, Sam?"

"What makes you think I'm bothered?"

"Come on, it's me, Rita. You can tell me." She put her arm through his to try to make him more comfortable.

"I don't know." He shrugged. "I'm just feeling sort of antsy, I suppose. I'm not used to staying in one place for so long, and I guess I miss the wandering life."

Rita didn't answer. Sam growing tired of her was not the issue as she'd feared—but it was just as bad. *He feels like moving on, but somehow I don't think a wife or a steady woman at his side fits into his plans.* The thought depressed and saddened her. Any emotional ties to other men were nothing compared with her feelings for Sam. She was deeply afraid she was in love with him, and now she had to face the cold reality that the emotion might not be mutual. *But I have to find out.*

Trying to smile, she asked as lightly as she could, "What will you do after you're through here?"

Sam shrugged again. "I don't know—maybe try to find an acting troupe to link up with. What about you?"

"I haven't thought about it much," she lied smoothly. "I'll find something, I suppose." Rita found herself wishing desperately for Sam to ask her to marry him. The thought leaped in her mind, startling in its importance and urgency. She'd lived the same sort of life that Sam had—roving, independent, and adventurous, but now she felt the need for roots and a family. The idea of settling down had entered her mind a few times while she'd had nothing to do but think during her recovery. Apparently the desire was more deeply rooted than she realized.

"Rita," Sam said, stopping and taking her by the arms, "you can't go back to Dancy. You know that, don't you?" Rita didn't answer. "He's definitely involved with this business, and I'm going to take him down for it—hard."

"I know," she said. "Don't worry, Sam. I'll find something."

"Something besides saloons?"

What do you care? she wanted to say and realized how childish it would sound. "Yes," she answered more confidently than she felt, "I've had enough of that life."

"Good. A beautiful girl like you—" he smoothed the wind-blown hair out of her face and kissed her forehead—"will have no trouble at all." His tenderness brought tears to her eyes that she didn't want him to see, so she fell into his arms.

Rita knew what she had to do. *I'll miss you, Sam. More than you'll ever know.*

They clung to each other for a long time with the strong wind whipping at their clothes.

———

After Sam left Rita at the caboose, she found Ringo Jukes, and he made arrangements for her to ride into Cisco with a coolie going for supplies. Jukes tried to talk her out of leaving so soon after her surgery, but she kindly fended off his protests and swore him to secrecy. Rita made herself stay in bed for the rest of the afternoon, conserving energy she knew would be needed.

Rita had known Sam and Katy were planning to have supper

with Chang and his friends, so she was ready with an excuse of back pain when they asked her to join them.

"Are you all right?" Sam asked worriedly.

"Yes, I think we just walked a little too far today."

"We'll have to watch that tomorrow."

There won't be a walk tomorrow, Rita thought. But she smiled and said, "Yes, we will."

"We'll bring you some supper—you may be hungry later," Katy said. "Maybe that'll help the pain go away." Her tone was light, but Rita detected a hesitation in her manner. *Have I given myself away?* "Are you sure you won't come?" Katy asked.

"I'm sure—go have a good time." Rita watched them through the window as they walked away, but then she saw Katy stop and say something to Sam. They both looked back at the caboose, and for a moment Rita thought they'd decided to come back. But to her relief they went on their way. *Katy knows. Or if she doesn't know exactly what's going on, she's figured something isn't right.*

When the wagon arrived, Rita found that the coolie could barely speak English. This suited her fine—she didn't have to explain her tears.

Rita had the coolie drop her off a block away from the Shamrock. She would have to dodge Red Dancy in order to sneak in and get her clothes. To her relief, she saw him standing outside the saloon talking to some men. Going around to the back door, she was relieved that Ray, the bartender, wasn't in the back room getting supplies. She ran up the back stairs, packed what few belongings she had into a small bag, and was creeping down the stairs again when she heard the door to the saloon area open and Red's voice directly below her. She could see Red but not the man with him.

"So, you finally decide to show your face, eh?" Red asked. "Why don't you go ahead and tell me your name?"

The visitor was standing in a corner of the room that was

blocked by the stairs. The thickness of the construction blocked his answer so that Rita couldn't make out his words—only a murmuring sound. He must have told Red to hold his voice down, because she suddenly had to strain to hear Red.

"Still want to keep your secrets," Red said, shaking his head. "Well, now that we're face-to-face, I think it's time you stopped ordering me around like a—"

The man interrupted him, his tone suddenly dangerous.

"Bronte's too slick—I told you that!" Suddenly, Red stiffened and slowly raised his hands in the air. "Now, wait a minute! D-don't shoot! I'm sorry—I'll—" Red turned his head away from the stranger, his face pinched in a mixture of horror and fear. Rita heard the hammer of a gun falling on an empty chamber with a loud *clack!* After a pause, she heard a low, evil chuckle from the stranger, followed by a comment.

Red's whole body was shaking. Rita couldn't help but feel a small satisfaction as she watched her tormentor reduced to jelly, but the gratification was mingled with fear of the sadistic stranger. When Red looked back in the direction of the stranger, his face was shiny with sweat, and he mumbled something about doing "anything."

The stranger spoke, and Red exclaimed, "Blow up the tunnel! Tonight?" The stranger shushed him and said something else. A thick packet of money landed at Red's feet, apparently thrown by the visitor. Red toned down his voice until Rita couldn't even hear him. They talked for a few minutes, and the only words she could make out were "dynamite" and "meet later."

The stranger left, and Rita started to make her way quietly back to her room to hide until she was sure Red was out of the way. On the second step she took, the floor creaked.

"Hey!" Red called from downstairs. He had apparently stayed in the room after the man left. "Who's up there?" Rita dropped her bag and made a dash for her room down the hall as she heard heavy boots pounding up the stairs. By the time she'd closed and locked her door, he was right outside. Backing away from the door, she was trying to gauge whether she could muster the courage to jump out the window when the door came crashing open.

All signs of the tremulous and cowed man Rita had seen before had vanished. Red was breathing heavily from the run up the stairs as he walked slowly into the room, clenching and unclenching his fists. His eyes were wild and staring. The lamp in the room reflected off of them, making them seem a vicious red. "Rita," he uttered, as if confirming what his eyes were seeing. "What have you been doing, girl? Eavesdropping?"

"N-no, Red—I swear I—"

"Didn't your mama teach you not to listen in on other people's conversations?" A small smile touched Red's lips, and to Rita it was worse than the dark and vindictive streak she knew. He had a look in his eyes that could only be described as insane. Rita was still backing away and realized she had to be getting close to the window. When she turned to glance behind her, Red seized her arm, pulled her toward him roughly, and slapped her. Rita's head snapped to the side, and she felt him take her by the arms and push her against the wall. Her back screamed in agony where she had been wounded, and for a moment she thought she would pass out as the room swam in her vision.

Red's stale breath reached her as he growled, "Think you were going to run to your boyfriend with a little information, Rita? Huh? Is that what you were thinking? Well, Uncle Red has a little surprise for you. You ain't going nowhere!" He turned his head and bellowed, *"Buurrrll!"* at the top of his lungs. Then he stayed right in her face—watching her, breathing on her—until the sound of Burl Overmire's heavy steps stopped at the door.

"Yeah, Red?"

Red slowly released his grip on Rita and faced Overmire. "I

want you to watch Rita until I get back. She's not to leave this room. I don't care if you have to sit on her. Is that clear, Burl?"

"Sure, Red."

Red cast Rita one last glare. "We've got a date later, Rita. I think I'll enjoy it, but I'm not so sure you will."

Burl closed the door behind Red and grinned vacantly at Rita. "Why's Red mad at you, Rita?"

Rita shook her head and sat at a small table with assorted liquors on a tray, thinking wryly, *I don't know what Red's going to do to me, but sticking me in a room with Burl Overmire is the start of a pretty painful torture. The man hasn't got the brains God gave an ant.* "I don't really know, Burl. He wouldn't tell me."

"Well, that's not very fair! He should've at least let you know." Burl had spotted the liquor tray and unconsciously licked his lips. Rita saw the hungry look, and a plan formulated instantly.

"Would you like a drink, Burl?"

"Uh—I don't think I better, Rita."

"Why not? It's just you and me—and I won't tell Red if you won't. Sit down."

This inviting offer, once it had soaked in, was too much for Burl Overmire to turn down. With an eager smile, he sat down and helped himself. When the tip of the bottle touched the glass, he stopped and asked seriously, "You really won't tell?"

"Cross my heart," Rita promised and did so.

That was all the reassurance Burl needed. Rita watched round-eyed as he filled one glass with the worst whiskey in the house, downed it in one gulp with a satisfied "Aaaaahhhhh," and repeated the action immediately. Wiping his mouth with his sleeve, he asked, "Ain't you gonna join me?"

"Now, Burl, you know I don't drink," Rita said, batting her eyes at him. Her cheek hurt terribly where Red had hit her, and her back was on fire, but she knew she had to hide the pain and charm Burl.

"That tray's for Red. He likes booze all over the place so he doesn't have to go all the way to the bar to get it."

"Well, OK." Incredibly, he picked up the bottle and repeated his ritual two more times. Rita was starting to have doubts about her plans to slip him a sedative. She always kept a potent mixture of powdered opium in her table drawer in case a man got out of control. But with Burl's massive size and obvious tolerance of alcohol, she began to wonder if the mixture would do the trick.

After Burl poured another drink, she interrupted him before he brought it to his lips by saying with a shudder, "Burl, honey, I'm cold. Could you go get my shawl out of the bag I left in the hall?"

"Sure, Rita." He stopped suddenly and gave her a suspicious look. "Hey, you won't try to escape or nothin', will you?"

Rita kept a straight face, saying, "Cross my heart," and performed the childish gesture again to his delight.

"You know, Rita," Burl said, beginning to slur a tiny bit, "I've always liked you."

"Why, thank you, Burl! I like you, too." With a slight blush, he left to do her bidding. She quickly reached inside the drawer and brought out the envelope, emptying the contents into Burl's drink. After replacing the envelope, she picked up the glass and swirled the liquid a few times to dissolve the opium, setting it down just as he entered the room.

Burl placed the shawl around her shoulders with a shy grin, sat down, and instantly gulped the drink. When he set the glass on the table, he closed one eye and formed an *o* with his lips. "Whew! That'n had a kick!" he exclaimed, picking up the half-empty bottle and blearily studying the golden liquid. "So, this's Red's secret sh—schtock? Boy, try that one on for size! Secret shtock—whoa, I did it again!—Stock." Then he again carefully pronounced, "Stock."

Rita was glad to see the alcohol start to take effect. "Yep, that's Red's secret shtock," she drawled. "Here, have some more, Burl."

"Don't mind if you do," he said agreeably, unaware of his mistake. *How many is that?* Rita wondered. *Five—six? I can't wait around much longer. I've got to get word to Sam and Katy about the plan to blow the tunnel!*

Burl was pondering his food-stained shirt front, but he apparently was having trouble focusing on the fabric. "Thish here's bean juice!" He raised his head to look at Rita, and she saw that his eyes were slightly crossed. "Thought you shaid you washed this shirt, Ma!"

He's hallucinating! Rita thought, and then Burl's head fell forward onto the table with a thud and a rattle of glassware.

"Finally!" she breathed. She snatched up her bag and hurried out the back door, hoping fervently the coolie was still at the mercantile store getting supplies. Her back pain had become a constant dull throbbing, and when she tried to run, the ache was too much. What little strength she had was ebbing fast, but she was determined to make it to the rail line to tell Sam and Katy about Red's plan.

———

Katy stepped into the dark caboose after dinner with Chang, when a hand clamped over her mouth and a strong arm circled her waist. Her immediate attempts to struggle out of the grip were met with failure as the breath was nearly squeezed out of her lungs.

"Shhhhh, not a sound, Katy. Not a sound."

A muffled moan escaped her when she recognized Michael Yeats's voice.

"Now, I'm going to ask a question. Where's Sam?"

The pressure on her lips loosened a bit, and Katy answered, "With Cole and Strobridge." Her words came out garbled since most of her mouth was still covered.

"OK," he breathed softly. "I'm not going to hurt you, Katy. Do you understand?" She nodded as best she could. "Good. Now, I'm going to set things right around here because they've gotten awfully haywire."

In the back of her mind, Katy heard the rattling sound of a wagon pulling up outside the caboose. *Sam, help me!* she thought. Michael kept his grip on her as he pulled her to the side of the window, and Katy's heart sank when she saw Rita weakly climbing down from the buckboard with the help of a coolie.

"Let her come in, Katy—don't try to warn her. I'm not going to hurt *anybody* unless they get in my way." He pulled her away from the window to the darker shadows.

Rita entered slowly, in obvious pain and discomfort and exhaustion. Katy watched her go to the oil lamp, fumble for matches, and light the lamp with her back to the two onlookers. At the moment she turned and saw them, Michael said, "Don't say a word, Rita. You don't want Katy to get hurt."

Rita's hollow, tired eyes were wide open as she stifled a scream with her hand and took a step back. Katy felt herself pushed to stand beside Rita. "Don't try to pull that gun you keep over there, Katy. I don't want to use this." From inside his coat appeared a large Colt .44, and he pointed it somewhere between the two women. His clothes were filthy and disheveled, and his features were as drained and wasted as Rita's.

Surprising both Katy and Michael, Rita suddenly collapsed to the floor with a groan. Katy ignored the weapon trained at her and went to her knees beside Rita.

"I'm sorry—I—can't—," Rita gasped, breathing heavily.

"It's all right, Rita," Katy said, putting a hand to the girl's forehead.

"The tunnel . . . They're going to blow the tunnel!"

"What! What are you talking about?" Katy asked, alarmed. She felt Michael's presence behind her, but her mind was locked with Rita's statement.

"Red and another man . . . I heard them talking, and they're going to blow up the tunnel tonight!" Rita licked her dry lips, and her eyes rolled back for a moment. Katy knew she was very close to passing out.

"Michael, get her some water—quick!" She felt his hesitation and half turned her head. "Go, Michael! She needs help. I keep water over there by the stove." She heard him move and considered a way to overtake him, but she couldn't *think*. His hand appeared in front of her holding a cup of water, and she gave Rita a drink. "Now, who was this man Red was talking to?"

"Couldn't see or hear him, but he was giving the orders."

Katy slowly turned and looked Michael in the eye. He looked at her, puzzled for a moment. Then a light dawned on his face. "It wasn't *me,* Katy! That's why I'm here—to convince you I don't have anything to do with what I'm being accused of!"

"Then why the gun, Michael?" she asked, her eyes automatically going to the pistol. He didn't answer, and with a shake of her head she turned back to Rita. "How long ago was this, Rita? Can you tell me?" But her head had gone to the side, eyes closed, as she breathed deeply through her open mouth.

Katy put her hands under Rita and tried to lift her. "Help me here!" she barked at Michael, and after a moment's hesitation, Michael put the revolver in his waistband and helped Katy move Rita to the bed.

He backed away from Katy slowly when they'd completed the task, his face uncertain as he drew the gun again. "I'm leaving," Katy announced, going to her coat and starting to put it on. "You can shoot me if you want to, Michael, but I've got to go try to stop this."

"I'm going with you."

"Going with me? You may be the one behind this!"

Michael's face was a war of indecision, and he finally replaced the gun yet again. "I'm trusting you not to try anything, Katy. All I want is to clear my name. *Please* give me the chance!"

Katy couldn't deny that he seemed totally sincere. He stood flexing his dirty hands, and his face cried out for trust. She sighed from uncertainty and indecision, then abandoned all caution with an impatient shake of her head. "I don't have time for this. Let's go."

CHAPTER FIFTEEN

Race with Death

M ichael drove the horses unmercifully. Katy couldn't help but wonder what would happen if one of them stepped in a gopher hole, and the image that came to mind was one of screaming horses, flying humans, and splintering wood.

All thoughts of grabbing the gun from him were gone. Katy was too busy holding on for dear life, but her mind was considering one possibility after another with lightning quickness. *What if Michael is telling the truth? What if the real murderer is up there? Can I shoot him if he's trying to kill me? Then again, what if I'm riding with the killer? Can I shoot baby-faced Michael?* Right before they'd left, she'd sent a man to find Sam and tell him to drop everything and meet her at the tunnel. There was no telling how far behind he was, if he even got the message.

Her immediate problem was Red Dancy, for she *knew* he would be there, if he wasn't already. Katy hadn't liked him from the minute she'd met him, but she had nagging doubts about whether she could trade gunfire with him. The thought terrified her. *Enough of this! Lord, you know the situation. Please grant me the strength and wisdom to take whatever action is necessary. I leave it in your hands.*

Michael was forced to slow the team down when they reached the winding, uphill road to the tunnel. They passed the site of the explosion, and Katy could see the large clearing that had been formed by the blast. She remembered innocent, smiling Key Sing and how one of his last acts on this earth had been waving frantically to her from the nitro wagon before starting up the mountain. *So many deaths caused by these despicable men—so much waste!* She felt her lips tighten with pure determination. *It's time for it to end!*

Reaching the mouth of the tunnel, Michael stopped the horses and looked questioningly at Katy. "Should we leave the wagon here and go in on foot?"

Katy looked around, trying to adjust her focus in the shadows. The moonlight was strong enough to illuminate the areas with no tree cover, but that mainly consisted of the road itself. "I think we should—"

"Drop your weapons and don't move!" Red Dancy called from behind them. "That's what *I* think you should do!" The sentence was punctuated with the sound of a pistol being cocked. "Go ahead—drop 'em!"

Michael stiffly threw his Colt to the roadside while Katy merely raised her hands to show that she was unarmed. "You won't get away with this, Dancy!" Katy announced, sounding more confident than she felt.

"Shut up, Steele! Both of you get down on this side," Dancy ordered as he appeared on Katy's side of the wagon. His gun was pointed straight at Katy's face, and she tried not to panic, though it was the first time she'd had a gun aimed in her direction. "And as for your opinion, *Detective* Steele," he snarled, "I will get away with this because there won't be any witnesses."

The moon above shed enough light on Dancy's face for Katy to see he was in a hurry and meant business. "Now, you and your boyfriend—" Dancy stopped, seeing Michael for the first time. "Hey, don't I know—"

The pounding hoofbeats of a horse approaching at a dead run cut off conversation as all three turned to see the rider. "Hold it right there, Dancy!" The white hair of Cole Price gleamed in the moon-light along with the barrel of the rifle he was pointing.

Oh, thank you, God—it's Cole! Katy thought. His horse came to a stop, and Cole dismounted with the rifle trained in Dancy's direction. He wore a cool, victorious smile on his face, as if he were actually enjoying the tense moment. His dark eyes left Dancy and locked on Katy for a moment. With a quick movement, he threw the carbine at Dancy and said to him, "Bronte's about ten minutes behind me. Take the rifle and kill him."

The action and words took a moment to translate in Katy's mind. When they did, she felt a corkscrew of ice move in her spine. "Cole?" she breathed, having trouble making her mouth work.

"Price, have you lost your mind?" Michael asked incredulously.

Cole removed bulging saddlebags from his horse, saying, "Shut up, Michael."

"Didn't think I could get the job done right?" Dancy asked Cole with a sour grin.

"Why shouldn't I think that, Dancy? You've botched the last two assignments." Cole regarded Katy, still wearing the look of tri-umph. "Sorry, Katy. Wrong place, wrong time." He shot Dancy a stern gaze. "Are you still here? Move!"

Dancy glared at Cole as he walked by him. "When this is over, we're gonna settle a few things," he pronounced as he mounted, then rode back down the road.

"Yes, we are," Cole murmured as he watched Dancy ride off.

Michael had been as shocked as Katy upon discovering Cole's betrayal, but the surprise quickly faded to be replaced by outrage. He'd been watching Cole's every move and saw that he'd forgotten to cover Katy and him with a gun after Dancy left. When he saw Cole was preoccupied with Dancy's threat, Michael leaped at him and felt his fist connect solidly behind Cole's ear.

Cole staggered back, but Michael was right on him, wrapping his arms around the bigger man as both of them fell to the ground.

Michael aimed a punch at Cole's back—right in the kidney area—and Cole's yelp of pain made Michael feel deeply satisfied.

Katy's reaction was slowed by the swiftness of Michael's attack, and by the time she'd turned to search for Michael's gun, a shot ripped the night air. Katy jerked at the explosion and spun around to see Michael, who had been sitting astride Cole's prone figure, slowly topple to the earth at Cole's side.

"Michael!" Katy screamed, but before she could rush to his side Cole cocked his pistol and aimed it at her.

"Right there, Katy!" Cole ordered, gasping from the blows Michael had delivered. "Stay—right—there!" He rose to his feet, holding a hand to his side in obvious pain, and with his boot turned Michael on his back.

Katy looked helplessly at Michael's still form and watched with horror as a stain, appearing black in the dim light, slowly spread over his chest. Her grief was overwhelming as she moaned, "Oh, Michael!"

Cole looked down at the still figure. "Michael was pretty dumb, pulling a stunt like that," he observed matter-of-factly. "But he hasn't been too smart all along, letting me frame him like that." He walked to his saddlebags, bent over with his gun still pointed at Katy, and threw them over his shoulder. Motioning with his gun, he commanded, "Into the tunnel, Katy. We don't have time to mourn a fool."

Events had unfolded so quickly that Katy hadn't had time to put everything in perspective, and a thought occurred to her with sickening clarity. "You murderer!" Katy shouted, unable to contain her anger and hurt any longer. "You killed my father, didn't you?" She knew what his answer would be, but the knowledge didn't stop the tears of anger and grief from coursing down her cheeks in fiery rivulets.

Cole didn't meet her accusing eyes when he said, "He was onto me—I didn't have any choice." When he looked at her, his face had softened somewhat. "I'm sorry, Katy. I enjoyed our times together, but I had to court you to find out what you knew. I didn't mean to hurt you—"

"Save your apologies, Cole. Maybe someday I'll forgive you, but not right now."

Cole smiled sadly. "All right, Katy. I wish I had time to explain everything to you, but I don't. Let's go—into the tunnel."

With the pistol aimed at her from ten feet away, Katy had no choice but to enter the dark opening. The construction crews were about a mile and a half into the tunnel—much too far away to hear cries for help. Torches were set in the walls every three hundred feet or so, and Katy stumbled along on the rough granite floor in the darkness. After a few minutes, she heard the striking of a match and turned to see Cole lighting a torch she hadn't even seen in the gloom. The light stabbed into the thick darkness, scattering shadows, and she could see far enough ahead to make out the next one to be lit.

Cole walked silently a few feet behind Katy. She asked, "You're going to kill me, aren't you?"

"There's no other way, I'm afraid."

With contempt Katy said, "You're insane, Cole." Every sound was magnified by a deep echo, and Katy started to wonder if maybe the workers would be able to hear her scream.

He seemed genuinely surprised. "Why do you say that?"

"You're responsible for so many deaths, and now you just decide to murder someone you've befriended. Don't you find that the least bit strange? I've read scientific articles about men like you—men with no conscience whatsoever. Killing a human causes no more grief than stepping on a bug."

"Katy, you have no idea how much money I'll be paid for tonight's work. Or how much power will be at my fingertips."

"Is that all you think there is to life—money and power?"

"You mean there's something else?" Cole asked. To Katy, the

saddest part of all was that she wasn't sure whether he was serious or not. Either way she knew he was seriously sick. If he wasn't joking, he had no idea what she was talking about and, therefore, truly had no remorse in him. If he *was* playing with her, that also required an insane mind. She heard him strike another match saying, "Not much farther now," as if he were consoling her instead of informing her that life would end shortly. *Give me strength, Lord.*

They walked a little farther, the only sounds being their breathing and footsteps, which echoed hollowly. Katy could think of many questions to ask, but the only important one had already been answered. She felt a strange calmness now that she knew what sort of person she was dealing with. Upon reaching a natural crevice in the wall, Cole ordered, "Stop right here," and dropped his saddlebags on the ground. Opening the flaps, he turned the bags upside down. Katy's eyes widened when she saw the contents: rope, fuse string wound around an oversized spool, and eight-inch-long tubes wrapped in two groups of ten that looked dull brown in the dim light. Each stick had a long fuse, and they all came together in a small gathering a few inches from the bundles. When she figured out what the tubes were, a nauseous feeling twisted her stomach.

"Mr. Alfred Nobel's newest invention—dynamite!" Cole announced grandly, raising one of the tightly wrapped bundles so she could see it better. "One of these little sticks could tear a fair-sized hole in this tunnel. This may be a bit much—but then again, you won't feel a thing, I promise. Turn around and put your hands behind your back, Katy."

Katy did so, thinking, *Is this how I die?* She cast glances down both ends of the tunnel, hoping to see a savior charging to her rescue. The urge to scream arose, but she was afraid Cole would only knock her unconscious. *I'm really scared, Lord. If I'm going to die, please give me peace in my last moments.*

"Now, sit down in the opening."

The crack was about four feet deep and two feet wide, and Katy grimaced when she sat on a particularly large stone. She shifted her position, but Cole warned, "Don't move!" and tied her ankles together so tightly she moaned with pain. Cole finished by tying her hands and ankles together, and Katy found herself in a painfully strained position with her back and shoulders bent sharply backward. Movement was out of the question, and she felt her fingers and toes growing numb from the restricting cords.

Katy watched him squat down and set the two bundles of dynamite directly in front of her, halfway inside the breach. "You'll probably just see a brilliant flash of light, and then it'll be over," he said thoughtfully, his mind on his work.

"I guess that's supposed to make me feel better."

Cole looked at her, surprised. "Yes, it was." He attached one end of the spooled fuse to the nest of dynamite fuses and stood. In the murky light, she saw that he looked genuinely sad. "I'm really sorry it has to end this way, Katy." On impulse, he came toward her, bent down, and kissed her on the forehead. Katy tried to avoid the kiss but was too confined to evade it. He ignored the sickened look on her face and whispered, "Good-bye, Katy." She watched him disappear, playing the fuse out from the spool as he left.

Cole had brought two hundred feet of the kerosene-soaked fuse with him, but as the spool emptied he wondered if he had shorted himself. When he turned and peered back the way he'd come, he thought he could vaguely see the crevice, and that was too close for his taste. *Or maybe I'm just imagining I see it.* Mentally shrugging, he struck a match, bent down and lit the fuse, made sure it started burning, and took off at a dead run for the safety of the road outside.

Just as Cole emerged from the tunnel and caught sight of stars shining, a large, black object entered his vision. Less than a second later, pain exploded like a piercing white light, and a shattering impact to his nose filled his whole being with pain. His world

217

turned upside down as the momentum from a dead run carried his lower body into the air, while his head and torso had stopped forward motion instantly with the collision. He realized dully as his back slammed to the ground that the cracking sound that accompanied the blow was the crunch of his nose splintering to pieces.

Sam had timed the swing of the rifle butt perfectly. Cole's face had met the hard wood at the very apex of the combination of force and accuracy. Sam had stood out of sight, listening intently to the nearing footsteps, and then had taken two broad strides before bringing the rifle butt around in a whistling arc with all his considerable strength.

Cole lay on the ground moaning through a mask of blood. It continued to pour out of his shattered nose, turning the dirt under his head black and staining his white hair. Sam dropped the rifle, grabbed Cole's coat lapels, and bellowed, *"Where's Katy?!"* into his face at the top of his lungs. The only answer he received was a strangled, choking sound and wide-open, pain-filled eyes.

"Sam!" He wheeled to see Michael turned on his side, holding a beseeching hand out to him. Sam threw Cole back to the ground and ran to Michael.

"Michael, I thought you were dead!"

"Katy," Michael croaked in obvious pain; "she's in the tunnel! Hurry, Sam! Hurry!"

Sam had jerked his pistol out of its holster even before Michael had finished speaking and handed it to him, saying, "If Cole moves an inch, shoot him! Do you understand, Michael? Shoot him!"

"I understand. Go—go!"

Sam shot a glance at Cole as he ran by him and saw he was still incapacitated and moaning. He could only hope that Michael would stay conscious enough to keep an eye on him.

Sam ran as he'd never run before. He stripped off his coat and felt the cold tunnel air like a dash of ice water, but he didn't care. His legs pumping like mad, he prayed he wouldn't step on a large rock or into a hole and break his leg. Dancy's attempt to bushwhack him had failed, and after Sam had wounded him, Dancy told of a white-haired man's plan to blow the tunnel. Sam had had to use a little persuasion on Dancy's wounded shoulder to get the story, but when Sam heard Dancy's description, there hadn't been any doubt about who the villain was.

Icicles of fear pierced his heart as he understood that he might be running straight into an explosion so vast that he couldn't comprehend the destruction. And Katy was in here somewhere— for all he knew that maniac Cole had strapped it to her somehow. For the first time in years Sam prayed: *Dear God, please let me get there in time! I know you don't have any reason to listen to the likes of me, but I beg you to hear me this one time if never again.*

A cramp developed with alarming pain in his left side, but he only redoubled his efforts and tried to block it out. *I've got to be close—Cole wouldn't have endangered himself by shortening his escape too much.*

Over his tortured breathing, Sam heard the most beautiful sound in the world: a woman's scream. And it sounded close. Fatigue made his legs feel like two wooden stumps, but he willed them to pump harder, and finally he saw the fuse glowing ahead, sparks dancing in a small arc. A cry escaped his lips, whether from relief, fear, or pent-up anxiety, he didn't know.

"Katy!" he called and heard "Sam!" screamed back instantly. *Thank you, God.*

Twenty feet.

Ten.

Five.

Sam skidded to a halt, snatched up the fuse in trembling hands, five inches from the tangle of dynamite, and desperately wrenched the burning end of the thread from the main body. Sam nearly collapsed from exhaustion and relief.

"Oh, Sam!" Katy sobbed, and he went to her without a word,

pulled the knife from his boot, and cut her bonds. Taken into his arms, she could only repeat over and over again, "Sam . . . Sam . . ." as her traumatized emotions let go completely. She'd been staring at the burning fuse with a fascinated, hypnotic stare as it had seared its way to her destruction. Sam's voice had sounded too far away to reach her in time, and her only thoughts had been that he would die with her and never know what had hit him.

Sam, still gulping air to calm the fire in his lungs, crushed her to him and panted fervently, out loud this time, "Thank you, God. Thank you!" Katy's face was buried in his shirt, and her words were muffled as she sobbed and laughed and wept at the same time. "I thought I'd lost you," Sam whispered to her again and again. She clawed at him desperately, her nails digging into his back, but he didn't care. She was alive, and that was all that mattered. They sat there in the gloom, two huddled figures as one, greedily drawing comfort from each other, yet providing relief and solace at the same time.

Sam suddenly remembered Michael and told Katy gently, "We have to go. Michael's out there with Cole, and he's pretty bad off."

"Michael's alive?" Katy asked incredulously.

"Yes, but barely, I think."

Katy found that her legs were in no shape to hurry since they were nearly asleep from the tight binding. Sam helped her until the feeling completely returned to them.

"What about Dancy?" Katy asked.

"He's tied to a tree with a bullet in his shoulder." Sam gave Katy a strange look. "God must be watching out for us tonight. Dancy had me dead in his sights and missed."

The crack of a gunshot echoed through the tunnel. Sam said immediately, "Michael!" and they took off running. "If Cole's shot him, Katy, I'll kill him! I don't care if I have to shoot him in the back while he's running away—I'll kill him!"

When they reached the entrance, they could make out the figures on the ground. Relief flooded over them as they saw Cole prone and unmoving, while Michael was weakly struggling to stay propped on his side.

"Michael, what happened?" Katy asked as she rushed to him.

Sam went to Cole and held two fingers to his wrist, then his neck, finding no life at all. "He's dead," he called over his shoulder.

"He pulled a gun from his boot," Michael said, pale faced. "I had to shoot him."

Katy inspected his wound, amazed that he had lost so much blood and was still alive. The bullet had hit him high in the chest area, missing his heart, but Katy didn't know how much time they had left. She saw that the blood around the wound had congealed in the cool air, but some still seeped slowly down his chest. "Sam, we've got to get him help—fast!"

Lost in thought, Sam hovered over Cole's body. In death, he appeared as his true self—a human monster. His face was twisted in a pained, dying grimace, white teeth exposed in the visage of a growling, diseased animal. There was no trace of the handsome and elegant gentleman.

And Sam thought that was fitting.

CHAPTER SIXTEEN

Endings and New Beginnings

Theodore Sedgewick?" the tall, stern man asked him. A badge winked from his chest, the armor of a U.S. marshal. Three men stood behind him, silent watchers armed to the teeth.

Sedgewick's heart fluttered. He'd been ten minutes from taking off for the East Coast when the knock had come at his door. Thinking it was his carriage driver, he'd instead found his worst nightmare. "Yes?" he croaked.

The expressionless man held up a sheet of paper. "I have a warrant for your arrest. Murder and conspiracy to commit murder. You'll have to come with us."

Somehow, without Sedgewick noticing a movement, the guns of the other three men were suddenly pointed directly at him. There was no way out, and he knew it. *Well . . . maybe one way.* "Please allow me to get my hat."

"You don't need your hat. Just come with—"

But Sedgewick had turned and dashed back inside the house, his quickness surprising even the seasoned marshal. The four men rammed through the closing door as one entity, seeing Sedgewick's back receding into an adjoining room. Rushing headlong into the room, they stopped, amazed, as the slim, hollow-eyed man they'd been sent to arrest turned his gun not on them but on his own head.

The explosion was enormous in the small room.

James Strobridge would never admit the fact to anyone, but he liked Michael Yeats very much. When Ringo Jukes informed him of Michael's brush with death, his face paled, and he ran to Michael's side immediately. Rumor had it that tears had actually formed in Strobridge's eyes when he'd seen the pasty-faced Michael lying on the sweat-soaked bed after the doctor had taken the bullet out. Of course, no one knew how the rumor had started, and if a man were brave enough to ask Ringo Jukes about it, he would give the questioner one of his rare smiles but no answer.

The rail construction had moved much deeper into the Sierra Nevadas, and the distance compelled them to move the tent city. When Strobridge was told by the doctor that Michael couldn't be moved when they were ready to strike the tents in a few days, Strobridge gladly gave up his office to serve as Michael's quarters until he was up and around.

Katy picked her way toward Michael's temporary home through the mud created by a soft rain the night before. Someone had left a pick handle beside the door for the obvious purpose of scraping mud off of one's boots before entering. Katy worked on her boots for a few minutes, but the results were less than satisfying. Shrugging her shoulders, she knocked on the door, heard a "Come in!" and entered.

Michael was alone, propped up on pillows reading an old magazine. His chest was heavily bandaged, and he had dark circles under his eyes, but the liquid brown eyes were clear of fever.

"Good morning, Michael. How are you feeling?" She was still uncomfortable being around him. Though many apologies had been made from everyone from Stanford on down for the mistaken arrest, Katy was left with guilty feelings.

"Better every day."

"Trying to catch up on your reading?" Katy asked, leaning over

224

and seeing "OCT.–NOV. 1864" on the cover of an *Atlantic Monthly* magazine. She whistled softly and said, "You've really got some catching up to do!"

Michael grinned. "Mr. Strobridge must have left it. It's a good magazine—here, want to read an article on dynamite?" He held out the magazine, and she cringed away from it as if from a snake.

"I don't even want to hear the word!"

"And I don't blame you." His kind face turned serious. "Still having nightmares?"

Three days had passed since the events at the tunnel, and Katy had finally confided to Michael and Sam that her nights had been filled with horrible dreams. In a particularly bad one, she was sitting in the crevice, hearing Sam calling her name, but he stumbled and fell. She couldn't see him fall, but she could hear the sound as he flew through the air in slow motion after tripping over the iron rail. Immediately following was an "oof," right before she watched, horrified, as the twenty fuses burned into their individual sticks of dynamite. She mercifully woke up before the blast, but her gown was drenched with sweat, her breathing tortured.

"Not a one last night," she said proudly.

"Fantastic! I was hoping they would end soon." Michael adjusted his blankets. "Any news on—what was his name? Sedgewick?"

Katy pulled a chair beside the bed and told him of Sedgewick's suicide. Michael showed no remorse or horror. Instead, he adjusted his bedclothes, not meeting her eyes when he commented coldly, "Saves the trouble of a trial, I suppose."

Sam and Katy had gone through Cole's belongings. He had left an "In the event of my death" letter tucked away in one of his many engineering books. It contained dates, messages, and the name of his boss. In the last entry, Cole had written of Sedgewick's reasons for sabotage and of his suspicions of the madman murdering his father. Apparently, in an ultimate act of selfishness, for which Sam and Katy were very glad, he hadn't wanted to go down alone if he died carrying out someone else's plans. Sam had asked, "What if Cole had been run over by a wagon or some silly accident like that? Sure would've left Sedgewick out in the cold!"

Sam and Katy simply turned their findings, along with a detailed final report of their investigation, over to Leland Stanford and Collis Huntington.

"And Dancy?" Michael asked.

Katy shook her head. "There's no doubt about that. He'll hang."

Michael nodded with no comment; then his eyes went to the window. "There go Sam and Rita."

Katy looked out and saw them walking hand in hand, Rita talking to him and gesturing with her other hand. She was still pale and weak, but she always became animated when she was with Sam.

"Have you decided what you're going to do, Katy?" Michael asked quietly.

Katy's eyes fell, but Michael had seen confusion for a moment. "No, I haven't." Since the rail was nearly completed on the eastern side of the mountains, Sam and Katy's job would be taken over by the company detective in Reno, Nevada. The man had been with Stanford's private security detail during his years as governor. Stanford couldn't let him go and didn't have the money to keep Sam and Katy on.

He patted her hand. "Something will come up for you."

"Michael," Katy started, staring at her twisting hands in her lap, "I'm so sorry I slapped you—"

"Shhhhh. There've been enough apologies. You thought I was responsible for your father's death, and to tell the truth, I think I got off easily. I'm just glad you didn't shoot me!"

"How can you joke about it?" she asked, amazed that he was laughing.

"Because it's over, Katy, and I hate to hold grudges."

"Thank you, Michael," she breathed, and for the first time felt really forgiven. "You're such a good man."

"Well, I don't know about that, but I'm glad you think so." His expression turned to concern. "Katy, I'll say it again; something will come up for you. I know that."

Katy wished she were as confident as he was and put on her best smile. "Look at it this way, Michael. No matter what happens, you'll have your caboose back in a day or two."

Michael didn't return her smile.

By noon of the same day, Katy had decided to go back to teaching. After seeing to Michael's needs, she'd told herself enough was enough. The dismay she was starting to feel over what to do next was not worth it. Teaching was the only profession for which she was trained, so she would go back to Sacramento and ask for her old job back.

Katy's time spent with the Central Pacific had been exciting and challenging. She'd met many different kinds of people and grown fond of several of them. But she couldn't very well force Leland Stanford to keep her on.

After lunch, she heard a knock on her door and opened it to find Sam and Chang. "Come in, gentlemen."

Chang wasted no time getting to the point of his being there. "Miss Kahtee, Chang smile, but there are tears under. Chang work gang leave for other side of mountain tonight."

"Oh, no! But it's so sudden! Then this will be the last time we see each other—for a while, anyway," Katy said with earnest regret.

"Yes. Chang want to tell you—" he turned and included Sam— "tell both of you how much he will miss his friends."

"Thank you, Chang. We'll miss you, too," Katy said. "And your wonderful cooking."

Sam took Chang's small hand in his and shook it, saying, "God bless you, Chang, wherever you go."

"Tank you, Mistah Sam."

When Chang turned to Katy, his eyes were wet. He held out his hand, and she grasped it in both of hers, leaned over, and softly kissed him on his leathery cheek. Looking into his eyes, she said, "I believe God sent you to me to be my comfort in a time of sorrow. I couldn't have asked him for a better friend."

Chang was so overcome by what she said that he couldn't speak. The tears that had been welling in his eyes spilled over and slanted down into his gray chin whiskers. He nodded over and over, then bowed, found his voice, and said, "You a shining stah in God's universe. Chang never forget you, Miss Kahtee."

"You'll always be in my heart, too, Chang." He turned to go, and they stood at the window and watched him walk away, back bent with age and slow of foot but with the unmistakable dignity that radiated from the whole Chinese people. "I'll never see him again, will I?" Katy asked quietly.

"Never say never, Katy. It's a big world out there."

"Yes, I suppose it is." She turned away when Chang walked out of sight, and sat down at the desk. Sam continued staring out the window, and they were quiet for a few minutes, lost in their thoughts. Finally, Katy asked, "What's the matter, Sam?" His mood had been reserved for the last day or so, very much unlike the normal, carefree Sam.

He walked to the chair opposite her and sat down, saying, "I'm losing another friend, too. I wrote to a man I got to know pretty well in San Francisco who owns a string of clothing stores." He picked up a nearby pencil and paper and doodled as he talked. "He's agreed to hire Rita," he finished, stealing a glance to see her reaction.

"Well, that's wonderful news—for Rita—isn't it?" Katy asked awkwardly. She didn't know how Sam felt about her—if he was in love, if they were just friends—but he seemed sad.

"Yes, she'll be able to start with a clean slate. Meet a man, marry him, have kids . . ."

Katy waited for more, then asked carefully, "Do you want to be that man, Sam?"

He looked up, put down the pencil, and ran his fingers through his hair, as Katy had seen him do many times when he was contemplating something. He started to speak, stopped, then started again. "No. That's not me." He suddenly stood, went back to the window, and said, "I'm not in love with her. It's just hard letting a friend go. You know that, Katy—just look at Chang."

"Yes, I know," Katy said softly.

Shaking his head in confusion, he said, "We should be happy for these people! Chang fits the life he's chosen. He just—fits, do you know what I mean?" Not waiting for an answer, he added, "And Rita will fit, too." He nodded his head again, this time as if he'd just convinced himself of something. "It's nice to see a happy ending sometimes. I'm happy—are you happy, Katy?"

"I'm going back to Sacramento, Sam. To get my teaching job back." Katy didn't know why she blurted the news to him at this particular time, but there it was, hanging in the air like a circus balloon.

"What? Why, Katy, that's ridiculous! You'll be buried in the same old grave you just crawled out of!" Sam's eyes were big, blue marbles of bewilderment. He spotted a mirror by the bed, quickly retrieved it, and brought it back to Katy, thrusting it in her face. "Look at you. Take a good, long look at yourself. You're beautiful, Katy! Your hair is gorgeous, your face looks healthy and alive." He put the mirror down and held her eyes with his. "What are you going to do? Go live with Aunt Agnes and make yourself homely again to please her?"

"That's enough, Sam!" Katy shot out of her chair and started for the door. "I don't have to listen to this. I'm confused enough as it is!" She left him staring after her and slammed the door. *Please don't come after me, Sam, please!* She listened for him to call to her to come back, but she heard nothing except her footsteps and accelerated breathing.

Katy didn't know where she was going—she only felt the need to move. She hadn't gone far when she remembered it was time to check on Michael. *Past time!* she thought, squinting at the noonday position of the sun. *I hope he's all right!* She hurried to the old office, once again fighting the mud, but this time didn't bother with the mud scraper. Calling, "Michael?" she started to open the door but found it being opened for her by Ringo Jukes.

"Ringo! What are *you* doing here?"

Jukes touched his hat brim in greeting. "Morning, Katy. Come on in." He held the door for her. "I was just about to head your way. Just stopped by here first in case you were tending to ol' gimpy here."

Katy looked at Michael and saw an amused smile. "I'm sorry I'm late, Michael. Are you all right?"

"I'm fine. I got a little thirsty and was ready to throw a boot through the window when my hero showed up and rescued me." When Michael saw Katy's anxious face, he amended, "I'm just joshing you, Katy. I was asleep—until I was rudely awakened." He eyed Jukes with a mischievous grin.

"Here, Katy, this is for you," Ringo said, ignoring Michael and handing Katy a folded, light blue piece of paper that she recognized as a telegram. *Now what?* was her first thought, and she knew she didn't want to open it. *The way this day's going, it can't be good news,* she said to herself moodily.

"I've got to get to work," Ringo continued. "Getting ready to move all these tents is a pain in the neck. I've turned into a mother telling her children to pick up all their toys." He favored Katy with one of his small smiles and left.

Katy went to the chair by Michael's bed and sat down heavily. Michael noticed the dejected expression and asked, "Aren't you going to open it?" Katy only shook her head. "You look like your dog just died! What's the matter?"

Sighing, Katy answered, "That Sam! He really knows how to get under my skin."

Michael chuckled and said merrily, "You two are such a pair! Bickering and fighting like a couple of schoolchildren." He then commented seriously, "He cares for you a lot, Katy."

"Well, he has a funny way of showing it sometimes."

"Say, could you fit me for a pair of those wings on your back?"

Katy shot him a dark look, but when she saw the boyish grin, she couldn't help but laugh. "Oh, Michael, I'm going to miss you!"

"And I'll miss you. Now, what's the late-breaking news?" he asked, nodding at the telegram. "Or is it none of my business?"

Katy started tearing it open, eyeing him with mock seriousness. "You sure know how to ruin a perfectly good session of self-pity."

Michael watched her examine the note, her eyes growing wide with excitement as she read. "Michael!" she breathed. "You won't believe this—it's a job offer! I've got to show Sam!" She was on her feet instantly, heading for the door, absently tossing a "Talk to you later!" over her shoulder before slamming the door in her haste.

Katy ran through the mud to the caboose, praying that Sam was still there or close by. Before she reached it, Sam appeared at the door, his eyes wide with wonder as he watched her stomping through the muck.

"Sam!" Katy called breathlessly. "You won't believe this. We just got a telegram from Stanford about a new job!"

231

"What? Let me see," he said excitedly, holding out his hand. He read the telegram quickly:

TO: SAM BRONTE
KATHERINE STEELE

FROM: LELAND STANFORD PRES CP

HAVE JUST BEEN INFORMED OF AUSTRIAN PRINCE AND PRINCESS KESSLER INTENTION TO VISIT AND SETTLE IN TEXAS STOP HAVE REQUESTED ESCORT TO RANCH FROM NEW ORLEANS STOP GOOD PAY STOP ARE YOU INTERESTED STOP

"Are we interested!" Sam bellowed, eyeing Katy with wide eyes. He stopped abruptly when he remembered Katy was upset with him earlier. "Are we interested, Katy?"

Katy let out a whoop of joy and practically jumped into his arms. "You bet we're interested!"

Sam held her at arm's length and asked with a big smile, "Can you put up with me?"

"Maybe it's the other way around."

"Well, now that you mention it—," he said slowly, good-naturedly rubbing his chin and gazing into the sky.

Katy hit him in the arm, exclaiming, "Sam!" and he picked her up with a laugh and spun her around.

When he set her down, he asked, "Are you ready to learn to ride a horse?"

"Now?"

He spread his hands. "No time like the present!"

Katy took his hands in hers and said seriously, "Sam . . . I couldn't have done it without you." She remembered her father's words to her the day they'd left the meeting with Stanford and Huntington. "Two really are better than one."

Sam swept her in his arms yet again, but this time he planted a solid kiss on her lips with a smack. "I like that—and I always kiss the boss after a job is over!"

Katy laughed with pure joy. "Oh? We'll see about that."